Fire
Fight

K. WILD

From the Chicken House

Real adventures are hard to come by, but this
page-turner will keep you on the edge of your seat.
Freedom and Java are facing a threat with more than
a touch of the supernatural and, being the awkward
characters they are, they never react predictably.

Brilliant action, fantastic characters and a
nail-gnawing climax! Enjoy!

Barry Cunningham
Publisher

K. WILD

2 Palmer Street, Frome, Somerset BA11 1DS

Text © Kate Wild 2008
Cover illustration © Kev Walker 2008
Cover design © Steve Wells 2008

First published in Great Britain in 2008
The Chicken House
2 Palmer Street
Frome, Somerset BA11 1DS
United Kingdom
www.doublecluck.com

Designed and typeset by Dorchester Typesetting Group Ltd
Printed and bound in Great Britain by CPI Bookmarque

1 3 5 7 9 10 8 6 4 2

British Library Cataloguing in Publication data available.

ISBN 978-1-905294-67-1

For my two boys, OJ and Jordan

Warning: most things you think you know about the world are a lie.

Previously in my life ...

Three months ago I was just another gypsy boy – moving from place to place, earning a crust of bread here and there, and maybe getting into a few scrapes. The next thing I know I've got an undercover police operation called Phoenix on my tail. It turns out they're the ones who deal with other-world crime – rumours of monsters in the sewers, laboratories letting mutants loose, secret troops of genetically modified soldiers ... if it's weird, they investigate.

You have to be crazy or a freak to work for Phoenix. That's why they wanted me – I've got the craziness. I spend my free time running across roofs, or finding ways to get into tunnels below the city streets. And any bit of trouble that's around usually sticks to me.

But mostly they came after me because I'm a freak. I have something called the Hercules gene. My great-great-great-granddaddy, the champion bare-knuckle fighter Hercules Smith, had a rogue gene that gave him phenomenal strength, and I've inherited it. That's why Wren, Phoenix's mission controller, contacted me three months ago. They wanted me to close down an underground fight club where kids are born and bred to fight all their lives.

And that's how I came to meet a rich girl called Java Sparrow and rescue her brother Johnny from the fight. After that, I thought I'd done my share of saving millionaires' kids from a fate worse than death, and Phoenix would leave me in peace to get on with my ducking and diving.

But this is my life we're talking about. Instead I got recruited full-time into the organization by Wren, so that I could risk my life on even more missions. Which wouldn't have been too bad, but I swear to God, no one – especially not Wren – mentioned anything about demons.

Part One
England

Chapter One

I f anyone caught me I was in big trouble.

In the light from the monitor I tapped out the instructions I'd memorized. An email flashed on to the screen. It said:

Hey, mates, watch this video clip closely. It's a scream!

I clicked on the attachment. A picture filled the screen. It was a figure in a black robe, the sort monks or martial arts fighters wear. He'd got his head bowed, as if he was praying.

So this was what all the fuss was about? A guy with his head down. This was the email I wasn't supposed to look at, or even breathe near. Jeez, what sort of baby did they take me for?

Skritch!

I froze. A faint scratching to my left, coming from the corridor. I waited to hear it again. Nothing. A mouse, maybe. This place was ancient, and probably full of rats, mice, deathwatch beetles and ghosts ready to rattle their chains.

Thing is, what I was doing was against the rules. I knew it.

But I was doing it anyway. So maybe it was my guilty conscience making me hear things.

Skritch!

No, that was definitely not my imagination. I crept to the door and peered out.

The corridor was pitch black, except for strips of bright light coming through gaps in the curtains, like laser beams. There was just enough light to show up the nightmare statues lining the walls. A two-metre-tall winged horse on my left, next to a marble lion and a unicorn.

I listened for a second or two. Nothing. So I went back to the monitor.

The man in the robe still had his head down. *Big deal,* I thought. But maybe I was missing something, so I leaned forward to get a better look. Which meant my nose was right near the screen when suddenly – *the hood lifted up.*

Wham! There was a flash view of a nightmare demon face. Glittering insect eyes. A thin slit of a mouth. A long forked tongue flickering out between needle-thin fangs. Then it screamed in my face.

I swear to God my heart nearly stopped. *Danger!* said my brain and I went into a crouching, heart-pounding stance, ready to fight, ready to run, ready to defend myself. And then, just when I'd managed to convince myself that this demon was on a computer screen and not breathing fire in my face, a hand thumped down on my shoulder.

'Don't move a muscle, boy.'

I could've whirled round in a fraction of a second and power-kicked whoever had got hold of me. But I didn't, because it was Wren. And he was worse than the demon. He was a giant of a man, but he'd appeared out of the shadows as if he'd got a cloak of invisibility or something. He was also my boss, this was his office in Phoenix Headquarters, and it was on his orders that the Screamer email was off limits to me.

'Want to know why I told you not to touch it, Freedom?' he growled in my ear.

I didn't answer, just stood staring out into the darkness with Wren's hand still gripping my shoulder. He told me anyway.

'*Because kids who watch it disappear without trace within twenty-four hours.*'

So that was me in trouble again.

Chapter Two

'Cut it out, Wren,' I said. 'It's just a joke. It can't hurt anyone. Put "screamer" or "prank flash" into Google and there's loads of 'em to download.'

Wren pushed me down into the office chair. It was like being shoved by a bulldozer. He loomed over me. The Screamer demon had been bad, but this was worse. He punched one of his big mitts at a control panel on the wall. The blind behind him slid up, letting the midday sun flood into the room.

'Some joke,' he said grimly. 'Except that eight other kids haven't found it funny.' He gave me his cop's stare. 'They've disappeared off the face of the earth. Who knows if they're even still alive?'

I blinked in the bright light. I wished he'd left the blinds down. It's easier to tell lies when your face can't give you away. And anyway, Phoenix HQ looked better in the dark.

It was an old haunted mansion squatting way out on the

moors. It was just the right place for a freaky organization such as Phoenix, because it'd been built by a mad earl. His hobby had been collecting statues of Greek gods and mythical creatures. He was allergic to sunlight, so the place was short on windows and big on tunnels and dark corridors. Turn a corner in Phoenix HQ and you were more likely to come face to face with a one-eyed giant or a mermaid than another human being.

There were dungeons and cellars, as well. Last week something had started howling down there, all night long. It sounded like they'd locked up the king of the wolves.

Wren began pacing up and down. He was wearing his usual cowboy hat, with an empty shoulder holster showing under his jacket. Usually it held a Magnum. He gave me a hard look.

'Tell me what you know about Screamers, Freedom.'

I pinned the innocent look back on my face.

'They're the sort of thing you email to your mates as a prank,' I said.

Java, the girl I'd met on my first Phoenix mission, had taught me about them. She was a marvel when it came to computers.

'It's a short movie, of something funny or puzzling, and when you lean forward for a better look it suddenly screams and makes you jump out of your skin.' I began to sweat. 'You've got it all wrong, Wren. They're harmless.'

Wren narrowed his eyes. 'Not this one.'

'An email can't make a kid disappear,' I said, sweating some more.

'We think there's a message hidden in the scream.'

'What? Like "run away"?'

'Exactly. And then the night before the kids disappear, they have a visit. They wake from a deep sleep to find they can't move a muscle. Imagine how terrifying that must be.' He paused. 'And then the Screamer appears in their rooms. We don't know what happens after that. But the kids go missing.'

I laughed. I swear I thought he was joking.

'The Screamer?' I said. 'The demon on the video, with the pointy teeth and the black eyes?'

'Yep.'

'The Screamer's not real, he's computer-generated!'

'That's not what we've heard.'

My heart began to beat a tattoo. I swear to God, I hadn't known it was dangerous. I couldn't meet Wren's eyes. But he bent down until we were eye to eye.

'So who did you forward it to?'

'I wanted to frighten my little nieces with it,' I said, after we'd stared at each other for a while across the desk. 'I was just messing around. I sent it to my laptop.'

Which was half true, but half a lie as well. Sometimes you have to lie to protect someone you're crazy about.

I'm talking here about Java Sparrow. She's nothing but trouble, but I'm mad about her. And I think she feels the same way about me. Unfortunately her rich and powerful daddy hates me, even though I saved his son's life. So me and Java aren't supposed to see, speak or even exist anywhere near each other. Me being on the same planet is enough to make her father see red.

'That's all? To no one else?' said Wren.

I looked away. Two days ago me and Java had talked on MSN. She showed me some Screamers she'd downloaded off YouTube. But I had to go one better, and say, 'That's nothing. Phoenix've got a Screamer that Wren's forbidden me to watch, it's that bad.' Which I shouldn't have done, because Phoenix stuff is secret. I was trying to impress her, I suppose.

Worse luck for me, she went, 'Oh my God, I have just got to see it!' and nagged and nagged me until I agreed to sneak into Wren's office and forward a copy to her laptop.

For a rich girl, Java was pretty good at breaking the law. But I couldn't tell Wren I'd disobeyed him.

So I said, 'Honest. Just my laptop.'

It was a small lie, compared to some of the whoppers I've told in the past, but it sealed my fate.

'Anyway, it's no big deal. I'll delete it straight away. Honest.'

I pushed my chair back. Wren must have thought I was going to make a dash for the door. His hand thumped down on the desk.

'Don't even think about leaving,' he said. 'Snow wants a word. You're on your last chance to start behaving like a member of a team, and not like a spoilt brat.'

In answer I swung my chair back on to its two back legs and stared out of the window.

When Phoenix had moved in they'd left the inside of the mansion much as they'd found it, but now the gardens were full of rifle ranges and physical training courses, with fun little items like a flooded tunnel, six-metre-drop jumps over spikes, and climbing walls with hardly any footholds.

I began flexing my muscles. Something told me I'd be needing to run very soon. I'd had enough of being indoors, and being told what I could and couldn't do.

'So do I get fired?' I said eventually. 'Can I go home?'

Two little lines appeared at the side of Wren's mouth, which I'd learned meant he was smiling. 'No. You don't get to just run away from your mistakes. Life doesn't work like that here.'

I could've pushed past him and been out of that room in seconds. But I didn't. A silence stretched between us. Then his mobile rang.

'Wren here. Yeh, I'm dealing with the Screamer email.' He shot me a look that warned me not to make any sort of move. 'You've got the footage? Is the quality good enough? Right, patch it through to me.'

Wren grabbed a remote and pressed a few buttons. The blinds slid back down.

He turned to me. 'You think the Screamer's not real?'

There was a click as a digital projector came to life. A beam of light shone on a screen on the far wall.

'Well, we've caught him live on camera kidnapping a teenager.'

Chapter Three

'**H**arvey King, aged fifteen, disappeared a few hours after this was recorded on a security camera.'

Wren settled himself on a corner of the desk, then aimed the remote. An image appeared on the screen. It showed a scruffy bedroom with four beds.

'Poor kid. Is he in a council care home?' I said.

'No, it's an expensive boarding school in Devon.'

There was a boy in one of the beds. He was lying totally still, as though he'd been turned to stone. I swear I've never seen such a look of terror on anyone's face. I watched as he put something up to his mouth. I thought maybe it was some sort of alarm, like a whistle. Then I realized it was a puffer. The sort of thing one of my sisters had for her wheezing. He kept sucking on it, his eyes wide. It looked like he was having an asthma attack, but his eyes were tracking something in the room. Something that was terrifying him. Something that was creeping towards him.

I squinted at the screen. Dear God, a patch of darkness was moving towards him. The puffer fell from his mouth. Then—

'Sweet Jesus, what was that?' I leaped back, my chair squealing on the floor.

The shadow had moved and become solid. A figure in a black robe, eyes glinting, was gliding forward.

The Screamer, reaching out for the terrified boy!

From the dark corridor behind me, there was a muffled 'Mmmpph!'

Wren glanced over. 'Ssh. Did you hear something?'

Now I knew what had disturbed me earlier. I glared at the door. 'No,' I lied.

We both turned back to the screen. Worse was to come. Suddenly the Screamer twisted its head round towards the camera. Towards us. It was as though those black eyes were looking right at me and Wren. I had to fight the urge to turn away, or cover my face.

Then—

'Jeez!' I ducked.

One second the Screamer was by the boy's bed, looking at us. The next he was centimetres from the camera lens. His face filled the screen. I could see the forked tongue, the mad eyes, and a dribble of spit on a pointed tooth. And then a scaly fist coming at the camera lens.

The screen went black.

'He smashed the camera,' said Wren. He pressed a button. The blinds came back up.

'It's a hoax,' I said, wiping the sweat off my brow. 'Special effects, that's all.'

18

Wren shook his head. 'No. It's come straight from the security office at the school. All that was left in the boy's room was his inhaler.'

My skin crawled. 'So that's going to happen to me, because I've opened the Screamer email?'

'Not necessarily. Only some kids are affected. The hidden message is programmed so that only certain brain waves will hear it.' Wren began pacing again. 'There are alpha brain waves for relaxing, beta for working, theta for daydreaming, and delta for sleep.'

'Yes, I know all that,' I said. 'We all have them at different times of the day.'

He came to a stop in front of me. 'But in the last fifteen years a new type has been found in a few kids. It's much faster than any of the others. It seems to be some sort of evolution of the mind. It's called Indigo.'

Indigo. I'd heard that word before. Java had used it. My stomach began to sink.

'Only someone with Indigo brain waves can hear the message. And they are the ones who disappear.'

He dug into his pocket and pulled out a pair of sunglasses. 'Our techies have invented these.'

He handed them to me. They were normal Black Fly shades, but with yellow lenses and something like an electrode on each earpiece.

'They have pinacyanole bromide lenses, and electrodes that put the brain into Indigo,' he said. 'Go and look in the mirror.'

I did. I had a halo around my head that was glowing blue-purple.

Wren came up behind me.

'The electrodes have speeded up your brain waves, and now they are Indigo for a few seconds. That's why you can see the blue halo.'

I took the glasses off. 'I didn't feel any different. What's so great about having Indigo brain waves?' But I think I knew. My stomach couldn't sink any further, so it began to churn instead. This was bad.

'It opens up parts of the brain we don't usually use,' said Wren, watching me, closely. 'And gives the Indigo kids paranormal powers.'

'You mean, like reading minds and making spoons bend?' I said. 'And talking to spirits?'

'So it seems.'

I gave a short laugh, but there was nothing to laugh about. 'There's no such thing,' I said. 'There's millions of pounds in prize money on offer for anyone who can do that sort of stuff. It's not possible.'

Wren raised an eyebrow. 'Really? Maybe there's even more money on offer to keep it secret. Remember, the world is nothing like you think it is.'

This was getting worse by the minute. And it was all my fault.

I reached for the glasses. 'Let me put them on, and see what happens when I listen to the Screamer again.'

Wren shook his head. 'No, one of our Psi team will try it first.'

'They're freaks,' I said. These were the agents who'd been trained in stuff like telepathy and remote viewing.

'No, they just use mind power, instead of brute force, like you. They're used to dealing with the paranormal. Accept it, this isn't your case.'

That didn't surprise me. Nothing exciting that happened at Phoenix was ever my case, it seemed.

I'd been promised action and adventure by Wren, but all I got were lessons in the headquarters classroom. I expect he thought he was 'civilizing' me, but what he didn't realize was that I didn't want civilizing. I'd lived fifteen years without school lessons, and I wasn't about to start now.

Wren glanced at me. 'You look worried about something.' He folded his arms. 'Want to tell me who you really sent the email to?'

I wiped the sweat from my face. 'I've told you already. I sent it to myself.'

'You'll tell me the truth in the end. I can wait,' he said, and walked over to the screen. Which gave me the split second I needed to say bye-bye to him and all the rules and regulations in Phoenix, and explode out of the room like a greyhound out of a trap.

It didn't matter any more that we weren't allowed to meet. I had to see Java and tell her she was in danger.

Chapter Four

Alarms went off straight away.

When I'd joined Phoenix, I'd thought I was signing up for the fun of it. That it was OK if I changed my mind. But it wasn't.

It seemed no one was allowed to walk out, not after they'd signed the Official Secrets Act. That was my mistake. I'd signed it, seen the secrets held at the HQ and now Phoenix owned me. If I made a run for it through the grounds and over the fence, they'd spot me from miles off. I had to be sneakier.

Ten seconds after I left the room, Wren strolled out into the corridor, flicked the lights on, then began shouting into his mobile.

'Security! Where the hell are you? The new recruit's done a runner . . . fifteen years old, medium height, dark hair, dark eyes, looks skinny but he's tough, never stands still . . . yeh, the one with the bad attitude, that's the one. OK, tell the gate to stop him if he goes through. My orders.'

My fists clenched. If I had a bad attitude, it was because the other cops didn't like me and gave me no respect.

Wren leant on one of the mad duke's giant marble statues lining the gloomy corridor.

I heard footsteps coming down the corridor towards Wren, but it wasn't Security. The footsteps were accompanied by a tap-tap-tapping. They belonged to Snow, the boss of Phoenix. I'd only met him once, when I first came here, but something about him made my hair stand on end.

The tapping was because Snow walked with a stick. There had been an accident a long time ago, Wren said.

The footsteps stopped. Wren nodded towards a gently swinging door leading out into the grounds. 'Freedom went thataway, I think.'

'Looks as if he's fed up with Phoenix,' said Snow, in his robotic voice.

When I first heard him speak, I thought he was talking through a scrambler, but that's how he always sounded – as if he was talking without moving his lips. He was.

I peered out from my hiding place. Snow was looking towards the door I'd set swinging. Beside Wren he looked small, because Wren was nearly two metres tall. But that's all you could say about Snow's looks.

Most of him was covered in a sharp black suit. And the bits that weren't were hidden; he wore leather gloves on his hands, and a plastic burns mask on his face. The mask went from his chin to his bristling grey hair. It made him look like an android. Wren said the accident had involved fire, but he wouldn't say any more. The techies had made the mask to replace Snow's burned skin, but the trouble was it wiped out all the expressions on his face, and if you can't see a bloke's expressions, you can't tell what he really has on his mind.

That's why Snow worried me. I didn't trust him, and it turns out the feeling was mutual.

'I want him back,' said Snow, still staring out of the door. He cracked his knuckles through his leather gloves.

Wren shrugged. 'Let him go. When he gets as far as the moors and slows down, we'll pick him up. Even he has to run out of breath sometime.' He glanced around. 'And I'll get some of the guys to do a search of the building in case he's hanging around.'

I kept very still.

Snow's voice came from below me. 'No, I want him found. Put Bigley and Gabriel on to it.'

I heard Wren sigh. 'Why the fuss about the kid, anyway? We don't normally hold every recruit's hand.'

'I want him kept here until he's learned a bit of discipline and can be trusted.' Snow's knuckles cracked again. 'There's something about that boy I don't trust,' he continued. 'The Hercules gene is too risky to have roaming the streets. And the boy knows too much about Phoenix now.'

'Freedom's sound,' said Wren. 'He's headstrong, that's all. Doesn't think before he acts.'

Snow shook his head. 'I think he's capable of being turned against us. Or it's possible he's got a secret reason for being here.'

I gritted my teeth and forced myself not to move. All my life I haven't been trusted. It's the gypsy thing again. People don't trust any of us. We arrive out of the blue, stay a while, and then disappear into the night. We're the eternal strangers that no one wants around. But I was sick of it.

Wren leant against the flying horse. It was a massive thing, with wings that soared nearly to the shadowy ceiling. He rubbed a hand across his eyes.

'This is all I need,' he said, wearily. 'We've got the Hound of the Baskervilles down in the cellars keeping everyone awake all night. We've got the Screamer email spreading—'

'And an unidentified life form in the sewers, apparently,' interrupted Snow. 'It's just come in. Eye-witness reports vary between a yeti and a large mutant gorilla. Anyhow, it's said to be big and dangerous.'

'Really? That's a new one. It's usually alligators and snakes in the sewers.'

'Never mind that for now. Get on with finding Freedom. He's your responsibility; you're the one who recruited him.'

Wren sighed. 'OK. I'm on to it.'

With that, he went one way and Snow went the other, leaning on his stick. When the corridor was quiet again I dropped down from between the wings of Pegasus, the flying horse.

Skritch! Skritch!

Ssssh!

That noise again. And I knew where it was coming from now.

I hopped over to one of the thick moth-eaten curtains over the windows, yanked it aside, and dragged a small kid out. He was in black Prada, just like me. Except I wasn't wearing a tablecloth nicked from the dining room as a cloak.

He didn't look too bothered that I'd caught him.

'Mayday, Mayday!' he said into his communicator. It was one of my old mobiles. 'The boss is on to us!'

His name is Ant. I'd rescued him from a fight club a couple of months ago. He should've been adopted by now and living the life of a regular little kid. But Ant is like one of those unwanted pets that no one claims from the RSPCA. He'd had foster homes, but they brought him back, or he ran away. He always ended up near me, hanging round Phoenix HQ, playing with the other pesky kids who were stranded here after being rescued. There were about five of them running round the place who couldn't fit into the outside world yet.

I caught a movement behind another curtain, and moved fast. This time my haul consisted of two more kids. A boy and a girl. They had cloaks too. Oh, and a green tint to their skin, emerald eyes and three shades of green highlights in their hair. You'd probably think they'd gone mad with a box of face paints, but you have to remember that we were in Phoenix HQ and nothing is normal. Wren reckoned the twins had been exposed to something toxic, but it was only a guess. They'd been rescued from the smouldering remains of an isolated building, and they couldn't remember anything about their former lives.

'Is Robotman gone?' said the girl. The little kids were frightened of Snow. They didn't mind Wren, who they called Giantman.

'Didn't I tell you lot to leave me alone?' I hissed. I'd only got a few minutes to work out how to get out of the place without getting spotted. I didn't need the little kids giving me away.

Ant looked at me. 'We're the Tunnel Crew, boss. Our mission is to track you at all times.'

They held out their tiny fists. Each one was tattooed with the word Tunal across one set of knuckles, and Kruw across the other. In biro, I hoped.

'We screwed up,' said the girl to the others.

'You're hardly silent. I heard you snivelling when the video was playing.'

The green boy wiped his nose on his sleeve. 'Don't like the Screamer,' he said.

But then we heard footsteps coming our way.

'You stay,' I said to Ant. I looked at the other two. 'You others, vamoose! And don't say a word to anyone, or . . .' I pulled my finger across my throat. They both grinned happily, then skipped off. So much for my frightening reputation.

I grabbed Ant. 'You say you're called the Tunnel Crew?'

'Yep.'

'What tunnel?' I said urgently.

The cellars beneath the mansion were off limits to me and the other kids. When I'd tried going there before, I'd been chased away, but this time we made it down the stone steps without being seen.

'There's a tunnel down here that leads to the church,' he said, skipping along happily at my side. 'We could play Dungeons and Dragons!'

'Not just now, Ant.'

Thank God for the mad duke! And thank God for little kids who could come and go without anyone taking any notice of them.

The duke had done himself proud down here, with the sort of big arched ceilings you'd see in a church, and a row of dungeons, only now they'd been turned into laboratories, and filled with bleeping and humming pieces of kit. Except the last one, which was locked.

'Oh no. It's through here,' said Ant, clinging to my hand. 'It wasn't locked last week.'

'No problem, I can get it open,' I said, and gave the bolt a mighty kick. The wood around it splintered and the door groaned inwards.

'See, we can get in now!' I said, and led us both into mortal danger.

Chapter Five

The dungeon was pitch black. The hairs on the back of my neck stood on end. I froze. I felt Ant shiver. I hadn't seen or heard anything, but a little voice in my head said, *Danger!* I knew the voice well.

It's like this: the shivers down our spine, and the hair standing on the back of our necks, and the fight-or-flight plan running like quicksilver through our minds in times of danger, all come from the old part of our brain. The part that looked after us when we were slimy reptiles slithering about in the swamps, the part that would make us fight to survive at any cost.

We've still got the reptile brain from back then, hiding under our human brain. And it's ready to defend us at a moment's notice. So when it comes down to our survival, that's the bit that kicks in, if we're lucky. And mine had just given me a big warning.

There was something in this dark old dungeon that was my enemy, even though we'd never met.

'Ant? You OK?' I said, quietly.

There was no reply. Instead there was the click of claws on the stone floor. In the darkness, something growled, low and menacing. It was a sound that sent chills right down my spine, and made me crouch and freeze, as if I was a caveman and I'd heard a sabre-toothed tiger outside the cave.

Slowly, slowly I reached up, fumbled around, then pulled the cord by my ear. The light came on. Sweet mercy, I wished it hadn't when I saw what was snarling.

Seemed I'd found the thing that howled in the night.

It was part Pit Bull, part Rottweiler, part Mastiff, and judging by its black tongue there was a bit of Chow in there too. But it mainly looked like a bow-legged killing machine, put together out of the worst bits of other dogs, and covered with short brown fur. Only its mother could've called it hand-some.

It was the Pit Bull part that was growling at us, its neck fur bristling, its eyes like lamps, swamped with hatred. It was ugly and scarred and had half an ear missing.

Its teeth were wrong too: the fangs that showed as it snarled were several centimetres long, but stuck out oddly, making it look goofy. When it stopped snarling for a moment to silently snap at me, I understood why. There was another line of razor-sharp teeth inside.

That's when I realized what I was facing. This was another of Phoenix's freaks, a new arrival I guessed, because I'd heard nothing about it from Wren. A genetically modified dog, probably confiscated from an illegal lab. Whatever it was, it had been bred for no other reason than to fight, and just for a split second, as our eyes met, I knew how it felt.

I'd been born to fight, too. The boys in our family have been fighters ever since my great-great-great-granddaddy Hercules Smith got the rogue gene. The best boys were trained to box or wrestle, but in each generation there was always one who was even better, quicker, stronger, the one with the Hercules gene, me in this case, and they usually came to a sticky end. I looked into the eyes of the hound in front of me, and knew I'd found my equal.

And its name, according to the label on its gigantic food bowl, was Spike. The bowl was made of steel, and it seemed Spike had been having a bit of fun chewing chunks out of it. I began to worry.

'What do I do, Fred?' whispered Ant. He'd nearly walked into the dog in the darkness. Now he was standing frozen, his eyes wide.

'Don't move!' I hissed.

The snarling stopped, but don't think that Spike was about to come up to have his belly rubbed. Dogs like this are deadliest when they go silent, it means they're about to attack. Worse still, it had taken its eyes off me and was looking at Ant as though he was a tasty morsel.

'It's got staring eyes. Don't like staring eyes,' whispered Ant, looking as if he was going to run. If he did, it would be deadly. A dog like Spike would chase down anything running.

I'm fast off the mark but I can't outrun a dog, even a heavy dog like a Rottweiler.

'Stay still, kid,' I said.

'Don't like it!' Jeez, any second he was going to panic, and

Spike would have him.

'He wants to play,' I said, inching forward. The dog had its eyes on Ant's throat. I swear its dripping jaws were only a leap away.

'So let's play hide-and-seek with him,' I whispered. 'Put your hands over your eyes and count to fifty, and whatever you do, don't take them away.'

Dear God, he looked at me with such trust, even though I'd just walked him straight into a killer's den. 'OK!' He put his tattooed hands up over his face and began counting.

I let out a small breath. At least his throat was now covered by his arms, by bone. It wasn't much, but it was something if Spike decided to leap at him. And his eyes were covered as well, because nothing winds a dog up more than staring at it. I looked away too.

Ever since Hercules' day the Smiths have kept dogs. We've had all sorts, from lurchers for rabbiting, to silly little things with long floppy ears that Whitney Jade calls 'spangles', and everybody else calls spaniels. We've even got pictures of Hercules with a dog. It looked as if it was part wolf and every bit as wild as he was. So handling the animals was in my blood.

Stare at a dog and he thinks you're threatening him. I wanted Spike to think we were no threat. I kept my hands down too; I didn't want him to think I was about to strike out.

Then I got into a fight stance, one leg in front of the other to maximize balance, and because I might need to use my foot to keep him away if he leaped for Ant. Although by the look of Spike's maw I might lose the foot if I tried anything like that. But the stance was solid and it meant I wouldn't fall, because the only thing going for me at the moment was my height advantage.

It worked. Spike took his mad red eyes away from Ant and focused on me. Time froze down there in the dungeon. On one side there was me, looking away but keeping the dog in my peripheral vision. And, on the other side, Spike staring at me with hatred in his eyes and his hackles bristling.

There was a bench next to me, and on it I could see a leather gauntlet. Whoever had been trying to handle Spike must have left it there. It had a splash of blood on the cuff, so it looked like Spike might have been the victor in that encounter. I needed that gauntlet. But if I moved too fast he'd go for me.

So I began to edge my way slowly towards the bench. Spike stared at me and curled his lip. And then, slowly, without looking away, he started to circle me.

I swivelled smoothly, keeping him in my sight. Believe me, Spike was not the sort of dog you'd want to turn your back on. And slowly, slowly, I backed into the bench, reached for the leather gauntlet and put it on my arm.

If Spike had been professionally trained as a guard dog, he would go for my arm first.

I glanced at Ant. He'd still got his arms in front of his throat, thank goodness. If this went wrong he'd need them there.

Ten paces across, on the other side of the dungeon, was a small door. I guessed this was the entrance to the tunnel.

'OK, Ant,' I said quietly. 'You're going to run for the tunnel door, when I tell you. Don't look back — just run and close the door behind you. Then wait there for me.'

'OK, Freedom,' he said.

'NOW!'

In one move I lunged for Spike as though I was going to attack him.

Eyes blazing, he went straight for the crazy, puny human who was waving an arm in front of his massive snout, and clamped his jaws around the gauntlet. Even through the leather I could feel those teeth digging in, like my arm was in a vice.

With all my strength I pulled back as though I was trying to drag my arm away. It was futile. I felt Spike tighten his grip. But that's what I wanted. It was my only chance.

When his jaws were clenched and all his attention was focused on biting my arm as hard as he could, and when I saw Ant disappear through the tunnel door, I twisted and fell on top of him, kept my arm jammed in his mouth and got him in a stranglehold.

Now he couldn't let go of me even if he wanted to. He had me and I had him. But it meant I could drag him over towards a rack near the door. And hanging there was a catch pole, a long stick with a loop at the end. Once you catch a dangerous dog with one of those, he can't reach to bite any more.

Spike was smart, I'll give him that. He realized I was up to something and resisted, his claws clattering on the tiles and his body jerking as he tried to get out of the neck lock. But he was too late. Using my teeth, I got the catch pole off the rack and dropped it over his bristling head and neck. Got him.

Now all I had to do was get him to let go of my arm.

So I rapped him on the nose with my knuckles. His red-rimmed eyes met mine and I swear if he could talk he'd have said, 'Don't even bother trying, pal, I ain't letting go for no one.'

The problem was, he still thought he was the leader of the pack and I still thought I was. One of us was going to have to back down.

I was getting desperate now, you understand. My arm was killing me. So when I saw the pepper spray on the bench, I grabbed it. Seemed like the dog handlers here had never encountered anything like Spike before, and weren't taking any chances. I sprayed it at him.

Bad move. The big dog's eyes grew redder and he winced, sneezed without letting go of my arm, and then gave me an evil look that clearly said he was going to chew it off for that.

His jaws began to squeeze even further and I felt my arm go numb. This was deadlock. I couldn't let go of him and he wasn't going to let me go, not after the tap on the nose and the pepper spray.

But I had one last thing to try. There was a stick on the rack, a short thing, like a cop's truncheon. I was going to have to prise his jaws apart.

'Bad dog,' I said in my sternest voice. 'Bad dog. NO!' and I picked the stick up and tried to fit it in the side of his mouth.

But I didn't have to, because suddenly I was free. Spike had let go of my arm and was cringing, his belly on the floor. I quickly pulled the catchpole loop tight. Now I had hold of him, but he couldn't reach me.

My arm began to come back to life and I breathed a sigh of relief. But I didn't feel any triumph.

This dog wasn't just a savage creature, it had been trained. Not by kindness, but by the shouted command and the boot. Spike had seen the stick approaching and he'd thought he was in for a beating, so he'd backed off.

Someone had ruined this dog with cruelty.

I edged my way towards the tunnel, Spike sliding after me as I dragged him along on the other end of the pole. When he saw where I was heading he started barking. I knew I'd bested him then. 'Barking dogs don't bite', goes the saying, and to some extent it's true. A dog barks to warn you or to hide his own fear.

I got myself right up to the door to the tunnel, then let go of the pole and leaped inside. As I slammed the door closed Spike threw himself at it, splintering the ancient wood.

Then he gave a solitary howl that echoed through the tunnel. I knew what it meant. Me and him had unfinished business. But that would have to wait.

Chapter Six

'**W**here are we?' I whispered.

'Near the end of the tunnel, I think,' said Ant. He was holding on to my hand. 'I've never dared go any further. I keep thinking the knight's gonna stand up and chase me.'

The knight was made of stone and lying on his coffin.

I shone my tiny key-ring torch around. It looked as if we were in a vault beneath the church. In the corner I could see a set of stone steps.

'Do you think the Screamer demon might be down here?' whispered Ant, as we fumbled our way upwards.

'There's no such thing,' I told him. 'No ghosts, either. The dead are dead, and that's it.'

From there it was a short trip to the church door, then out into the fresh air. In the distance I could see Phoenix House and the training grounds. There seemed to be a few cops searching the grounds. Between the HQ and the church there were fields. In the one nearest to us, a kushti painted horse was grazing. When it heard us it looked up and snorted a few times.

I turned to Ant, who was squinting in the weak September sunshine.

'Run back, and don't tell anyone where I am, for as long as you can. OK?'

Ant nodded and ran back across the fields, doing little skips every now and then, and flinging his arms about. Poor kid, he'd spent too much time underground, and now he loved being free and running where he wanted. He was like me; I needed sun and fresh air as well. And living in Phoenix HQ wasn't doing me any good. The central heating was getting to my throat and I couldn't breathe. I needed a trailer and fresh air, not stuffy rooms and radiators.

I put my fingers in my mouth and whistled. The black-and-white horse trotted over with his ears pricked.

'Good boy, Fury.' I scratched his ears and found him a Polo to crunch.

This was my brother-in-law's horse. Joe's a good horse trainer, and Fury's a vanner, the favourite gypsy horse, black and white with a mane and tail that stream out like flags when he gallops. In the old days he'd have pulled the wooden wagons of gypsy folk. Nowadays we have Mitsubishis and Land Rovers to pull the trailers, so Fury's just for riding and showing off at fairs.

He was in the field outside the Phoenix grounds because my sister, Crystal, lived not far away. She'd come into a bit of money, thanks to my last mission with Phoenix, and invested it in land.

And since not everyone likes to sell land to travelling people, she'd negotiated with Wren and bought an acre or two of Phoenix land that they weren't using. Then her and Joe'd put their trailers on it and moved the horses in. She'd called her new home Costalot. Phoenix hadn't exactly given it to her at a knock-down price.

Fury snorted at me over the fence. I gave him another Polo. 'Hey, fella, fancy a gallop?'

He snorted again, which I took to mean yes. He already had a halter on, but I needed a rein. I had a quick search along the fence and found a tattered old piece of rope wrapped round a broken post. It was just long enough to knot on to the halter. That's all I needed. I always ride bareback. Then I grabbed his mane and swung myself on to his back, just as a police siren started up from the grounds of Phoenix HQ and began wailing towards me.

I turned the horse towards the moors, and then I only had to touch him with my heels and he was off like the wind.

The siren got quieter and I risked a glance over my shoulder. The four-wheel drive had bounced on to the moor, but was hitting every hill and hollow, not flying over them like I was. Soon the siren faded away altogether and there was just the sound of Fury's hooves drumming on the peat and the snorting of his breath.

When I was sure they weren't following me any more I turned towards the main road into town and let Fury gallop alongside it, jumping the hedges that got in our way.

I went by Costalot and saw Crystal and Joe's trailers pulled up and the washing hanging out and the little girls playing around, and my heart ached for the life I'd left behind: the travelling, moving around the country, following Joe's work, or just visiting our family. The little kids playing out all day long, until they got chased into bed at midnight.

And as Fury ran and jumped and ate up the miles into town, I breathed the fresh air deeply. This was better. I'd been suffocating in Phoenix House. Now I was free.

Chapter Seven

The iron gates in front of me were huge, and had a decorated shield on each one. Part of the design was a small bird, a sparrow. Jeez, the Sparrow family even had a coat of arms.

I was waiting in the shadow of some bushes by the gates. I'd tethered Fury on the grass verge further down the road. Then I'd had a look round and found that the grounds were surrounded by a high wall with an intruder alarm wire running along the top. Daddy Sparrow certainly didn't like unwanted visitors.

It looked as if there was a party going on in the garden. I could hear music and laughter. But I didn't think ringing her daddy and asking if I could have an invite would work. Instead, I'd made a different phone call. That's why I was waiting at the front gates. After a bit, a van turned the corner. The driver leaned out and rang the entry phone.

'Pizza delivery.'

The entry phone squawked a few times.

'Well, someone ordered them.'

Yep. I had.

The entry phone squawked again.

'Yeh, tell me about it. A bunch of kids not ordering pizza. Now that would be unusual.'

The gates slid silently open, and the delivery van swept in. In less than a second I'd caught hold of the handle at the back and was standing on the bumper, getting a free ride in.

Jeez, Java's house was big. As we rounded the bend it reared up in front of us, covered in ivy and with so many windows I hadn't time to count them.

I couldn't imagine living in it. It wasn't like a trailer – you knew where everyone was with one of those. But with a house like this, you'd have all that empty space around you, where anything could be happening.

Then we rounded another bend in the drive, and I saw the swimming pool, the hot tub, the tennis court and the Hawaiian bar with its thatched roof. And a whole load of beautiful people.

Above the bar was a big banner saying, Bon Voyage Java.

The pizza van drew up beside the pool. I leaped off and faded into the crowds.

Java had told me, last time we met, that she was off to Malta this evening. Not just for a holiday, but to a private school.

I hadn't had an invite to the party, but it looked like I was going to have a chance to say goodbye. As long as I wasn't seen. Her daddy would have me arrested on sight for going anywhere near his precious daughter.

He was standing by the pool bar, holding half a coconut with a straw sticking out of it in one hand, and a cigar in the other, watching Java and her friends having fun. He wore Ray-Bans, and a Hawaiian shirt that was open at the front to show off his hairy chest. He didn't look as if he was made of flesh; more like he'd been carved out of corned beef with a chisel.

But he didn't matter, nor did the big house or the pool, because I'd spotted Java. My heart began to pound. The same pointed impish face, the same bird bones that I remembered from when we'd been side by side fighting for our lives . . . and the lives of all the kids in the fight.

She'd been born into a life of private schools, nannies and holidays on sunny beaches. Her daddy didn't think I was fit to shine her shoes, but if he'd spoken to my mammy he'd have found out that she thought the same about his daughter. Java was no sort of girl for me; not when I had proper gypsy girls to fall for.

She was in a bikini, sitting on the edge of the pool dabbling her feet, and talking to a boy in flash clothes.

A girl walked by me and noticed me staring. 'Don't they look good together?' she said, swigging something blue out of a bottle.

I nodded. Even I could see they 'fitted'. 'Who is he?'

The girl's eyes widened. 'Duh! It's *Jamie Champion*. Where've you been hiding? He came up with the idea for that computer game, Sixth Sense. He's loaded and he's only eighteen.' She gave them an envious stare. 'Lucky Java.'

She handed me a bottle of the blue stuff. 'Want one?'

I shook my head. My sister drank alcopops, but I didn't

touch them. Stuff like that could seriously slow you down, and I wanted to keep my edge.

The girl shrugged and wandered back to the sun loungers round the pool. The rest of the guests were basking on them like seals on a beach. Daddy Sparrow had certainly not spared any expense on his troublesome daughter's farewell.

I waited for a couple of minutes, until the computer wizard had cleared off to get them some drinks, then I grabbed one of the pizza boxes stacked on the bar and made my way over to Java. No one took any notice of me; they were too busy wolfing down the pizza. It must give you a terrible hunger, sitting around on a sun lounger all day.

'Pizza, ma'am?' I said. 'Jalapeños and pepperoni OK?'

Java turned round. And straight away it all went wrong.

Chapter Eight

If she was pleased to see me, she hid it well. She looked like someone who'd been caught out. She got up from the edge of the pool, looking everywhere but at me. 'No thank you,' she said, slowly, staring over my shoulder. 'I'm a veggie.'

'Wouldn't you know it,' I said, grabbing a pizza slice and wolfing it down. The five-mile ride had made me starving. 'The girl's a freak.'

She stared at me, then tried to joke. 'You're very bold for a waiter.'

'That's me,' I said.

Her body language was all wrong. She'd got her shoulders hunched and her arms folded, like she was hiding something.

'So what's wrong?'

She looked around nervously. 'I'm worried my dad'll see you.'

Maybe, but that wasn't all. I couldn't stop watching her, but she couldn't meet my eyes at all. It was as though we hardly knew each other.

'I need to speak to you, Java.'

She looked around. 'There's people everywhere. It's too risky.'

I gave her a smile. 'Not everywhere. Follow me.'

We skirted round the pool, making sure her father didn't see us, then made our way behind the Hawaiian bar. It didn't take me a minute to stack up a few crates, climb on to the thatched roof and hoist Java up after me. I stayed low on the sloping thatch so that no one would notice us.

'Old times' sake,' I said.

She almost smiled back. The first time I'd met her had been on a roof; only then she'd tried to kick me off it. This time she rested on her elbow and frowned at me. I took this as a good sign, because when she was mad she looked like an angry pixie.

'I'll have to go soon,' she said. 'There's lots going on at the moment, and I'm a bit edgy.'

'I thought that was why you had the Buttercup Syrup and roll-ups?' When we'd first met she'd been attached to her tin of tobacco and a bottle of cough mixture for comfort.

She looked up quickly and smiled. 'I've given them up for good. I don't need them any more. I've got other things in my life now.'

For the first time her eyes got that laser-beam look I remembered from the first time we met.

'I thought Buttercup Syrup reminded you of your mum,' I said.

She began fiddling with a bit of straw sticking out of the

thatch. 'It used to. But things change,' she said, looking away across the garden.

Did I mention that, as well as the tobacco and the cough syrup, she believed she could talk to her dead mammy? But not any more, she couldn't. Her ma's helpful whispers had fallen silent, she claimed. Maybe she'd just imagined it all along, to comfort herself, and now she'd grown too old for imaginary chats. Or maybe the dead have got better things to do than talk to us.

'There's this Indigo group I belong to now,' she said, looking into the distance. 'It's made me think differently about things.'

Indigo. My heart sank. 'So what's that?' I said, as though I'd never heard the word before.

And it was like the sun had come out. 'It's the best! We all meet up. We're all the same, all Indigos. Jamie got us all together.'

Jeez, I might have known he'd be part of it.

'We train our minds. We can do these amazing things just by thinking! Jamie's really cool. He's a black belt in Kwan Sool. That's Korean fighting.'

Bully for him.

She lay back on the thatch and smiled. 'It's hard to describe, if you're not Indigo. But it's as though you've felt a freak all your life, and then suddenly you meet others who are the same, and you don't feel odd any more.'

'Aw, that's right, love,' I said. 'Me, I'd never understand about feeling like a freak.' She must have forgotten about the Hercules gene that'd given me so much grief all my life. Cool

Jamie Champion must've shoved everything else out of her mind.

She looked down, embarrassed.

'Look, let's not argue. It's good to see you again before I go away,' she said, slowly.

But I got the impression that she wasn't exactly telling the truth.

'You didn't look like you were missing me.'

From where we were hiding I could see computer wiz Jamie walking round the pool with two drinks in his hand, looking for Java.

'He's just a friend.' She glanced at me. 'So what're you doing here?'

'I'm in trouble because I sent you the Screamer email.' I kept my gaze on her, gauging her reaction. She began breaking the straw into pieces.

'Oh, God. Sorry, that's my fault. They'll never trace it to here; I was careful about that. They'll never know where it was sent.'

'Never mind,' I said. 'The thing is, don't watch it. It was on the Phoenix computer for a good reason. It's dangerous. Some kids who watch it disappear. Just get rid of it, delete it.'

Java gave her impish smile. 'Too late. I've watched it, and I'm still here. Not a bad screamer. But I promise I won't send it to anyone else. In fact,' she began to slither down the thatching, 'I'll delete it this minute.'

But she wasn't going to walk out on me now. The smile hadn't fooled me at all. I slithered down after her, catching up with her as she walked off towards the pool.

'You knew it was dangerous, didn't you?'

'No.' But her face said otherwise.

'Stop lying! You knew it wasn't just an ordinary prank email.' Then a horrible thought occurred to me. 'When we talked on MSN, you mentioned Screamers first. It was like you knew Phoenix had the Screamer email. Is that why you kept in contact with me?'

'No!'

But she stopped and pulled me into the shade of a big sun umbrella, so that we were out of sight of her father. Then she looked at me for the first time.

'OK, this is the truth. The Screamer email started in Malta last year. I tried to get a copy, but it got banned. Then, when I came to see you at Phoenix Headquarters, I saw a memo about it on a notice board.'

'And you knew it made kids disappear?'

'No. Honest.' She looked away.

'So what did you think would happen?'

She began fiddling with the fringe on the umbrella, so that she didn't have to look at me. 'If you watch it and you're Indigo, the Screamer demon comes to you. Everyone in my group wanted a go. I sort of told them I could get a copy.'

'So you lied to me,' I said, quietly. 'Want. Take. Get. Is that how you work now?'

She looked away again. 'I couldn't tell you; you'd say it was too dangerous. But I have to try and speak to it.'

'Speak to the demon?' She was driving me mad, but I kept my voice down. Some of the beautiful people on the sun loungers were giving us sidelong glances and listening in.

'You can't speak to that thing!' I said. 'It's a hoax, or clever special effects. It's not real.' But her face came alight again.

'No! I've heard about it,' she said. 'If you can overcome your fear, it'll give you access to something amazing. Something that will expand your mind. Imagine that, Freedom!' Her eyes glowed.

I'd thought it was about thrill-seeking. Her and her friends in the group finding ways to scare themselves silly. But now I was beginning to suspect something else.

'Expand your mind? Like drugs?'

'No.' But she wasn't looking at me.

'So, did anything happen when you watched it? Did the Screamer demon come out of the screen and get you?'

Java's eyes looked everywhere but at me. 'Nope.'

She was lying, but I didn't have time to ask her why, because Jamie Champion found us.

'Java, I got you some pizza. Where have you been?' he said, standing in my way, like he was the alpha male round here. 'Are you OK?'

Jeez. Of course she was OK, he could see that. But it didn't stop him giving me a dirty look.

'You're the pizza boy, aren't you?' he said, looking me up and down. 'Why are you still here?'

Like he owned the world just because he had loads of money.

'None of your business,' I said.

That didn't go down well. 'Java, do you want me to get your father?' he said.

Panic came into Java's eyes. 'No! Just leave it, Jamie, OK?'

'So, did you open the Screamer email?' I asked him. 'Or did you let Java take the risk?'

His face went red. Which, I suppose, answered my question.

'I think you should leave,' he said, giving me a push.

He'd got himself a bit of an audience now. A few of the sunbathers were sitting up and having a good old look at us. So he gave me another push. Except he didn't realize he was pushing a Smith. We might look skinny, but we have bones made of iron to give us ballast. I never even budged a millimetre.

'Sorry? Was that a Korean fighting move?' I said, all innocence. 'Should I have taken a fall?'

'Stop it,' said Java, scowling.

We both ignored her.

'No, that was a push,' said Jamie. 'But this is Kwan Sool ...'

He hooked my foot and then did an open hand strike. Boy, he was quick. So quick that no onlooker would have noticed. I stumbled backwards and ended up crouching, unhurt except for my pride.

He looked down at me.

'People like you need to learn some manners.'

I sprang up and took a hold of his stupid shirt. And pushed him in the pool.

'Very clever!' said Java angrily. 'Just leave it, can't you!'

I watched Jamie surface and start spluttering. 'Your friends shouldn't judge people so hastily.'

'You're as bad,' she said, her voice shaking with anger. 'You look down on anyone who isn't a gypsy. I think you'd better go, Freedom.'

The guests sat up on their sun loungers and adjusted their sunglasses as though they couldn't believe what they were seeing.

'Shush!' I said, but it was too late. She shouldn't have said that so loud. Or maybe she meant her daddy to hear.

In any case, Mr Sparrow spun round when he heard my name, as if he was on the alert for the sound of it, however far away it might be. Like heat-seeking missiles his eyes found me straight away. I heard him say 'that gypsy boy again', but he said it like you'd say 'trash' or something.

His face went an even darker red, and the expression chiselled on it was one of hatred. It was a look that said he'd really like to take a shotgun and let me have both barrels.

Jamie was struggling out of the pool, looking furious. A few of the other guests seemed to have decided I wasn't wanted, too. They began to come towards me with mean looks on their faces.

So what could I do? Give a dog a bad name and all that. I waited till they reached me and then I pushed them in the pool as well. Afterwards I went over and saluted Java, who was standing with her arms folded, tapping her foot, her eyes blazing with anger.

'Me and you. We're finished,' I said.

She glared at me. 'Fine.'

Then I left them in peace before they called the police. I knew what I was going to do now. I had a plan. I was going to sort this Screamer business out once and for all. But in my own way.

I'd had enough of working for the cops. Gypsies and cops didn't mix. And nor did girls like Java and boys like me. But we'd been to the brink of death together and she helped me get out of a very tight spot, so I owed her.

I'd investigate the Screamer email in my own way, and make sure she was safe. Then we'd go our separate ways.

I unhitched Fury, leaped on his back, spurred him into a gallop, and went back to the only life I wanted. Costalot. My sister's little plot of land and the trailers.

But there was no peace even there.

Chapter Nine

'**H**eavens above, boy, if you run out on something, don't just head for home!' said Wren, disgusted. 'It's the first place we look. You wouldn't believe the number of murderers we find having tea at their mum's.' He was sitting on a deck chair by a crackling campfire, chatting to Crystal. I ignored him and handed Fury's halter rope over to Joe.

'That's a good horse, Joe,' I said to my brother-in-law. 'I've walked him the last mile, so he's nice and cool.'

Joe was more friendly with me now I didn't live with them any more. Me and my daddy had argued badly a while ago, and we'd had a fight. It's the Hercules gene. My daddy was a good fighter but he hadn't got the mutant gene like me. If we'd carried on with the fight I would've bested him. So I left and went travelling with my big sister Crystal and her family to make sure we didn't fight any more.

I looked around Costalot and breathed deeply. This was better. This was the life I knew. There were little kids and ponies everywhere. Since they'd moved on to the site, the girls'd even started at school. Usually we're too free-range for classrooms and it takes superglue to make us stick to a desk and chair. Maybe the girls would have it easier.

They were playing with the miniature ponies, tiny Falabellas that Joe bred, combing their manes and tying ribbons in them, like real-life My Little Ponies. Two of the kids came over and fixed themselves to my legs.

'Fwed! We missed ya!' This was Whitney Jade, my niece.

The other was Ant. If he wasn't hanging round Phoenix HQ, he liked to scamper across the fields and stay with Crystal and the girls. Maybe he'd got a lift with Wren.

'I didn't tell no one,' he whispered. 'Giantman guessed you'd come here, boss.'

'Whitney Jade, fetch me your tom tooter!' I said.

They ran off. I sat down beside Crystal. She was polishing her Waterford glassware out in the weak sunshine. I kept away from Wren, who was warming his cowboy boots by the fire. I figured that if I didn't acknowledge him, it'd encourage him to leave me alone and go back to Phoenix.

It was late afternoon and the heat had gone out of the day. You could tell autumn was coming. And when the weather shifted there was nothing Joe liked more than a yog, as we called it. He'd set an iron hook over it, with a pot hanging from the hook. The pot was steaming and bubbling. It smelt like stew, so he must've been out rabbiting.

I was home.

I slumped down on a deckchair. 'I've left Phoenix, Crys, I'm coming back here.'

Wren lit a cigar and smiled to himself. He probably thought I was joking. But I'd have liked to see him try and get me to go back.

Crystal looked at me and frowned.

'Daddy's coming down tomorrow with some new horses.'

I shrugged. 'I'll make myself scarce.'

'He wants to talk to you.'

'I'm busy. I'll sort it later.'

Whitney Jade came back lugging the new laptop I'd got for them. If travellers didn't start getting to grips with computers, they were going to get left behind. Luckily we're very quick at learning new things. We've had to be.

I flipped it open, powered it up and sat my mobile next to it. Java hadn't just given me heartache, she'd given me computer skills as well.

When Wren glanced over and saw what I'd got up on the screen, he sat up. 'So you did send the Screamer email to yourself?'

'Yeh.' Let him think that. It would keep Java well out of the picture.

'What the hell do you think you're doing, boy?' he growled, as he watched me tapping the keys. 'We've just had another report in. Two more kids have disappeared.'

'I've got a debt to pay,' I said, not looking at him. 'Whitney, Ant, go away and play.'

They both went back to fighting over a quad bike.

'Why're you doing this?' said Wren.

'Classified.'

'It won't work on you,' he drawled. 'You're not Indigo.'

I took something out of my pocket.

'What the—?' he said, sitting up.

'It will now,' I said. I put on the modified Black Fly shades I'd 'borrowed' from his desk as I'd run from his office.

'You're quick.'

I shrugged. 'Isn't that what you all think back there anyway? Hide everything, Freedom's about, he'll steal it?'

'No.'

'Snow doesn't trust me.'

'Snow doesn't trust anyone.'

'Nobody gives me any respect. I just get pushed around and treated like a kid.'

Wren raised an eyebrow. 'You have to earn respect in Phoenix.'

'I'm not going back, Wren. I feel like an alien living in a building, going to school; I don't understand the rules.'

'You were doing fine.'

'Why all the maths and English lessons?'

Wren groaned, as if I was stupid. 'Because why teach survival to a born survivor? But you need discipline, you're too quick off the mark, and it might get you – or someone else – into trouble before long.'

He didn't know it, but it had already. I should never have forwarded that email to Java. Wren was right. I hadn't thought it through. I'd been told not to go near it. I'd been warned away. But I'd still sent it to her, without finding out why it was classified as dangerous.

'So seeing if you can sit through a maths lesson is hardly asking too much,' finished Wren.

But he was never going to change my mind. I clicked a couple of times and the demon screamed, and once again my life changed direction.

So did my chair. It went over backwards.

Crystal dropped the Waterford vase and said, 'For Christ's sake, Fred, what the——?' and Joe shot round the trailer trying to hold on to Fury, who was skittering all over the place, his soup-plate hooves churning the ground.

I sat up. 'That was different.'

Wren put down the bitten remains of his cigar. 'Fascinating. You activated something pretty massive there.' He held out a hand to help me up. I ignored it. 'You OK, boy?'

I shrugged. 'I suppose so.' I felt as though my brain had been in a hurricane. 'I thought I saw the Screamer come out of the screen and leap at me.'

Wren lit another of his foul little cigars. 'Certain frequency waves can produce hallucinogenic images. It's what's behind a lot of the hauntings and poltergeists we investigate.'

He stood up and gave Crystal a wink that made her eyes sparkle and made Joe give him a dirty look. 'Thanks for your hospitality, but I'm thinking I'd better get your brother back to base.'

I couldn't believe the bloke. He never listened to a word I said. It was like he owned me.

'I'm not coming, Wren. I told you, I've quit,' I said. 'And don't even think about saying I've signed the Official Secrets Act. I don't care. I'll just go away, and you can ask as many travellers as you want; no one will ever tell you where I am.'

Wren squinted down at me. 'After that little stunt you've

just pulled, you're in danger, Freedom. I want to monitor you and see what happens.'

'You told me this wasn't my case. Nothing is my case, it seems. So I've got myself my own mission, and I don't need your protection.'

'You could be helping to save some of the kids who've disappeared,' he said.

'I'm not interested.'

Wren shrugged. 'Well, we wouldn't want you with that attitude,' he said. He gave Crystal another wink and strolled off without a backward glance as the sun sank behind Phoenix House in the distance.

Now all I had to do was wait and see if the Screamer would come to me in the night.

Chapter Ten

'What you looking at?' said Ant.

'Nothing,' I said. 'Now get to sleep.'

I was staring out of the trailer window. High up I could see the lights of a plane going over. I thought maybe it was Java on her way to Malta, flying out of my life. I'd thought I'd lost her once before, then we managed to meet up again. But this time it was over between us.

Moonlight shone down on the other trailers, the horsebox and the cars. A couple of Joe's miniature Falabellas grazed around the trailers, their outlines no bigger than those of Labrador dogs. I scanned the horizon. Nothing was moving anywhere. In the distance the bulk of Phoenix House rose black against the moonlit sky.

Ant was on the floor in a nest of blankets. For most of his young life he'd slept under the boxing ring at the fight club in a nest of old clothes. Since then the carers at his foster homes kept trying to get him into jimjams and a proper bed, but it never worked. His favourite place was a nest beside my bed.

We'd had a feast earlier, a takeaway Thai red curry, sticky rice and a tub of Häagen-Dazs Mint Choc Chip. Now he was nodding off to sleep, smelling of curry and spearmint. I'd tried to make him sleep in one of the other trailers for the night, but he kept coming back here. I'd come to the conclusion that he was probably safer by my side than roaming round Costalot when there might be an intruder hanging around.

Of course I'd set up traps. There were trip wires and string everywhere. If Crystal sleepwalked her way into my trailer, she'd make enough noise to wake the dead.

I was trying to stay awake. If something was coming to get me, then I wanted to see it before it saw me.

Midnight came and went.

What did I think was going to happen? To tell the truth, I didn't know, but if the Screamer was a man, then I'd deal with him.

I lay on my bunk, squeezing my muscles, doing bicep curls, anything to keep moving so they wouldn't stiffen up. Nothing was going to stop me bursting into action at the sight of an intruder, real or demonic.

An owl hooted in the distance, toowit, and then another answered, closer, toowoo. I sat up to look out of the window at them. I like owls; they're stealth birds. But I was too tired. My eyelids drooped. Maybe I slept.

'Let me in,' hissed a small voice in my ear. My eyes snapped open. 'I won't hurt you.' Which vexed me at first, but I told myself it was probably only Joe, so I stepped over my booby traps and unlatched the trailer door.

My reptile brain was screaming, Don't do it, Fred! sounding a red alert, but I told it to shut up.

I got back into bed and went back to sleep.

'Wake up,' said a voice.

I opened my eyes. The clock by my side said two-thirty. It was freezing. I watched my breath cloud in front of my face. Sweet mercy, it shouldn't have been that cold. I tried to get out of bed to fetch myself another quilt.

That's when I found out I couldn't move.

Blind panic swept over me. I was paralysed. Not a finger, not a toe, not an eyebrow would move. I tried to shout out, warn Ant, but my throat was frozen. My breath was coming in short wheezes, like I was suffocating. Then I felt the hairs start to stand up on the back of my neck.

Something was in the trailer.

I could feel its presence. And it was getting nearer.

I swear, at that moment I believed in ghosts and demons and monsters. Fear swamped my brain. I couldn't think straight. I couldn't think at all. I was like one of those bunnies that get themselves in the middle of the road and freeze when a car comes towards them, and then bang!

The door to the bedroom creaked.

Did I say that the dead don't concern themselves with the living? I was wrong. Hadn't I heard old Hercules, my great-great-great-granddaddy, talking to me when I was in peril before? Hadn't Java said she could speak to her mammy who died when she was a baby?

Now the undead were in my trailer.

'Most of what you know about the world is a lie,' Wren

had told me when I joined Phoenix.

The door creaked open a little more. A thin hand covered in scales, with a gold signet ring as big as a knuckle-duster, slid into view. The ring was fashioned like a coiled snake. Jeez, maybe I was dreaming it. I prayed I was. I clenched my neck muscles and tried to move my head. Nothing!

I tested my leg muscles, then my arms. Nothing moved. Not even a fingertip. From outside, Fury began neighing and clattering about. Maybe he'd sensed the intruder. I swivelled my eyes back to the door.

The Screamer was there!

Hell!

It glided forward.

No, no, no, stay there, I screamed. But no sound came out. Then, out of nowhere, it came to me to say the Lord's Prayer in gypsy, how Great-granny Kate used to say it, how old Hercules would have said it. Even if I couldn't say it out loud, it might help.

'Meery dearie Dad, sauvo jivves drey the tem oprey,

Be sharrafo teero nav, te awel teero tem—'

The Screamer began to raise its head as it came towards me, hands held out before it, gliding. I prayed some more, but still it came towards me. Then it looked up, its hood falling back, and there was the face I'd seen on the screen, the same needle-sharp fangs, the same mad eyes.

Meery dearie Dad! I shouted in my mind, but there was nothing I could do. Even the Hercules gene couldn't save me now.

Down below, by my side, Ant muttered, 'Gerroff, boss!'

Just that. But a tiny glimmer of hope squeezed through the panic that was flooding my mind.

I held my breath and listened. Ant whimpered again, and moved in his sleep as though something had kicked him. 'Gerroff!' he muttered again. And, dear God, I knew! I knew the truth.

'Meery dearie Dad!' I said again, and this time the smallest whisper of a sound came out of my mouth.

Because I'd broken the spell. And it wasn't magic, it wasn't supernatural. It was man-made trickery.

The Screamer's foot had touched Ant and he'd moved in his sleep! This was no demon, this was a man, a man wearing a robe, not an entity from another dimension.

He hadn't got the power to paralyse me. I reckon there'd been some sort of hidden message in the email. A hypnotic suggestion that bypassed my ears and went deep into my brain, telling my muscles to lock up at a given signal.

All I had to do was convince my mind that I was in control again.

'Meery dearie Dad!' I said again, louder this time.

And the Screamer hissed. He'd heard, and he didn't like it. I gave him a closer look. Those weren't fangs, they were teeth filed to points, and the scales on his skin were tattoos. This was a man.

And if he was mortal, I could beat him.

The little finger on my left hand twitched. The Screamer noticed. He hissed again, his sharp filed teeth glinting, and for a split second our eyes met.

'You are not Indigo, you are impostor!' he spat.

I don't know how, but he knew I wasn't like other kids who had disappeared. But he was too slow.

'Gotcha!' I said and broke the paralysis.

I was out of bed and leaping for him before I could even draw breath.

But he was fast, too. In one lightning movement he'd grabbed Ant's foot, swung the boy towards him and leaped through the trailer door. I was alone.

Chapter Eleven

Outside, the moon lit Costalot as though everything was outlined in silver wire. Nothing moved except a patch of shadow: the Screamer fleeing with Ant over his shoulder. And something was very wrong there, because by now Ant should've been screaming loud enough to wake the whole site. Two steps and I was right behind him and reaching out. My fists itched. No one was going to take Ant hostage. My fingers touched his robe and I grabbed on to it, but he was too quick.

He danced out of my grasp, put Ant on the ground and then began to spin towards me, like he was a deadly ballet dancer or something. I was so stunned I forgot to get out of his way. Three stripes of blood appeared across my cheek, the front of my T-shirt fell open and his teeth snapped close to my ear. Then he spun away a few metres and laughed.

'So you like to fight fancy, do you?' I said, softly. 'Fine by me.'

I moved like lightning and hit him. He fell back. My old

boxing coach would've been proud. Until the Screamer whirled back towards me and three more slashes appeared across my arms. This time I'd caught a glimpse of his hands. He'd got dagger-sharp steel claws embedded in his fingertips. And, going by the state of my T-shirt, the swinging ends of his rope belt were fitted with razor blades as well.

'OK, now you've made me cross,' I said.

It was like no fight I'd ever had in the past. I could have been sparring with smoke, whirling smoke with hidden claws. He spun towards me again and I tried to fend him off, but his steel claws slashed my arms and the razor blades sliced across my chest.

One of his spins sent me crashing to the ground. I rolled, and ended up near Ant. The little boy never moved. He was lying crumpled on the ground, his eyes closed. The Screamer had done something to him, I hadn't the time to think what, but it made me see red. I don't go looking for fights, though if anyone insists on one, or wants to do me down, I'll oblige.

But you don't take little kids hostage, and you don't do things to them that knock them out cold.

I got up, my heart like stone. I let him spin towards me. I let him think I was going to stand still or cower back out of his way. He'd be ready for that; it was what he'd expect. So instead, when he was a step away and his hand was already beginning to swing round, I stepped forward into his face and attacked him instead.

He wasn't ready for that. His weapons were his feet, for kicking, and his hands, for chopping. Which is OK if your opponent keeps his distance. I'd moved too close and my weapons were my elbows and my head. And he had no defence.

Up close I struck like lightning. A headbutt to his chin, then an elbow to his ribs. He staggered for a second, and came back. But I'd made sure I was off to one side, so I could deflect his slashing claws and flying razor blades. Then I struck again, an elbow to the side of his head.

That made him back off, but only to come back even faster. So I stepped towards him again, and this time he ricocheted off my foot as I aimed at his knee. The force of my kick spun him round like a top, then he tripped and fell close to Ant.

'Had enough yet, fella?' I said, softly, hoping Joe and Crystal hadn't heard. We were right near their trailer. 'Try screaming now and see where it gets you.'

But he wasn't there. And nor was Ant.

'Nice try,' I said, creeping forward.

I think he was hoping I'd get the holy horrors and believe he'd disappeared into another dimension with the little boy. But he hadn't fooled me this time.

I reckoned he'd rolled, grabbed Ant under cover of the darkness and slid under the trailer. Which meant he was probably going to appear on the other side. I glued myself to the side of the trailer, then slid round towards the back.

Three small shapes trotted out of my way, then carried on grazing a moment later. The little Falabellas didn't look spooked, which worried me. Usually even a butterfly flying by could send them into mini bouts of rearing and bucking.

So maybe I'd been wrong and the Screamer hadn't come

out this side. Maybe he was quicker than I gave him credit for. But he wasn't fast enough to have got clear of Costalot, which meant he was here somewhere.

Over by Joe's horsebox, Fury whinnied.

One baby step at a time I made my way over, then faded into the shadows around the horsebox. And, bingo, I'd got him. He was crouched behind it, his robe spread around him and his scrawny white hand across Ant's mouth.

'Not so supernatural now, are you?' I said, dancing over to him with a view to grabbing Ant. Once the little fella was alright I could go all out to beat the Screamer. But I don't think fate liked me that night, because the next minute he came racing towards me and roared in my face, and something that felt like a flame burned my skin, as if he'd turned into a dragon or something.

After that I felt his fist hit my cheek, and I went flying back across the grass. And that shouldn't have happened, because I know about punching and I know how hard a punch should be, and that was ten times the norm. It was harder than mine, and I'm a freak, a throwback.

He was flesh and blood. He wasn't supernatural. It must have been a fluke. So in a second I was up and racing back to him. He'd picked the fight, not me, and now I was going to be the one to finish it.

He hadn't gone far. I don't think he'd expected anyone to get up after that punch. But he didn't know I had a chin as hard as Desperate Dan's.

He was hiding near the hedge, as though he was getting his breath back. He was just squatting there, hissing through his pointed teeth and holding on to Ant, who, thank God, had his eyes open now. The Screamer didn't expect me, and he didn't hear me either, because he was muttering quietly to himself.

'No, this is not good! Must escape. Nothing matters but the safety of Draconis, only Draconis, always Draconis . . .'

In the moonlight his face looked white and older. Much older than it had been a few minutes ago. It rang a bell in my brain. So did the fact that he was drinking something from a small silver flask, like the ones men keep in their back pockets and fill up with whisky on cold days. I don't think his was full of booze, though. It smelt more like chocolate milk.

'Fred! He's burning me, he's hot!' squealed Ant.

The Screamer glanced down and said, 'Sleep!' and Ant sagged again in his arms. Then he glared up at me. 'Stay back, gypsy, unless you want another blast of Dragon Fire,' he hissed.

'Neat trick,' I said, carrying on towards him. I was banking on the fact that I might know how he'd thrown that mammoth punch. It was something I'd heard whispered about in fighting circles, but never believed.

'You're not looking so good now,' I told him. He cringed back. 'You look like you've just run out of energy.'

There was another waft of chocolate milk as he swigged from the flask again. Then he scurried back along the hedge, out of my way.

'It was a good punch. Do it again,' I said, approaching him.

He scuttled back again, dragging Ant. 'Stay back,' he hissed. 'Next time I'll scorch your face off.'

'OK, do it,' I said, following him. I held my hands out wide. 'Go on, then. Let me feel the Dragon Fire again.'

The Screamer hissed, his forked tongue flickering.

'You can't, can you?' I jeered, hoping that it was true, and I hadn't made a mistake. 'You've got no energy left. You're empty.'

See, we're all designed to have our energy on drip-feed, a little bit at a time. We don't burn, we smoulder. But I reckon he'd managed to make all the energy stored in his cells burn at once. That's why he'd got really hot, and when he'd breathed out ready to punch me, his breath was as hot as a dragon's flame. Now all I had to figure out was how he managed to download all his energy in one go. That was a trick I'd have liked to know myself.

'Try it again, creep,' I said, but I'd miscalculated. The chocolate milk had done its work faster than I thought, and all I saw was his fist coming towards me. I felt his hot breath in my face, and then I was rolling again.

'If you want to see the child again, keep back!' he hissed.

When I picked myself up a moment later, he was gone.

In front of me his silhouette fled down the avenue of trees near Costalot's entrance, the moonlight flickering over him as he ran, Ant struggling under his arm. He went straight over Joe's Range Rover and then leaped the gate on to the road. I was right behind him. He was a free-runner, an acrobat, amazingly good. But human.

And he knew how to use all his energy in one go. Dragon power. I wanted it.

We fled down the road towards Phoenix House like bats

out of hell. Until a motor glided silently up beside me. A black BMW.

'Get in,' said Wren, and then gunned it down the road.

Chapter Twelve

'What the hell is it?'

'Human, believe it or not,' I said, hanging on to the dashboard as Wren put his foot down. 'But he gave me the screaming habdabs when he appeared. He got into my mind somehow. He asked me to let him in and I did. I somehow made myself think it was Joe calling out. When he appeared I couldn't move. That's why the kid with the puffer never moved.'

'Sounds like there were subliminal commands in the email attachment.'

I nodded. 'That's what I thought. But it felt real at the time.'

'Perfect abduction scenario. Paralysed victim. And if it goes wrong, who's going to believe that the kid nearly got taken by a demon?' Wren looked over at me. 'What's up with your jaw?'

I was wiggling my chin trying to get my top teeth and bottom teeth to fit together properly again and stop clicking. 'He's got a punch like a sledgehammer. He called it

Dragon Fire, but it left him all over the place, and drinking chocolate milk-shake. I think he can use all his energy in one go. He was burning up.'

Wren's eyes widened and he whistled. 'Total cell-burn? I've heard of it. It takes a lot of training, a few of the men on our combat team can do it to a degree.' He peered down the dark road. 'So he's skilled as well as hideous.'

We were closing on the figure. But as we screeched up to him, and Wren stood on the brakes, with me hanging off the door ready to leap out, the Screamer jinked to the right and went up and over the four-metre electrified fence surrounding Phoenix House as easily as if it was a garden gate.

Wren thumped the steering wheel. 'Yay! We've got him now. There's not a blade of grass that's not covered by CCTV cameras.'

I swung myself back into the motor. 'You've not got a camera on the Pegasus horse in the corridor,' I said.

Wren thumped the wheel again. 'Damn! So *that's* where you were.' Then he got on his mobile. 'Security, we've got an intruder. Just gone over the east fence. I want him tracked. Patch me through to the main cameras. But leave the capture to us. He's got a hostage.'

The video screen on the dashboard flickered on, and then we were scanning the grounds. 'There he is!' I shouted. 'He's up by the house.'

Gates opened before us and we roared into the Phoenix grounds.

'OK, we've got him,' said Wren, his head out of the

window as he craned to see the Screamer. 'Aw, for heaven's sake, he's suicidal! He's going up the side of the house. Who the hell is he, Spider-Man?'

'I'll get him,' I said, and leaped out of the motor as Wren screeched on to the gravel car park in front of the mansion.

Picked out in the moonlight a robed figure, with another over his shoulder, bounded up the ivy and on to the roof as though gravity meant nothing to him. That was OK by me; gravity didn't bother me much, either.

'He's on the right front tower.'

Phoenix House had a round tower at each corner, like something out of a fairytale, except that these towers were bristling with gargoyles. The mad earl had loved gargoyles.

I went up the ivy using my hands and feet, like a chimp going up a jungle tree. I got over the roof turret by getting a handhold on the outstretched claws of a stone serpent that snaked a metre out from the turret wall, and then putting my foot in its gaping jaws. The rest of the flat roof of the mansion was filled with more stone monsters. But the one monster I wanted to find was gone.

'Can you see him?' I shouted.

A couple of cops bounded out of the door over by the chimney stacks. One of them was Gabriel, who I knew from my first mission. 'He hasn't come this way!' he shouted.

I spun on my heel, surveying the roof. It was too dark to see properly, but I was using eagle vision and making the most of the fitful moonlight. Eagles don't focus on their prey. They lock on to the whole area, so that wherever the mouse runs they'll still be able to fly down and casually pick it up.

That's what I was doing: letting the whole of the roof into my sight, so I'd pick up any movement, any fleeting shadow.

But there was nothing. The pale stone of the gargoyles stood out against the black sky. Heat rose from the tiles beneath my feet. Nothing stirred except a couple more cops, one of them Wren, who ran on to the roof.

And a slight breeze, scented with peppermint and curry – Ant! Thank the Lord for Häagen-Dazs and Thai chicken.

He was close by, too. I looked around. There were gargoyles everywhere, all shapes and sizes. In the darkness any one of them could be a crouched human or a stone statue. But stone doesn't budge when you kick it.

I kicked out at every gargoyle within reach, until one moved. Its cloak twitched. I grabbed the Screamer as he tried to leap away. Ant's limp body was lying close by.

'I've got them both,' I shouted, and the cops began haring towards me across the roof. 'And we need a medic!"

But the Screamer wasn't in the mood to wait and be caught. He pulled away from me and began going through his fancy fight moves.

Like I was going to fall for that again.

He came out of the dark, the razor blades flashing in the moonbeams. But I held my ground. I'd got the measure of him now.

Here's the rule. The showier you fight, the more someone's going to dodge under your guard whilst you're getting into a karate stance or deciding to whirl about, and then they'll knock you for six.

Spinning about can be lethal when you're armed with

pointed teeth and nails like steel talons and a belt tipped with flying razor blades, but you can still be tripped easily.

I'd had my fill of those claws and blades. As he came at me I moved at top speed, and caught him with an oblique kick to his shin, knocking him to one side. He rebounded into the statue of a centaur, a half-man, half-horse with a bow and arrow. He hit the edge of the arrow, squealed and spun away holding his side.

That was my chance. I grabbed him and got an arm lock on him, but I hadn't got a good hold. Our eyes met in the moonlight, then he pulled out of my grasp and leaped away. I was a nanosecond behind him as he raced for the edge of the tower, tripping and leaping over gargoyles and air shafts.

'Princess Lato, Dragon Goddess of the world, save me! Smite the unbelievers!' he shouted as he sprinted for the edge.

Then, with a smile that showed his needle-like teeth, he leaped for the turret wall and dropped, grabbing out for the ivy to stop himself plummeting all the way.

But he only dropped a metre or so. I had a hold on his hood, and before he even knew what was going on I had heaved him back up and hooked the hood on to the stone serpent's iron-clad claw.

'There you go – a dragon has saved you!'

He flailed and hissed and swore and howled, then suddenly clasped his hands together as though to say the Lord's Prayer. I knew why he'd stopped flailing around.

'Keep praying, or you're going to drop right out of your robe, unless you can fly.'

Wren came up behind me, out of breath. He'd have to quit

those cigars.

'Not good news, Wren,' I said, without taking my eyes away from the Screamer.

'What?' he wheezed.

'If he falls, he's going to land on your motor.'

Behind him, Gabriel was tending to Ant.

'He's awake,' he shouted.

The little boy was gazing around. He must have thought the old days were back, the days when he lived in the fight.

'You OK, kid?' I shouted over.

Ant blinked at me. 'The baddie said "Sleep" and I did!'

We turned and looked at the Screamer turning and twisting in the breeze, hissing and snarling.

'Well, let's ask the baddie a few questions, shall we?' I said. And sneezed.

Chapter Thirteen

'Hang on to this, will you?' said Wren. He handed me a shotgun.

'I don't mess with guns,' I said, trying to hand it back to him and wipe my eyes with my free hand at the same time.

He ignored my protest. 'Keep it; you'll need to use it in a minute or two.' He glanced at me. 'And that's an order.'

I doubted it. I was allergic to guns, and already my eyes were itching and my nose twitching like a bunny's. I'd done target practice down at the range behind Phoenix House, like all the other recruits. But I was the only one wearing swimming goggles and a clip on my nose.

'So, let's have a word with Mr Creepy,' said Wren.

The moonlight shone down on the Screamer as he hung from the claw of the stone serpent, his feet dangling above the three-storey drop. His red eyes were fixed on us.

'Princess Lato, strike down these puny mortals!' he screamed.

'Less of the puny,' said Wren, striking a match on the sole of his huge cowboy boot.

Under the cover of the parapet wall, I broke the shotgun open at the hinge. It was loaded with two cartridges, but they looked unusual. I tipped one out, but Wren nudged me.

'Who's this Princess Lato when she's at home?' he muttered.

'I don't know, but I'm getting fed up of hearing about her,' I said. I glanced at the stone claw holding the Screamer up. 'I'd stop all the cursing and answer our questions,' I said to him. 'Your hood is starting to rip.'

Wren perched himself on the parapet, smoke trailing from his cigar. 'So how about telling us who you are?'

The Screamer glared at us. 'I'm telling you nothing!'

There was a terrible ripping sound, and he dropped lower. His hood couldn't stand the strain. All that was holding him up now was a little strip of brown cloth. He panicked, which wasn't a good idea.

'Pull me in, you heathens, or my masters will—'

Wren unhooked a small police baton from his belt and flicked it out to its full length. Then he prodded the dangling figure, making him sway. The Screamer hissed in anger and fear.

'I'd start talking right this minute if I were you, or I might help that bit of material to rip all the way across!' urged Wren. 'Let's start with your name.'

'Never!'

A breeze twisted the Screamer around, and we all heard the cloak tear a bit more. He glanced down at the ground far below, and a whimper escaped from between his sharpened teeth. His forked tongue licked out nervously, and he shot us a look of hatred.

'I am Kanashibari Alexander Xavier Zane Xuereb Martinov Estrella Rufus Volchek Brill Bardias—'

'Enough. I think we get the idea,' interrupted Wren. 'OK, so now tell me, what the hell is going on with the email and the kids?'

The Screamer's tongue flicked out. 'I will tell you nothing more. I don't care if I die!'

'OK,' said Wren, with another grim smile. He poked his baton at the scrap of fabric holding the Screamer up. 'Don't let us keep you hanging around. I'll unhook you.'

'No! Wait, damn you!' The Screamer pushed the stick away, his face becoming shiny with sweat. 'Let me think about this!'

'I'd do as he says,' I said. Wren was beginning to scare even me. If the man fell, he'd be killed instantly. I didn't have much sympathy for him, but Wren handing me a gun had unnerved me. I'd never seen this side of him before.

The Screamer must have felt the same way, because his eyes grew round with fear and a dribble of spit escaped his fangs.

'You'll be sorry!' he said. 'I am the demon servant, come to strike fear and—'

'You're a bloke with your teeth filed,' I said, to shut him up. 'You're as human as I am.'

'I am otherkin!' he yelped.

'Skin tattoos, sharpened teeth, implanted fangs, surgically modified tongue, implanted claws. Why?' said Wren. 'Who are you working for? Who wants you to look like this?'

'You think I'd betray them? I would rather die!'

He didn't learn very quickly.

'OK,' said Wren. 'That can be arranged.' And he leaned out and jabbed with the baton again. There was another tearing sound as the cloth ripped all the way through. Like lightning, the Screamer grabbed the stone serpent's foot with his steel claws, and held on for dear life.

'Pull me in!'

'First I want to hear why you go round stealing children,' said Wren, leaning over as though he was going to rap the creep's knuckles.

The man's eyes flicked from left to right as he tried to think of an excuse. 'It's my own idea,' he spat out at last. 'I'm a pervert!'

'Nope, don't buy that,' said Wren. 'That email is an impressive piece of subliminal messaging. You didn't invent this on your own; it's bigger than that. So try again.' He held the stick over the man's whitening knuckles as he dangled pathetically from the stone gargoyle.

The sleeves of his robe had fallen back, leaving his skinny arms exposed. The scaly tattoos carried on all the way up, and I wondered whether his whole body had got the lizard treatment. On his left wrist he had a gold wristband. It coiled tightly round his arm, and was snake-shaped like his ring. Its tail was set with emeralds, and its eyes were rubies.

'Why are you abducting Indigos?' Wren demanded, then poked him with the stick. 'Hurry up – you've got strong hands and steel talons, but at some point you're going to let go. And the ground is still a long way down.'

The Screamer glanced down. That little movement was enough to start his claws slipping on the mossy stone, with a horrible noise, like fingernails down a blackboard. He gave a cry of distress, then managed to claw one hand back up.

'They have a special talent that we need,' he yelped, kicking his leg out desperately to try and get a toehold on the ivy covering the brickwork, so he could give his hands a rest.

'Is it just the email you use?' said Wren.

'Pull me in, damn you!' His foot kept missing the wall by a few centimetres.

Wren shook his head slowly. 'When you've told me everything.'

'Email's best,' he hissed, squeezing the words out between frantic clutches at the stonework. ''S only heard by the right ones!' His voice became stronger again as his left hand found a better grip. 'It's like a virus. It can't be stopped. It's everywhere! In homes, in schools!' His eyes burned with an unholy glee.

'See, Wren, I knew school wasn't good for kids,' I muttered.

I sneaked a look at the shotgun cartridge in my hand. It was longer and heavier than usual, and on one side was written: *Net Pro. Live Capture. Mark 2.* I slotted it back in.

'So how does the hidden message work?' said Wren. 'I'd hurry up if I were you: your fingers look like they're going to go dead any second now.'

'Go rot in hell!' The Screamer's face was contorted with fury. His body swung towards us, and I heard his foot strike the wall again. 'The email's got secret commands. The Indigos contact us. But they don't remember.'

Wren rapped his knuckles. I put my hand on the shotgun's trigger. 'Keep talking, creep. I ain't heard enough yet.'

The Screamer's breath was coming in painful gasps now. 'We – find out address – later I come round . . .' He stopped and tried to hitch his claws higher up the stonework. I think he was going to curse us again, but one look at Wren's face froze the words on his lips.

'Carry on talking . . . or die, it's your choice,' said Wren, in an ominously quiet voice.

A shiver ran down my spine. Up on the roof the darkness was falling away, and a rosy light was shining from the east. It lit Wren's face like he was an avenging angel. Or maybe a demon.

'I am the collector. I take them away with me!'

I breathed a sigh of relief. He hadn't taken Java, so it couldn't have worked on her. Her dad's security system may have stopped him getting in.

His nails screeched on the stone again. 'Damn you all!' He shot us a fleeting look of defiance. 'You're too late, anyway! We've got enough!'

'Yeh, yeh, yeh, whatever,' said Wren, grimly. 'And now for the million-dollar question. Who are you working for?'

'Not telling!'

That's when I heard his foot hit the wall again. And this time he found a toehold in the ivy – just enough to give him a lift and take the pressure off his hands and arms. A look of triumph flashed across his face as he let go with his right hand and clasped the snake wristband. A terrible glee came into his eyes, his cheeks flushed red.

'Aw, no, Wren, he's going—'

I didn't have time to finish. He did an impossible swing, one-handed, pulling himself up until he was squatting on the stone serpent like an evil grinning imp.

Wren took a step back. 'Whoa! What the hell—?'

'Dragon Fire!' I said. I got my finger on the trigger again.

The Screamer laughed in our faces. His breath was like fire. Any second now he was going to leap over our heads and be off across the roof. He thought he was invincible now.

He licked his lips with his forked tongue, and his eyes rolled upwards. 'At dawn when day and night are equal, then we summon the Dragon Goddess!' he intoned. 'Then the world will quake before my masters again!'

'Get ready for him coming our way!' I said to Wren.

The Screamer stood up on the serpent and laughed again. His breath scorched across us. You could see that he was burning energy the way a furnace eats coal.

'I'd love to stay and chat,' he jeered, and sank back on his haunches, ready to spring forward.

'Shoot!' said Wren.

'No!' All I needed was a few more seconds.

'Shoot!'

The Screamer grinned at us. He was coiled like a spring. 'Bye-bye!'

Ten seconds, eleven seconds. I needed more time.

'I know who your masters are!' I shouted. 'I'll tell them you've failed, that you told us everything!'

That made him hesitate. Twenty seconds. 'You know

nothing, gypsy boy!' he taunted. But I saw him grasp the head of the serpent to steady himself. His balance was failing.

'Want to bet?' I shouted. I leaned over the parapet. 'They are called Draconis.'

Score! His mouth dropped open. 'No!' he screamed. 'You can't know that! They will kill me!'

Twenty-five seconds. His foot slipped off the stone and he wobbled. He caught his balance, then tilted to the other side. Yes! He'd burned all his energy. Any second now he'd be as weak as a kitten.

His feet skidded and he fell, catching hold of the stone with his claws. Thirty seconds. There was the tortured screech of metal on stone before his hands began to slip. A look of horror crossed his face.

He fell. And I shot him.

Chapter Fourteen

The gun kicked against my shoulder. A split second later something like a giant spider's web exploded in the air, wrapping the Screamer in its embrace. An almost invisible cord, like fishing line, was still fixed to the gun. As the net tightened the shotgun was dragged forward, but I was ready for it, and braced my feet against the stone parapet and pulled.

'Hang on, kid,' said Wren, and put a hand on the gun as well.

A few seconds later we hauled the cocooned creep over the parapet. He lay on the roof, gasping like a baboon wrapped in a poacher's net.

I sneezed three times, then wiped my streaming eyes. 'You were risking it, Wren,' I said. 'What if I'd missed?'

Wren clapped me on the back. 'I've seen you on the firing range. You don't miss.'

He got a pair of handcuffs out of his pocket and handed them to Gabriel. 'Untangle him and cuff him.' He arched an eyebrow at me. 'Did you really think I'd let him die? We look after our prisoners at Phoenix. But he wouldn't have talked if he thought we were going to go easy on him. He's not the only one who's skilled at illusion.'

Gabriel hoisted the man to his feet.

'Take him away and put him in the dungeons. And make sure he has no access to the outside world or computers.'

'He's half unconscious,' said Gabriel.

'He ran out of energy. Don't give him any sugar and you'll be in for a quiet night,' I said.

Gabriel put the cuffs on him.

'Wait,' I took hold of the gold wristband. I pulled, and it unwound and came away in my hand. 'Can I check it out?'

Wren nodded. 'How did you know the names of his masters?' he asked, as if he'd got something on his mind.

'It was a guess. I heard him mumbling the word "Draconis" when we fought at Costalot. I needed to check I was correct.'

Wren frowned then smacked his forehead. 'Draconis! When you first said it, I had a feeling I'd heard it before. Now I remember. Years ago, we heard rumours about a family called Draconis who worshipped a dragon goddess. They were very rich and powerful. But there's been no news about them for years.'

'Wren, people don't worship dragons these days.'

He laughed. 'I'm telling you, boy, you wouldn't believe what people worship if they think it might bring them power or riches.' He rubbed his eyes. 'But I'm damned if I can see where kidnapping Indigo kids comes into dragon worship.'

Gabriel looked up. 'Black magic?'

Wren nodded slowly. 'Could be. We haven't had any mad, bad magicians for a while. But they don't usually go for hi-tech stuff like emails.'

'Yeh, it's letters written in blood and wearing goat's horns with that lot,' said Gabriel. 'And dancing round bonfires at midnight.'

Wren flicked his mobile open. 'Bigley, I want you to run a check on a family called Draconis. Look in the records and find out why we investigated them last time.'

'Wren,' I said. 'Ask her to find out when the day and night are equal and winter starts.'

'Did you hear that, Bigley?' Wren's phone squawked. He nodded. 'Yeh, of course, the autumn equinox. When is it?' The phone squawked again. 'The twenty-third of September. No wonder he said we'd never have time to stop whatever it is they're planning. But they don't know Phoenix. Two days? That's plenty of time for us.'

Wren's eyes had started to sparkle. He loved a challenge.

He clicked his phone off and looked at the lightening sky. Dawn was breaking. 'It's the twenty-first today. It's cutting it fine, but we can solve this. But for now, let's try and get some kip.' Then he thumped me on the back. 'Good work, boy. Shame you're not part of the team any more.'

I shrugged, and began picking my way across the roof. 'I'll be getting back to Costalot.'

He stared after me. 'Stay here, try and get a few hours of sleep. We'll talk in the morning.'

'No.'

'Well, then, let me show you something before you go. I think you'll find it interesting.'

I followed him reluctantly off the roof, down past the attic rooms where the servants used to live when the mad duke was here, and along the dark upper corridors where Snow had his offices. I'd never been along here before.

He clicked a switch, and wall lights illuminated a row of framed photos stretching all the way down the corridor.

Wren put his fingers to his lips and we crept along. Some of the photos were coloured and modern, some were black and white, and some were so old they were brown and faded and it was like looking at ghosts. But, then again, I suppose they were.

The men and women in the photos all had one thing in common: they looked like fighters. Even the women had cauliflower ears and squashed noses.

'The famous sons and daughters of Phoenix through the ages,' whispered Wren.

Two hundred years Phoenix had been going, Wren had told me, working in secret to uncover the strange and dangerous things that surround us. The secrets that we don't realize are there amongst us, the evil that has been around since the dawn of time.

We walked on down the corridor until we stopped by one old faded photo. I knew who it was straight away.

'Hercules?'

'The very same. Your great-great-great-grandfather.'

The Smith clan had photos of Hercules, but they were all of him in his fighting gear. He would enter the fighting booths with a lion skin over one shoulder, like the Greek hero he was named for. This photo had been taken in a studio, and he was wearing his best suit, but he still had the big handlebar moustache, the thick black hair and the cheeky smile that I'd inherited, and which sometimes got me into trouble – and sometimes got me out of it.

His long hair reminded me of Leon, the cloned brother I'd found in the Bear Pit. Poor Leon had been genetically engineered to fight all his life. It'd ruined his health and he'd ended up a monster. But underneath his matted hair and deformed face, you could still just about see the Smith features that came from Hercules. The last time I saw those features, he'd been standing in the Bear Pit as it collapsed around him. A sad end to a sad life.

I looked at my great-great-great-granddaddy, and he stared back at me. He had his arms folded and his chin up, and I could just make out his battered and scarred knuckles, the souvenirs of countless bare-knuckle fights he'd taken part in at fairs up and down the country. Until one day, Lord alone knows how, he'd been recruited into Phoenix and began using his skills to fight evil in Victorian England.

Wren pointed to a woman in the next photograph. She looked as tough as Hercules. 'That's Delilah Pain, a flyer, expert on the high trapeze, born in the circus. She was very close to Hercules.'

I'd never known who my great-great-great-granny had been. All our family ever talked about was Hercules. Could this woman have been his love, and my ancestor? It might explain the way I liked to run across roof tops. Maybe I'd inherited the genes of a circus flyer as well as those of a bare-knuckle fighter. Now that I looked closely, she did look a bit like Whitney Jade.

'Phoenix records show that he pulled off some of the most amazing missions,' said Wren quietly.

And I seemed to hear Hercules whisper in my ear, 'You can't keep walking out on things, Fredboy. You've walked out on your daddy, you've walked out on every school you've been to, you can't run for ever. You've got a chance to make a difference. You're a Smith. Now, look lively. I worked for Phoenix. They may be gorjers but they ain't so bad. If I can do it, so can you.'

I looked at Wren. 'OK, I'll stay here tonight. I'll give you a report of all that happened at Costalot with the Screamer, in the morning.'

And with that I went back to my old room in the dorm wing. In the green twins' room next door, they'd stuck pictures on the walls and filled the windowsill with toys and stuff they'd made in class, so that it had become their very own nest. My room was bare, just a bed and a chest of drawers. I'd never learned the knack of making a place look like home. When you travel, home changes all the time.

They'd put Ant in my room after checking him over, and he was curled up in his usual cocoon of blankets. He woke up when I came in.

'You OK?' I said.

'Yes, Fred.'

I looked around. 'It's too stuffy in here. I'm going to sleep outside.' I grabbed my quilt.

Which meant Ant took no time getting up, wrapping himself in a blanket and coming with me. We made our way to the roof, dragging our bedclothes like a couple of ghosts.

Once we'd got ourselves comfy, I got the wristband out and began fiddling with it. I bent it this way and that, I twisted it on to my wrist, took it off, shook it. Nothing. I examined every mark on it. It was just a gold wristband in the shape of a snake.

'Give us a go!' said Ant.

'There's nothing to have a go at. It's a wristband.'

'Let's see!'

'No. It might be dangerous.'

Ant wrinkled his nose at me. 'It's a wristband, boss. Wristbands aren't dangerous.'

'This one might be. I think it's got some kind of mechanism in it.' Every time the Screamer had gone into Dragon Fire, he'd grabbed his wrist first.

I got my penknife out and began trying to pry the golden scales apart. Nothing. I put it round my wrist and squeezed, like I'd seen the Screamer do. Nothing. I tried everything, until Ant had fallen asleep by my side, and my own eyes were beginning to close. It seemed like I'd got it wrong; maybe the Screamer grabbing his wrist before he went into cell-burn was just a fluke. And the wristband was just a wristband.

At last, as dawn broke, I slept, curled in amongst the gargoyles.

I thought I'd taken care of the Screamer and got Java out of trouble. But a few hours later, I found I was wrong.

Chapter Fifteen

I hadn't even opened my eyes when my mobile rang.

'You despicable, lying, son of—' It was Java's daddy bawling at me.

'Huh?'

'I want to know exactly where my daughter is this time!'

'She's in Malta, isn't she? I mean, that's the party I crashed, her going-away party.' I sat up. Dew had fallen with the dawn, and my bedding was damp and cold. Ant was nowhere to be seen. Nor was the snake wristband.

'Don't come over all innocent!' he bellowed. 'You know something.'

'I swear, I don't know what you're talking about. Last I heard she was getting the night flight to Malta.'

'Oh, yes, she got on the flight. And then she got off at Luqa airport. No one's seen her since. So where is she, boy?'

That got me up and pacing across the roof. 'Dear God, she's missing?'

Java's daddy nearly exploded. 'Don't play the innocent. You

know where she is! I know this has something to do with you! I'm warning you: I'll clear you and your family off their land, and I'll run you out of the county. I can do that, you know. I have the power. I want you and your raggle-taggle relatives away from here. I don't care if you *have* bought land, I'll still have you moved on, and I'll—'

I hung up on him. Java was missing and it was all my fault for showing her the Screamer email. I'd captured the Screamer, and still I hadn't saved her.

I had to find Wren.

He was in the canteen. It used to be the duke's dining room and had massive paintings of Greek gods and goddesses on the walls. All I can say is that men and women didn't wear a lot of clothes in those days. My mammy would've been horrified.

Wren was tucking into a massive plate of bacon, eggs and fried tomatoes along with the other cops on duty. I ran over to him.

'Wren, I've got to talk to the Screamer. Then you have to help me get to Malta.'

He wiped a hand across his mouth and swallowed. 'Why? And don't say "classified" or you'll be hanging from the stone serpent up on the tower like our spiky-toothed friend.'

I took a deep breath and then stepped back, just to be on the safe side. 'Java's gone missing.'

Wren froze for a moment, then slowly and ominously put down the crust of bread he was using to mop up the fried tomatoes. Then he said, 'What?' in a terrible, quiet voice.

I swallowed. 'Java's—'

'I heard what you said!' He flung his hands out in despair. 'But I didn't want to believe it. Please tell me I'm wrong, tell me you didn't give the girl a copy of the Screamer email, tell me she wasn't the one you forwarded the email to.'

I concentrated on some crumbs on the table. 'I did.'

He leaped to his feet, looming over me. 'Do you ever stop to think, boy, ever?' The canteen went quiet and everyone looked over at me.

No, of course I didn't. I'd made it my life's work to go shooting off at all angles. But I didn't like people shouting at me. I could've hit him. We could have fought. But I didn't. Wren was the first person I might not be able to beat. Not because he was the strongest and fittest person in the world – he wasn't. But he was more *real* than anyone else I'd ever met. When he walked into a room, everyone took notice of him. I think it was what the martial artists called chi. Life force. He just had it in spades. And I suppose I respected him.

'You knew she had the email, even after I told you it was dangerous?" he said.

The cooks doling out the breakfasts at the serving hatch were listening now.

I nodded. 'She watched it. But nothing happened, so I thought she was going to be OK. Then she got her flight to Malta, and disappeared. I've got to talk to the Screamer and make him tell me where she is.'

Wren shook his head. 'You won't get a word out of him. We've been trying since earlier this morning. He seems to have placed himself in a catatonic trance. We've stuck pins into him and he doesn't flinch.' He shook his head at me.

'How could you have been so stupid?'

I frowned. 'OK, I did wrong. It was stupid. But it's happened. Now I have to go and find her and make it right. I can do this with you or on my own.'

'Snow won't go for it.'

'I don't care. I'm going one way or another.'

Wren looked at me. 'You've disappointed me,' he said quietly.

But I'd had enough. He couldn't make me feel any more guilty than I felt already.

'If you don't want to help, say so,' I said, turning to go. 'Then I'll get on and find her on my own.'

'Oh no, you don't,' he said, slapping the remains of his breakfast between two doorsteps of bread, and then escorting me out of the canteen. 'This is a mission now, so you're going to do as you're told and follow orders. Comprende?'

'Aye, aye,' I said, giving him a mock salute. 'Where are we going?'

'To the Ops room.'

Wren's mobile bleeped. He answered it. 'Bigley, do me a favour. We need to find Draconis families in Malta as well, now – what? What!' The mobile squawked for a while. Wren's face dropped. 'OK, I'll be there in a minute.'

'What?' I said. Something about Wren's expression made the blood freeze in my veins.

'Bigley found out why we investigated the family before.'

I swallowed. 'What was it?'

'On the equinox of the twenty-third of September 1988, three bodies were found in the grounds of the Draconis family home,' he said, striding out of the canteen. I hurried to keep up with him.

'How did they die?'

'They'd been sacrificed, and their blood drained.'

Chapter Sixteen

The Ops room was a dead ringer for an underground bunker. The old duke really hadn't liked sunlight very much: this time he'd done away with windows altogether. At one end, between two fat marble cherubs, was a big projector screen. And a wall-sized blackboard sat at the other end with all the current operations chalked on it.

I followed Wren down the spiral stairs, using the banister and one hand to get me down in a single massive, curling leap. Worse luck, Snow was at the bottom, leaning on his stick, and staring at me with his soulless eyes from behind his burn mask.

Maybe he always looked at new recruits like that, but I didn't think so. He was probably down here to check that I didn't steal anything.

The rest of the darkened room was taken up by a massive oak dining table, big enough for the duke to hold banquets for fifty people. Now it was covered in loads of computers, piles of paper and empty coffee cups. Techie blokes were tapping away on computers, answering the ringing phones, walking round looking baffled and scratching their heads, or lying back in their chairs dozing. Some were laughing or talking to thin air, and then pounding away at the computer keyboards. I thought they were talking to themselves at first, but then I noticed the earpieces.

I gave the Operations board a quick scan. The Screamer investigation was fourth along, next to one about a monster in the sewer, codenamed Yeti.

'Phoenix are investigating a monster running round underneath the town?' I said to Wren.

'It's a genuine enquiry.' He gave me a funny look. 'There's a little voice at the back of my mind shouting at me to take a closer look at it. But we're just too damn busy at the moment. The Screamer case is going to take most of our manpower.'

Someone coughed behind us. 'I don't have much time, so can we get on with this?' said a stern voice.

'Bigley!' said Wren, and the two little lines shot up by his mouth, his version of a wide smile.

Bigley was a Phoenix cop. I'd seen her around, but she was like no cop I'd ever met before. She only wore turquoise and she carried a big chunk of crystal, the size of a baby's fist, on the end of a silver chain. She said it tuned into her tachyon energy or something, but don't get the idea that she was a peace-and-love hippy type – I reckon it was really a weapon. She'd once found me and the other kids messing around near her office, and she'd swung the crystal round her head like a meteor hammer and aimed it at us.

I think Wren fancied her. 'She's going to be the Psi operator on this case,' he whispered, giving her an admiring glance, but keeping his distance. 'The mind is a powerful weapon. But all the Psi team are a bit crazy. You have to know how to handle them.'

'What exactly do they do?' I'd seen the name on a door, but I'd never gone inside.

'Mainly we use them for remote viewing. They can locate kidnap victims or fugitives using their minds. But Bigley's become fascinated with this whole case. She's been chasing down info all morning.'

He rushed forward. 'Hey, well done on finding the—' he began, trailing after her like a puppy. But Bigley ignored him. She swept a corner of the big table free of papers. A few of the techie blokes began to complain, but when they saw it was Bigley they shut up quickly.

'Sit down,' she said to us.

We sat down, better trained than Spike in the cellars below. She was holding a stack of photos and shuffling them like a pack of cards.

'I've done some research on our family and come up with two very strange findings.'

'Occultists?' said Wren, trying to score more points with her, no doubt. She ignored him. I just wished she'd get on with it. Sitting down was driving me mad, but I kept quiet as I didn't want her chunk of crystal aimed at my head again.

'The Draconis family were petty criminals, living in slums, until the eighteenth century,' she began. 'Then a ruthless man called Black Michael became head of the family. A year later they'd bought a ruined, isolated castle in the north and turned it into a home fit for kings.'

She slapped a picture down on the table. It showed a wild-looking bloke with crooked eyes and long black hair hanging in ringlets.

'After Black Michael took over, they suddenly "found" themselves a fortune in gold.'

Wren looked thoughtful. 'Got to be a crime of some sort, then. What's the other strange thing about them?' Bigley began to deal out the photos like my great-granny Kate used to deal her tarot cards. The first one she laid down was an old black-and-white one. A group shot of lots of old people.

'This is Agnes Draconis celebrating her one hundred and fifteenth birthday. In the Draconis clan you were considered young at ninety years old.'

She dealt another photo. It was of a castle with a moat, sitting out on a windswept moor.

'They are also very secretive. No one is ever invited to their castle, and they never do business with anyone.'

Wren folded his arms. 'So, we've got a secretive family with lots of gold. And they all live for a very long time.'

'Yep,' said Bigley. 'Got any ideas?'

'Satanists,' said Wren.

I shrugged. 'Bank robbers?' This was driving me mad. I just wanted to get going.

Bigley laid down another photo. A satellite shot of the castle, with a crater where part of the moat should have been, like someone had dropped a Scud missile into the water. A massive circle of blackened grass surrounded it.

'The Draconis family carried on being fabulously rich up

to 1975,' she explained. 'Until the night thieves broke in. There was a massive explosion, and one of the thieves was killed. The other escaped, but must've been badly burned. Since then the castle has been falling to pieces. They've got no money. And a lot of them are ill.'

Wren was frowning at the photo. 'It's almost as if whatever was making them rich, and giving them long lives, was destroyed in the explosion.'

'Does it matter?' I said. 'Can't I just go to Malta and get Java?'

They both ignored me.

Bigley laid out more photos. 'We've got ten missing Indigos. And now Java.'

My heart sank when I looked at the row of photos. They were the sort that people get taken at school. The sort I'd never stayed at school long enough to get. The sort that get flashed up on the news when some poor kid gets abducted or murdered. These weren't rough, tough kids like me who might be able to fight back, but the kind who'd always do their homework, and line up nicely for the school photo, and not kick people in the shins if they tried anything on. Harvey King, the boarding-school boy, was there. I hoped he was doing OK without the inhaler he'd left behind. My sister used to worry if she lost hers.

'They're all fifteen or sixteen years of age. Police had them down as runaways until Harvey King's CCTV tape. Even now they think it's a hoax. So it's up to Phoenix.'

'We don't know where the kids are being kept,' said Wren. 'It could be the castle. It could be in Malta.'

I sprang up. 'Well, we know that's where Java is, so can I get going——?'

Bigley blinked at me, and wound the chain from her crystal round her fist. Wren just stared. 'This is a briefing, Freedom. You'll sit down and listen.'

I sat down, but I wasn't happy. It wasn't a briefing, it was a waste of time.

Bigley shuffled her photos and laid another one down. 'The Maltese family live in a small, isolated bay, hard to reach from the local towns, called Ras il-wahx. "The Bay of Ghosts".'

Jeez, it certainly wasn't anything like England. The sea was the blue of Java's swimming pool. It didn't look real. And the rocks surrounding the bay were the colour of honey cake, and crumbling. In between there were cactus plants and dusty-looking shrubs. The sky was the same colour as the sea, and the sand looked like vanilla ice cream.

'The family live in a *palazzo* on the cliff,' she continued. 'It's got an old temple attached to it. The castle has a temple as well. They worship a pagan dragon goddess.'

She put down a picture of a statue. It was a girl in a long dress with snakes for hair, a dagger at her belt, and a snake wriggling in each hand.

'The Screamer mentioned a goddess,' I said. 'Princess Lato.'

Bigley's eyes narrowed and she twirled her crystal round. 'That's her. In the old days her worshippers were very blood-thirsty.'

Wren stared at the statue. 'And three murder victims were found on their land years ago. They're sacrificing people, aren't they?'

Bigley nodded. 'Could be. The three victims were spoon-benders. Psychics.'

I frowned. 'Jeez, you mean they might be planning to sacrifice the Indigo kids?' I snapped my fingers impatiently. 'Come on, Wren, just let me go and find Java—'

Wren glared at me. 'Not yet. We have to infiltrate both homes at the same time, so they don't have time to warn each other.' He began striding up and down. 'We've got two days, two sites.'

He walked up and down a couple more times, then he slammed a hand on the desk.

'Here's how we play it. Me and Bigley, we go up to the castle.' He turned to Bigley. 'You do a spot of remote viewing. See if you can sense whether the kids are being held in there. Then we need to get someone into the Malta *palazzo* to do the same.'

I kicked the leg of the table. 'For heaven's sake, I said I'd go! All you're doing is talking.'

Bigley stared at me. I didn't care.

'She's one of eleven kids missing,' she said. 'We have to think of them all.'

'I don't,' I said. 'All I want to do is rescue Java.'

Next thing Wren grabbed my chair and turned it his way. There was nowhere to look but at him.

'It's called teamwork, Freedom. We work together. We look after each other. Then everyone gets rescued. No one gets left behind.'

'One moment,' said a cold voice.

Snow was sitting in the corner, leaning his hands on his stick. He'd been listening in.

'I don't think Freedom should go. You can see he can't play by the rules,' he said. 'Send the Maltese police in. They know the territory.' His eyes, behind the mask, found mine.

'I'm going,' I said.

A silence fell around us.

Snow brushed a speck of dust off his sleeve. 'No, I don't think so.'

'Why?' said Wren.

'He isn't capable of following orders.'

This was my fault. Me and my big mouth. I should've sat quietly. 'I will! Just try me out,' I said. 'If the local cops try to go in, the family'll close ranks. They'll smuggle Java out and then we'll never find her.'

Bigley looked from one of us to the other. 'Snow, we can send Freedom in undercover,' she said. 'The property is guarded, but we can get him in by sea. He can recce the place at night, hide up somewhere and get Java out when we give the word.'

'He's too much of a liability. The odds are high that he'll be caught,' said Snow.

'If he gets caught going in, he can say he's a scuba-diver looking for treasure and he got pulled their way by the current. They're not going to suspect a kid with romantic ideas about the famous sunken treasure.'

'What treasure?' I said. You'd think I was still about six years old, the way I got excited when I heard that word.

'There's a myth about a gold statue of Princess Lato

keeping watch over a hoard of gold,' said Bigley. 'It's that dragon worship thing again. It's supposed to be lost somewhere under the sea around Malta.'

'So Freedom can pretend he's a treasure hunter?' said Wren. 'I like it. It's the best plan we've got, Snow.'

Snow looked from me to Wren. 'This is too rushed. You don't even know if he can scuba-dive.'

'That's no problem,' I said quickly. 'When I was on holiday last year I got some lessons. It's a piece of cake.'

'There you go. He gets in, locates Java.' Wren turned to his boss. 'He needs to be challenged. He doesn't do well when life is too easy. What do you say?'

Through Snow's mask, his cold grey eyes stared at me. I felt like someone had put the air con on full blast. As far as I knew I'd never done anything to this man, but he didn't like me at all.

He stood up. 'Let him try if you must, but he's your responsibility, Wren,' he said, and walked out, leaning on his stick.

Some of the other cops had stopped to listen. They looked from Snow to me, and then muttered amongst themselves. From the few glances they threw my way I got the impression they agreed with Snow. They thought I was too big for my boots, that I'd fail. Well, I'd show them.

I took a deep breath. This was it, I had my mission. But the only thing on my mind was the thought of Java being sacrificed. I felt my fists clenching just thinking about it.

'We'll get you kitted out with a weapon,' said Wren.

I didn't even have to think. 'I'll have Spike.'

'Huh? A spike?'

'No. Just Spike,' I said.

Bigley pointed downwards. 'The dog that chewed halfway through the bars in the back of a riot van last week. And then ate a jumbo-sized Pedigree Chum without taking it out of the can,' she explained.

'The mutant mutt?' said Wren. 'No way. That thing's untrainable and as dangerous as hell.' He clapped me on the back. 'Sorry, kid, but it looks like we're going to have to humanely euthanize him.'

'Huh?'

'Put him to sleep. Destroy him.'

I walked off. We'd see about that. Contrary to what Snow might think, everyone and everything deserved a chance to prove its worth.

Chapter Seventeen

The door to the dungeon vibrated as something hurled itself at it. Spike welcoming me again.

I opened the door a little. The growling got louder and turned to snarling. A huge set of razor-sharp teeth bit a chunk out of the door, then Spike's maw appeared in the gap and snapped at me, dripping saliva.

I ignored him, opening the door a bit wider. Spike backed off a few paces, but the growling never let up. I took a deep breath, then walked in and closed the door behind me.

There was no going back now. It was just me and Spike.

'Listen, mutt, they're thinking of destroying you, so you can make this easy or hard,' I said. 'Are you going to be sensible?'

He answered that by leaping at me. But I was too quick. I dived, and his claws found the stone wall. He fell to the floor, his massive jaws rattling on the granite slabs.

He was up faster than a sunbeam streaking across a dark room.

'Jeez, Spike, let's be friends!' I said, but he wasn't having it.

He leaped, I dodged. He came at me with his teeth. I grabbed him by the scruff and sent him flying. He growled. I howled in pain as his teeth caught me time and time again. Someone had got this dog and taught it that its only purpose in life was to attack. He wouldn't stop until one of us was the victor. And I couldn't stop moving, because if I did he'd corner me. He had sharper teeth, but I could leap on to the bench out of his reach.

We dodged and sparred each other to a standstill. In the end Spike's tongue was hanging out so far it touched the floor, and his knobbly, bowed knees were shaking. So were mine. We squatted in opposite corners of the dungeon, panting and trembling. Spike sank on to his belly. His red eyes glared at me, offended. I'd ruined his view that he was the toughest creature in the world.

Now it would be the stronger of us who survived and triumphed. But then I got to thinking that maybe there didn't need to be a winner. Maybe we could come out of this as equals. One of us had to call a truce and it looked like it was going to be me.

Spike got up ominously slowly, his eyes never leaving me. I stood up and scuffed my feet around on the floor, pretending to be searching for something, letting him know that I wasn't going to invade his space, that he needn't protect himself from me.

The panting carried on, but the growling got quieter.

'Hey, I ain't going to hurt you, or grab you, I just want to be friends,' I said, still not looking at him, and walking in a circle, never approaching him directly. Ever seen one dog check out another dog it doesn't know? It walks in an arch. When we pull on to a new piece of ground and a local dog comes by to see what's what, he walks round our dogs in an arch, like he isn't bothered whether they meet or not. And our dogs yawn and look away, like they haven't seen him.

After a minute the growling stopped completely. I heard Spike sneeze and lick his chops, so I squatted down on my haunches and pretended to be very interested in a dog biscuit on the floor. I yawned a couple of times. In dog talk I was saying, 'You don't have to worry about defending yourself from me, because I mean you no harm.' I was hoping his yawning was saying the same thing to me. If it wasn't, I was in trouble.

There was a scrabble of claws on the stone floor, and Spike's huge shadow loomed beside me. Then a massive head nudged me. Jeez, it was like being rammed with a small tank. I took a deep breath, then put my hand out and scratched him behind his ragged ears.

He slumped on the floor, with a massive groan like a door creaking, and rolled on to his back.

'Hey, Spike. Want your belly rubbed?'

And so we became sort of pals. Two misfits together. He'd got a big collar round his neck, thick leather with studs to reinforce it. It looked like a joke collar for a cartoon bulldog, but when I got hold of it and tried to pull him towards the door, I knew why he needed such a big one. It was like trying to hold back an avalanche. Spike wasn't the biggest dog in the world, but like me he was ten times stronger than he looked. He didn't appreciate being controlled, either. His teeth snapped near my hand. I let go of his collar.

I bent down and looked him in the eye this time, to show him I meant business.

'Listen. Do you want an adventure?' I said. 'Or do you want to spend the rest of your days in here, like a lab rat, with the techies doing experiments on you? And after that they'll humanely euthanize you — it's on the cards, I heard 'em talking. Is that what you want?'

He couldn't have understood me, but perhaps he picked up signals and messages from my eyes and body language. Because he came and stood to heel by my side, of his own free will, and when I moved he walked beside me.

We made it upstairs together. There was no one about, so I opened a side door that led to a little walled garden. I think it used to be the kitchen garden where they grew herbs and stuff like that for the duke's meals. There were still pots of herbs around the edges now, for the Phoenix chefs.

'There you are, Spike, a bit of fresh air for you.'

Spike wagged his rat-like tail, then waddled off in his bow-legged way and peed on one of the flowerpots. I made a vow not to touch any meals with herbs in them from now on.

'Hey, Spike, you want a doggie treat?' I took a dog biscuit out my pocket. I'd found a box of them in his dungeon.

He ignored me.

'Spike, dinner!' I said. Still he ignored me. The biscuit had doggie chow written on it.

'Chow!' I said.

Instantly his ears went up, and he barrelled over to me and took the biscuit — and the rest of my hand, nearly. 'Spike likes chow. Good dog.'

Then he went for a serious sniff around the place, so I left him there. I felt good about his release. I didn't like to see any creature stuck in a dark dungeon and imprisoned.

Chapter Eighteen

I found Wren in the firearms room.

'Well, your name's on the board, Freedom. Now let's get you kitted out.'

I sneezed. There were shelves everywhere, stacked with guns of all shapes and sizes. 'I told you, I don't want a weapon,' I said.

'There's more than that here,' said Wren. 'Which communicator do you want?' He pointed to the table. 'They all work like mobile phones, via satellite.'

I stared blankly at a necklace with beads in the shape of little skulls, like Goth kids wear. Next to it were a couple of credit cards. Further along the counter was a pair of thin leather fingerless gloves like fighters put on when they don't want to bust their knuckles. And a bus ticket.

'I'd choose one if I could see one,' I said.

'They're all state-of-the-art communicators,' said Wren. He picked up the necklace. 'No need to dial a number. Just squeeze the right skull and you get straight through to

Phoenix. The bead acts as the mike as well.' He picked up the credit cards. 'These are mobile phones. One hour talk time, and a single connection through to Phoenix HQ.' He picked up the bus ticket. 'This is good. It's a phone, yet you can fold it like paper. Use it, then throw it away.'

'And the gloves?'

Wren picked one up. 'These are my favourites. Make a fist; that connects you. Then put the glove to your ear and you can listen and talk. At the end of the call, make a fist again to disconnect.' He laid it back down on the counter. 'Which one do you want?'

Jeez, was he joking? I wanted them all, of course.

Half an hour later I followed Wren to the accounts office, where a bloke slapped a bundle of cash in my hand.

'Go and get a wetsuit and beachwear,' said Wren. 'And don't spend it all, I want some change. And I'll need receipts for everything or Khampal here will be down on me like a ton of bricks. And remember, it's still hot out in Malta.' He paused. 'Ever been abroad?'

'Nope.'

'Think of our hottest summer day, when the heat's getting too much and there's thunderstorms on the horizon, and you're somewhere near a September day in Malta.'

I went straight to Costalot and my sister.

Her eyes widened when she saw me. 'Have you come to see Daddy?' she said, looking pleased.

Me and my daddy hadn't met since we had the fight and fell out. I always had plenty of excuses to get out of the way when our paths crossed, or when Crystal went visiting them. Now he was down this way buying horses, but I didn't plan on meeting him.

'No, I've got stuff to do,' I told her. 'But I need you to help me buy some clothes. I'm getting an all-expenses-paid holiday courtesy of Phoenix!'

I didn't have to tell her twice. Crystal loves to shop. First we got a wetsuit, and then she took me to the best clothes shops in town. She had a thing about Versace at the time. I don't know what she got me, because I didn't look at the labels, but after pushing me into loads of changing rooms and handing me armfuls of stuff, we were finally done. And I was standing there in camo shorts and a T-shirt that had cost more than half the money Wren had given me. I looked in the mirror. I looked fine, the ugly was still there, but there wasn't much I could do about that.

Anyway, I winked at the assistant and she smiled back, so I must've looked OK.

'And now the finishing touch,' said Crystal. And handed me some sunglasses that wiped out the rest of Wren's expense money. I didn't care – they looked good. Let him explain to Khampal in Accounts.

When I got back to Phoenix House, Armageddon was happening.

Chapter Nineteen

I could hear shouts and curses even as I walked up the gravel drive. Before I could punch in my entry code, the oak front door shook a couple of times as something heavy slammed into it from inside.

It sounded like a battle was taking place in the hallway.

As the front door swung open a couple of cops shot by me, one limping and missing a shoe, the other with his trousers shredded below the knee. Inside cops were perched every-where. A man with a tattered Kevlar waistcoat and a broom that was now missing most of its head was backed against one wall.

Wren was clinging to a statue of an eagle with four legs and the tail of a lizard, yelling, 'Someone get the dart gun!'

'It's OK, sir, I've got him!' said one of the techies. He slammed the door on a big pet carrier, the sort of thing you'd take Fido down to the vet's in, except this one was made of steel. 'Just don't mention the m-o-n-k-e-y.'

The carrier was lurching from side to side, and a furious

Spike could be seen chewing on one of the bars.

'Hey, what're you doing to Spike?' I said, going up and patting his nose through the bars. 'See, he's OK, really. You're frightening him, Wren, waving your arms about and shouting.'

'It's Gabriel's fault!' shouted Wren. 'He mentioned the monkey!' The cage went berserk, and began to vibrate across the floor.

The techie next to me said, 'When Spike was in the lab, he used to get terrorized by a small capuchin m-o-n-k-e-y. You only have to say the word and he goes mad and runs off.'

'And you want to take that thing to Malta?' Wren howled. 'It nearly had my leg off!'

'Hey, boy,' I said, and Spike squinted at me and growled low in his throat. 'It's just that he doesn't like bars and being shut in. He's like me. It's driving him insane.'

I popped the catch and Spike raced out and headed straight for the techie bloke, who leaped on to a cupboard in record-breaking time. When the dog'd cleared the floor, he cocked his leg and peed in the old fireplace, then came over and sneezed on me and sat down with a satisfied look on his ugly chops.

'Get a choke chain on it!' said Wren, climbing down, but staying well back.

'He's OK,' I said. 'He doesn't like chains, either.'

'The dog's a mutant menace,' said Wren.

'So am I,' I said, and grinned at him. 'But you gave me a chance.'

Wren shook his head. 'It's not safe. It's a potential killer.'

'He's OK. Watch this.' I bent down. 'Hey, Spike, want your belly rubbed?'

Spike's red-rimmed eyes swivelled towards me like two enemy guns. The look in them was clear. *Try that in front of other people,* he was saying, *and I'll have your arm off.*

I pulled my hand back quickly.

A door opened behind us. Bigley stuck her head out.

'Wren, I've got our itinerary ready for the Draconis case.'

'One moment,' he said.

He came and put his hand out to stroke Spike on the head.

'I wouldn't if I were you,' I said.

The dog curled his lip silently. For a second Wren hesitated. Then he bent down and looked into Spike's glowering eyes.

'If you want to get euthanized, then bite me,' he said.

Then he plonked his hand on the dog's head.

There was a frozen standoff for a few seconds, with Spike looking like one of the duke's marble statues and Wren not moving his hand.

Then Wren said, 'That's better,' and took his hand away. And Spike turned his back and began ignoring him.

'OK, Freedom, I haven't got time to argue,' he said. 'It's you and the mutt. But it flies cargo and you're responsible for its conduct.'

Chapter Twenty

efore I left I went on a hunt for the Tunnel Crew. I found them in a huddle at the farthest end of a far-off dark corridor. They glanced round when they heard me approaching, then there was a lot of passing things from hand to hand, like they were trying to get rid of the evidence.

'OK, give it me,' I said to Ant.

He held out two grubby hands to show they were empty, so I risked life and limb and felt in his pocket. Ant's pockets were notorious. There could've been anything in there. Dead slugs, half-eaten sweets, spiders in matchboxes. But this time, thank goodness, I pulled out the snake wristband.

The other thing they were trying to hide was a Barbie doll. Well, two halves of a Barbie doll.

'We know how it works!' said Ant, pointing to the wristband. 'We practised on Barbie. We know how to make it spiky!'

'Huh?' The doll wasn't looking too good. It had been

severed in two round the waist.

Ant took the wristband from me. 'It's like this, boss. You wind it round your wrist, except we wound it round the doll. And then you press its eyes and then turn its tail two times, and look!'

Ant put the wristband round Barbie's neck this time, then poked its eyes and twisted its tail.

There was a nasty little *shhhik* noise, and suddenly the wristband had grown a set of vicious needles on the inside. Barbie's head fell off and rolled across the floor. I began to sweat. Dear God, if any of the kids had put that round their skinny wrists and tried it, the needles would have pierced right through. Thank God they'd only tortured Barbie with it.

'Did we do good?' said Ant.

I took him by the shoulders. 'You did good. But you could have hurt yourself.'

I pocketed the wristband. I'd hand it in to the Firearms room for safekeeping. Then I fixed Ant with my best serious look. 'I'm going to be away for a while, so behave.'

Ant tapped his heart. 'Tunnel Crew always obeys the boss!'

They wandered off down another corridor, their capes trailing behind them, on the lookout for more adventures. I went back downstairs to the hall, shoved my wetsuit into a rucksack and picked up my fake passport from Admin.

'How am I getting to Malta, Wren?' I said.

He felt in his pocket. 'I've got you a holiday flight from Luton airport. The mutt goes in with the luggage.'

My heart sank. OK, this was my first foreign mission, but I thought it'd be a bit fancier than a package tour from Luton.

He led me through the house to the quadrangle, Spike trotting beside us. Phoenix House was built around a large courtyard. It used to be full of rose gardens in the duke's day, but now it had been tarmacked over. In the evenings, me, Ant and the other kids played football in there.

'So how am I getting to Luton airport? Bus?' I said.

Wren stopped with his hand on the door to the quad. Two lines appeared beside his mouth. Something must have amused him.

'Sorry, did I say package flight from Luton?' he said.

He swung the door open.

Chapter Twenty-One

Crouched on the tarmac were two black helicopters, ready for take-off.

Wren shoved me forward and I moved out into the quadrangle. 'What I actually meant', he said, 'was a helicopter to a secret base in the UK and then a jet to the Mediterranean, where there's a research station we can land on. Then you'll be transported to an area just off the coast, where you'll assume your identity as a treasure seeker who's got himself a bit lost.'

But I was hardly listening. I couldn't take my eyes off the helicopters. They were awesome. I felt like going up and stroking one. They looked stealth just sitting there with their blades spinning slowly.

'One for me and Bigley, one for you.' Even Wren was standing gazing at them.

'Kushti,' I said, trying to sound like this sort of thing happened every day of my life.

He put a hand on my arm, and looked at me. 'You get in,

locate Java. Check for other Indigos. Then report back. Do you understand? Surveillance only, until we all know what we're going to do. I don't want you putting yourself or Java at risk. Understood?'

'Jeez, Wren. Yeh, alright.'

He hesitated. 'Things might get weird, or deadly. I don't know what the Draconis clan are up to. They might think they're witches and wizards, they might be religious nutters who think it's their right to sacrifice kids to this Princess Lato.'

'OK, I get it. The world is much stranger than I can ever imagine.'

But Wren didn't let up. 'I'm serious. This is the first time you'll be confronting something that might be paranormal. No one will think any the less of you if you find it too much and get the hell out of there.'

I would, though. It was my fault Java was missing, so it was my responsibility to get her back.

'Understood,' I said.

In the distance I could hear a motor beeping madly. I recognized the beep. My heart sank. Sure enough, a cop came out behind us.

'Freedom, can you have a quick look on the monitor? We've got a disturbance at the gate.'

I'd been half expecting something like this. We went over to one of the security monitors. On the screen there was a view of the front gates. They were closed, but a white Hiace pick-up truck had swerved in front of them. And a dark man was limping up and down and shouting into the intercom.

I knew who it was. Hammy Smith. My father, come

looking for me.

'You want to go and have a word?' said Wren, looking at me curiously. 'We've got about seven minutes before take-off.'

'No, ta,' I said. 'It can wait. I'll catch him later.'

Then I slung my bag on my back, ducked under the blades of the chopper and got on board.

Part Two
Malta

Chapter Twenty-Two

The coast was a silver line against a black sea. Except at the Bay of Ghosts. You'd think it'd be dark and deserted with a name like that, but it was a blaze of lights reflecting out into the sea towards us.

And somewhere amongst those lights was Java, I hoped.

I'd never travelled so far and so fast. Wren seemed to have an endless supply of mates in the military who did him favours. Such as getting me aboard jets that could cover the journey to the centre of the Med in an hour. And then arrange for a powerboat with an engine as powerful as a rocket to blast me across the last few miles of sea. The Sportfish Cruiser was slicing through the waves, but in the last few minutes a terrible wind had got up and the sea had turned rough. Now we were bucking and rearing all over the place. Spike'd been sick twice, but I hadn't. My stomach was cast iron.

We'd spent the last few minutes manoeuvring towards land. If we went any nearer now, we might be spotted from the bay.

I was standing by the captain. He was battling with the wheel, trying to keep the powerboat on an even keel. Big tough Spike was sitting on my feet, shivering like my mammy's chihuahua. I'd tried to stroke him once, thinking maybe he was scared, but his double row of fangs had snapped a fraction from my hands. I'd gathered that he was concentrating on the boat ride and wished to be left alone.

Wren was on the phone to me again. He'd been calling on and off since I'd left the UK. Something told me Snow was giving him a hard time for sending me. I held my hand up to my ear, trying to hear what he was saying. The glove communicator was working perfectly.

'OK, listen up, here's the latest info about the Maltese Draconis,' he shouted. It sounded like he was still in the helicopter, travelling north to the castle. 'Most people are scared of them, even though they seem to consist of an old grandmother, an uncle who's some sort of chemist or scientist, and two kids.'

'How old?'

'A girl of ten. Angelina, who they call Angel, but she's anything but an angel, apparently. And there was a boy called Apollo, who would be about fifteen, but apparently he died seven years ago.'

'So one child, then,' I shouted over the noise of the wind.

'No!' said Wren's voice in my ear. 'Apollo's been seen recently. By all accounts the household is extremely odd.'

'You're not kidding,' I said. 'A kid who's dead but walks around?'

'No one has a good word for the family. But no one dares

say anything to their faces, because they've got their own army, apparently. And that's troubling me, because you might get picked up by them.'

The wind was so loud I wasn't sure I'd heard right. 'An army?'

'Yes, they guard the place, to make sure no one gets near. They call themselves Draks. And they've got a bad reputation for roughing up anyone who gets anywhere near the family.'

'OK. How's it going at your end?'

Wren gave a laugh. 'We're just landing on the moor. We have to make our own way after that. And it's raining. You don't know how lucky you are.'

Wren didn't fool me. It was a dream come true for him, alone in the dark with Bigley. I was going to say something like that to him, but the captain turned and gave me a shake. 'We're here. Are you ready?'

I put my hand back to my ear. 'Got to go, Wren.'

'Remember. Any problems and you call Phoenix. This is teamwork. You're not on your own.'

'Yeh, OK. I'll make contact when I have a chance. Bye.' I turned to the captain. 'What do I—?'

'Get over to the side of the boat. OK, on the count of five! One . . .'

I climbed over the edge and perched on the rim. Suddenly his boot hit me in the back and kicked me off. 'Five!'

I hit the water. 'Just jump,' the captain had said. *Just leap into that pitch-black sea and then it's a brisk swim to the shore. You've got the scuba gear. Easy peasy.* So why had I spent the last few minutes gnawing my fingernails? It was his fault. He shouldn't have told me about the sharks in the Mediterranean.

There was a splash behind me. It was Spike, baring his fangs and looking disgusted. I think the captain must've had to encourage him to jump, too, because a piece of Navy uniform was caught between his teeth. A low growl came from his throat.

'Aw, stop complaining,' I said. 'You needed a bath!'

The powerboat surged around us in a circle, making me and Spike bob about like rubber ducks.

'Scuba gear working OK?' shouted the captain.

I'd got the scuba tank on my back, a weight belt, face mask and life jacket. Last year I'd had a diving lesson while we were on holiday, and I'd taken a liking to it. It was like flying under water. But that was from a beach, with an instructor by my side.

Now I was far out, in the deep, and no one was going to hold my hand this time. But this was the Smith way of learning how to do things. Want to learn to swim? Then jump in and see how fast you can get to the surface. Ride a bike? Get on one and let someone give you a really big push down a hill.

I pulled down the face mask and put the regulator in my mouth. My heart started pounding. As my head sank beneath the waves, I fought the urge to battle to the surface, to save myself from drowning. My survival instincts had kicked in and were trying to rescue me. I ignored them and sucked in a lungful of air, then breathed out. I sank a bit lower. I took another couple of breaths and relaxed. I had entered a world of silence, broken only by the bubbles of air rasping in and out of the regulator, and a view from beneath of Spike's paddling paws.

I surfaced.

'Yep. The gear's OK.' But I didn't exactly like it down there in the dark. I kept thinking something was about to come out of the depths and bite me.

The boat was blowing sideways in the strong wind that was sweeping across the sea. 'I'd get moving if I were you,' the captain shouted. 'The biggest great white shark in the Mediterranean was spotted right outside this bay.'

'Great, I'll remember that for next time.'

The engine roared, lashing the sea into white foam. His laughter faded away beneath the howl of the wind. Then I was alone.

Wouldn't you know it, straight away something touched my leg. I swear to God I nearly died. Turns out it was Spike's tail.

'OK, dog, let's get going,' I said. 'And if you see anything that looks like a very big fish, eat it.'

I stayed just below the surface, Spike thrashing along overhead, following my bubbles. The wind was whipping the tops off the waves and slamming them into his muzzle, but as soon as we swam into the bay, the water got calmer and the waves smaller. Spike stopped snorting and growling so much.

Now I could hear music, and feel the thump of its vibrations in the water. I got my head above the water. Ras il-wahx, the Bay of Ghosts, was filled with floodlights and music. As a wave picked me up I saw a load of people milling about. It was certainly a popular place to be.

Not that I was thinking too much about the music and lights. I'd still got sharks on my mind. I couldn't keep myself from looking down into the dark, deep water beneath me. That's how, as we swam for shore, I saw the glimmer of light way down in the depths.

'Swim to the shore,' I said to Spike. 'Vamoose! Wait for me there.'

He gave me an evil look, his paws thrashing at the water. Then he paddled away with his chin high above the water and his legs pedalling madly as though he was trying to walk on the surface. I had the feeling he was going to get his own back for this indignity.

I put the regulator back in my mouth and headed straight down towards the light, trailing bubbles in my wake. It was another world, silent and dark. Fish hung asleep in the water, then suddenly woke and finned away. Something big went slowly by at the corner of my vision. I prayed it wasn't a great white.

At first I thought the light was coming from a cave. But no cave I've ever seen has a rectangular doorway. Things that are made by nature don't have straight lines. So what was a doorway doing six metres under the waves?

I kicked out and headed for it. Only, instead of going forward, I got jerked violently back.

Something had hold of my ankle.

Shark! said my reptile brain. *Flee! Shake it off! Flee!*

But I'd got something even worse to worry about. Whatever was hanging on to my ankle had got hold of the scuba tank on my back and ripped the regulator from my mouth.

I screwed my body round and caught a glimpse in the strange light coming from the doorway.

It wasn't a shark.

Chapter Twenty-Three

Great white sharks are killing machines, but humans are just as bad.

My captors were human, and intent on drowning me, it seemed. But they didn't stand much of a chance. My brain still hadn't figured out that they weren't sharks, so I went into a slamming, kicking frenzy that would've made a great white proud.

One of them was still hanging on to the scuba gear strapped to my back, so I flicked the quick release, wriggled out of it, and swam clear. The tank sank to the bottom with a thunk.

With my lungs bursting, I thrashed for the surface and took a massive breath. A heartbeat or two later, the water erupted around me, and I glimpsed tattooed scales on the backs of hands, like the Screamer's, and steel claws on fingertips. Then I was being dragged towards the shore. I kicked and struggled until I found my feet touching the bottom, and stood up in waist-deep water.

So much for surveillance only. I'd got a welcoming committee. A girl, with a serpent tattooed up her arm. And a fella, with piercings all over his face.

Except you could forget the welcome.

Everything about their movements was threatening. The girl crowded me, pushing at my shoulder, demanding to know who I was. The fella just laughed and then yelled, 'We gotta trespasser!'

So I blew the sea water out of my lungs and started shouting. If you're ever in trouble because some creep is trying to mug you or bully you, my advice is this: start shouting. Roar like a lion from the pit of your stomach. Shout crazy stuff like 'I'm gonna eat your head if you don't back off!' It can put the brakes on the fight and give you time to scarper.

'Get away from me!' I yelled. 'Or I'll scratch your eyes out and feed 'em to the sharks!'

The girl stood back. Even the fella relaxed his grip for a second or two.

'Yeh, right. Let me go, creeps,' I carried on, nodding and waving my hands about like a lunatic. 'I'm going to report you all, you see if I don't.'

But a whole load more tattooed, spiky people, all in black, had come up to join the fray. Some were just kids playing tough, but others were the sort of men you saw on pub doors acting as bouncers. They might as well have had *AGGRO* or *GBH* tattooed on their foreheads, because that was what they were looking for.

There were girls amongst them as well, mean-looking

ones like the serpent girl at my side. They were shouting to each other in Maltese and laughing. I think I'd made their night, turning up in their bay. But I don't think that was because they wanted me to join in the party.

'Get your filthy hands off me!' I yelled, playing the innocent for all I was worth, and trying to catch a glimpse of Spike at the same time. I was praying that he'd managed to get ashore. 'I've got a dog. You'd better not have harmed him, or I'll call the police!'

'Shut him up!' shouted one of the boys, switching to English.

'Sure thing,' said Serpent Girl, then thumped me in the face with the row of rings she was wearing on her knuckles. It felt like she'd left the imprint of each one on my chin.

I turned to the fella with the pierced face.

'Hey, are you the boss round here? If so, you're going to be in trouble when I report you to the cops!'

His face, glittering with metal, loomed in front of me.

'Tell the cops whatever you want, kid. I'm Pierce. I'm not the boss. You want Apollo.'

'Apollo Draconis? I heard he'd died young,' I said.

Pierce laughed. So did all the others. Seemed like I'd amused them all. 'Oh, yeh, he's dead all right! But don't take my word for it. Why don't you ask him yourself?'

They were making fun of me, and I hate that.

'You like having a dead boss, do you?' I said.

Pierce grinned. He waved his hand at the freaks around him. 'Haven't you noticed that we're the damned? Of course we like having a dead boss!'

Then they dragged me up the beach, like some dangerous fish they'd landed. I blinked the water out of my eyes and, under the cover of a whole load of swearing and cursing, took careful note of my surroundings. When you've put yourself into danger, it's a good idea to know where the nearest exit points are.

From what I could see through my wet hair, as they half dragged, half shoved me up the beach, there were only freaks out here.

Jeez, it was like something out of a sci-fi war film.

The whole place was floodlit. You could probably have seen it from space. The bay was a rocky half-circle surrounded by the crumbling honey-cake cliffs. On top of the cliffs I could just make out a high wall, topped with barbed wire, cutting off whatever lay behind it from the outside world.

Behind the beach, it looked like the Draconis family had decided that nature wasn't exciting enough: they'd put in ramps and platforms around the rocks and steep paths climbing up the cliff sides, and turned the bay into a hi-tech assault course.

And then let an army of ghouls and serpent people take up residence.

They dragged me up a steep, zigzagging path, heading for a high platform overlooking the bay. I took a quick squint around to see if I could spot Java or any of the other Indigos, but I didn't really expect them to be outside. They'd be hidden away somewhere.

We were halfway up when a scrabble of claws and a low growl from behind a rock stopped the gang in their tracks.

'Santa Maria!' yelped Pierce, backing off. 'Where the hell did that thing come from?'

Spike walked forward slowly, his eyes like headlamps and the fur along his back bristling. His gaze was fixed on Pierce and the gang flocking around me.

'I told you, he's my dog,' I said. 'He follows me when I go diving.'

Spike rumbled low in his chest. He fixed his red eyes on Pierce and lifted his lip, showing his fangs.

'Down, Spike!' I said, trying to make out I had some control over the mutt. 'It's OK, they're just creeps pretending to be freaks – that's all.'

To my surprise, Spike stopped growling, then waddled off into the bushes again.

It was true: the people in this bay were normal, except that they'd got themselves tattoos, studs, steel fingernails, pointy teeth and a few split tongues. The Screamer must have been their role model. I'd definitely come to the right place.

Most of them were on rollerblades. Something was going on in the bay, but I couldn't make out what. At first I thought it was a big fight, because there was lots of pushing and shoving going on across the ramps and levels. Then the music made me think they were dancing, that this was a rave. But now a basketball shot out of the crowd and skimmed past our faces, and a crowd of rollerbladers swooped after it. One of them fell, skidded across the concrete into a barrier and lay in a crumpled heap, groaning.

I got it now. They were playing some sort of game. A

dangerous game, by the look of it, one that didn't take any prisoners.

'Where are we going?' I yelled, as Pierce dragged me up the ramp.

He didn't answer; just threw me down in front of two pairs of expensive rollerblades.

I glanced up at their owners.

Seemed I'd just found Angel and her dead brother.

Chapter Twenty-Four

I was up in a split second and bouncing on my toes. 'You're going to be sorry for this,' I spat.

I thought I'd be able to size them up with a glance, that they'd be rich kids like Jamie Champion and the others at Java's party, but neither of them was anything like I was expecting.

Apollo was possibly alive, for one thing, even though he looked dead. He was about my age, and everything about him was black and twisted. Black combats, black T-shirt hanging from his thin twisted shoulders. Black hair over a pale face, with dark circles under the eyes, as if he'd been ill, or lived on a diet of biscuits and coffee. Even his smile was twisted further to one side than the other.

His hair was too long and the wind was blowing it across his face, and into his eyes. Which was an improvement, because his eyes were the worst things about him. They had no shine. Everyone's eyes shine – it's what makes them look alive. Apollo's were dull, like a shark's.

'Search him,' he said, in a flat voice, watching me through his hair. He'd got some kind of accent, like Italian, but rougher.

'Right, boss.'

Pierce waved a knife at me, then slashed the front of my wetsuit. I took the hint and climbed out of it. Then he patted me down and felt in the pockets of my camo shorts.

'Nothing, Apollo. No mobile, no weapon,' he said, putting his massive, tattooed fist on my shoulder and keeping it there. Hint taken. I wasn't to budge.

'Why the gloves?' said Serpent Girl. 'Does he think he's a fighter?' She laughed.

'I am, love,' I said. 'All my gang wear them. We don't want to bruise our knuckles on thugs like you.'

'Your gang?' she sneered. 'Where are they now?'

'You'll be sorry, when I tell them about you and—'

'Shut him up,' said Apollo. And Serpent Girl obliged. It took me a minute before I could stand again.

Apollo pushed his hair out of his eyes as the wind tore across the beach and scraped sand over our faces. 'You may have chosen the wrong time to gatecrash our party,' he said, giving me a twisted smile. 'This wind is called the Scirocco. It's been blowing for three days now. On the fourth day it brings madness and death.'

I winked at the young girl next to him. 'How's about telling your big brother to lighten up a bit, love?' I said.

Angel looked like the Mona Lisa, but younger and on skates. She had a secret smile, like she knew something that no one else did. But it was her eyes you noticed first. She never blinked; just watched everything through her long dark hair, like her brother. Except her hair hung all the way down her back, the way gypsy girls wear it. My sister would've approved. Especially as Angel was wearing D&G Junior, black trimmed with pink – the pink matching the bow on the little white fluffy dog at her feet.

Wren had said she was ten years old, but she was cuddling a doll, hugging it to her chest, like she was a little girl of three. It was one of those rag dolls, made from scraps of fabric, with buttons for eyes and woolly hair. It looked like it'd been in her hands since she was a baby; one of its eyes was hanging by a thread. Its woollen hair was in lots of little plaits like snakes. In each of the doll's cotton hands, there was a tiny toy snake. I recognized it straight away – Princess Lato, the Dragon Goddess.

Angel looked at me through her fringe, winding one of the plaits round her finger.

'Does he always treat strangers like this?' I said to her.

Her eyes became huge, and she hugged her doll tighter. Maybe she didn't understand me. But Wren had said that everyone in Malta spoke English as well as Maltese.

'What's up – love, cat got your tongue?' I said.

Apollo made a signal with his thin hand, and straight away Pierce slammed his fist down on my shoulder. It was a warning.

'Angel doesn't talk. She's mute,' Apollo told me. 'She hasn't spoken to anyone since she was three years old.'

He glanced at her as she brought the doll up close to her face and whispered to it.

'Except for Princess,' he continued, with a sly smile. 'She speaks to Princess, her doll.'

Serpent Girl sniggered, and hissed in my ear, 'Don't be fooled by Angel because she's little. Get on the wrong side of her and she'll put a hex on you.' She pulled her finger across her throat. 'Instant pain. That doll's voodoo.'

I could see where Angel had got the reputation. She was too still, too watchful. I wondered what had happened when she was three to make her stop talking, except to a rag doll.

'Well, thanks for the warm welcome, but perhaps you'd like to tell your goons to back off and let me leave peacefully,' I said to Apollo. 'Before I get angry.'

Apollo gave his twisted grin again. 'Goons? These aren't goons, they're my army of the damned, the Draks. And we are the Draconis family.' He paused, like he expected me to bow down at his feet when I heard this.

Instead I stared at him blankly.

He frowned. 'This is our own private army, dedicated to us. They do everything we say.'

I flexed my muscles. 'Bully for you. But if Pierce doesn't let go of me soon,' I punched my palm with my fist, 'I'll show you all why I don't need a personal army.'

A silence fell around us. Pierce's fist tightened on my shoulder. Apollo's eyes widened, like the eyes of a bored cat when it's just glimpsed something that might be fun to torment. 'Big talk,' he drawled.

'I can back it up.'

He narrowed his eyes. 'You were trespassing on our property.'

'I was hunting for the Dragon's treasure. And I saw some lights underwater.'

'Yeh, well, bad luck!' said Pierce, spinning me round and twisting my arm up my back. 'You won't be telling anyone about it because it's time you left—'

Apollo's thin hand moved again. But this time it was a signal to Serpent Girl. She lashed out and caught Pierce in the face.

'Shut up,' Apollo told him, his eyes glinting. 'I'm dealing with this. No one touches him for now.'

He glanced at Angel. She nodded slightly. I got the feeling that, even though she was only a kid and didn't speak, she had a lot of power.

'The lights you saw are off limits,' said Apollo. 'It's a very old doorway into the temple complex beneath the cliffs. We use the higher doorway now.'

He pointed to the top of the cliff, where there was an old mansion, painted pink, with a flat roof and shuttered windows.

'Can I investigate?' I said, like I was just a thrill-seeker. 'It could help me find the gold.'

He gave a cruel laugh. I got the impression that the last person who'd requested a tour through the property might be swimming round in Davy Jones' locker.

'No, this is Draconis land and my relatives wouldn't like it.' There was a movement behind me. '*Santa Maria*, what the hell is that?' he said, backing away.

I didn't even have to look. There was an eager snuffle, and Spike trotted up. I was praying he hadn't seen the little fluffball dog, but my prayers weren't answered. He licked his chops, stuck his tail high in the air, and made a beeline for the white pooch. I felt embarrassed for him. I wanted to tell him not to bother, that girls were nothing but trouble, but he was on a mission and nothing was going to stop him.

'He's my dog, he comes diving with me,' I said.

'What's up with its teeth?' said Apollo.

'I think he's part shark or something,' I joked, trying to get a hold of Spike's collar before he disgraced us all. 'He's OK. He's a pussycat really.' I crossed my fingers.

The little fluffy dog took one look at Spike, curled its lip and hid behind Angel's boots. But that wasn't going to deter loverboy Spike. He pulled away from me and eagerly followed her.

'Keep him away from Tinkerbell,' said Apollo. 'Or my sister will punish your dog.'

Yeh, right, I thought. *Little girl punishes killer pit bull freakdog.*

But I was wrong.

Chapter Twenty-Five

Right on cue, Angel hugged her doll tighter and her lips moved soundlessly. I don't know what happened next; I swear to God no one went anywhere near Spike. But suddenly he cowered down, gave a yelp like he'd been stabbed through the head, somersaulted in pain, shot off down the ramp and disappeared into the night.

'See?' hissed Serpent Girl beside me. 'Voodoo.'

A cold sweat broke out on me. This was getting dangerous. The only way I was going to stay in one piece was to keep on being interesting and relieving their boredom. The moment they thought I was a victim, I'd get mashed.

Well, if they wanted excitement . . .

'Hey, you tell your sister to leave that dog alone,' I shouted, breaking away from Pierce.

Jeez, they were well trained. Five Draks stopped lounging around looking cool in their black skater gear, and pinned me against the steel rails of the balcony.

Apollo skated up to me. No twisted grin now. Just

narrowed eyes. 'That was a big mistake. You don't walk in here and start shouting orders. We're the Draconis family. Haven't you heard of us? You've obviously not been in Malta very long.'

I could hardly breathe, they'd got me in some kind of neck hold.

'So?' I gasped. 'We've all got families.'

'Not like ours,' said Apollo, looking at me through his hair. 'Our family has a very dark side. So don't come looking for kindness here. You won't find any from me, I'm dead. And you won't find any from them.' He waved a hand at the Draks.

I gave a mocking laugh, pushing my luck. 'You look pretty alive to me. Dead people don't normally walk around.'

Apollo came close, invading my space, showing me who was boss. He gave me his dead black stare. 'I'm eternally damned. So I walk. But I don't have a soul.'

Our faces were close together now. I stared right back at him.

'I'm warning you: let me go, or I'll fight,' I said. 'I don't want to hurt you.'

Apollo's mouth twisted into a delighted smile. 'You don't want to hurt us?'

'Kick him out,' said Pierce, shaking me like a dog shakes a bone.

'No, hand him over!' shouted one of the Draks. 'He can play murderball. Then we'll see how tough he is.' He bounced a basketball and then threw it over to us.

'Is that what you call the game they're playing?' I said to Apollo.

He nodded.

I gave a snigger. 'Looks more like a girls' game to me. Looks more like cissyball. Call that tough?'

Apollo's thin hand signalled again, and Serpent Girl hit me. I fell to my knees.

'Hey, look, he's going to shine my skates!' she crowed. And then kicked me in the ribs. That made everyone laugh. I didn't get the chance to appreciate the joke myself. I was using all my energy to try and breathe through the pain.

'I'd still beat you all at your stupid game,' I gasped.

Apollo shoved Serpent Girl out of the way. He pushed the hair out of his eyes and squinted at me. 'You want to play murderball?'

'Yeh.'

The boredom faded from his eyes. One corner of his mouth twisted up. 'I tell you what: we'll play sudden death.'

Pierce gave a growl of laughter. I got the impression that the sudden death version of murderball might mean just that.

'And if you win, you're welcome to stay the night. I'll even help you look for clues to your treasure.' The smile became even more twisted. 'But fail, and you'll really regret swimming in here.'

Everyone laughed. But it was cruel laughter. These people clearly thought that if I said yes, I was going to get destroyed.

I picked myself up. So far I'd got bruised ribs, scratched knees and hurt pride, and I'd only been here a few minutes.

'Yeh, I'll play,' I said.

I had to, even though it was going to hurt. If I impressed Apollo, then I'd buy myself time to have a nose around, and to find Java.

'Everyone has wheels, that's the rule,' said Apollo. He nodded to Pierce, who stuck out a foot as one of the Draks skated by. The boy tripped, skidded and fell next to us.

'Give him your skates,' Apollo said to the fallen man. 'Then we play.'

I don't know why he kept including himself. He didn't look like he had any energy to play the game. But then, as if to prove me wrong, he said, 'I'll get the ball.'

Next second he was off down the slope at full speed. He grabbed the ball, and flicked it back to us. He arrived back before it had a chance to bounce.

I swallowed. Perhaps it wasn't going to be so easy to beat a dead boy and his army.

'Are you ready, Angel?' he said.

She tucked the rag doll into her belt and nodded.

'What team am I on?' I said, putting on the borrowed blades.

'There are no teams. You're on your own.' He pointed to the top of the terraces, halfway up the side of the cliff. 'You start up there with the ball.' He pointed down to the bottom, near the beach, where a black line had been painted. 'You have to get the ball over that line.' He grinned. 'We tackle you in any way we want to get the ball. If you knock any of us down, that person has to leave the game.'

Around me, on the paths, the Draks had skated to strategic spots, ready to draw first blood. They weren't worried – they knew the paths, they knew where the shortcuts were. They must have thought they'd got the newbie all sewn up.

He threw me the ball. 'Imxi!' he said.

'Imshy?'

His mouth twisted. 'Imxi! It means "Come on". Let murder begin.'

I felt the fear take hold of me.

'Snow? Wren here. We're about a mile away from the castle. Bigley is remote-viewing the place. Trying to find out where the Indigos are being held. But she's getting nothing. Either the kids aren't here, or she can't read the signal. She says there's loads of interference. So we're going to have to try and get nearer . . . '

Chapter Twenty-Six

It was twenty Draks against one. Me.

No wonder the fear had started. Dry mouth, eyes wide. Butterflies doing random somersaults in my stomach. My heart beating fast. Muscles shaking, ready to go. My brain in overdrive. Don't ask it to do maths, though, or write a poem. It was working full-time on surviving.

Exactly what I needed.

Fear and excitement are twins: we crave the excitement, but we don't like the fear. It makes us feel helpless, like babies again. Except me.

I liked the fear. It was the only thing that'd give me an edge. Because when you feel fear, adrenaline floods through your body. And adrenaline is a superfuel. It would make me faster and smarter.

The Draks were over-confident. They did this all the time. They saw me as the puny kid who was going to get mashed. There was no superfuel in their blood, poor saps.

I got into my position, overlooking the paths and terraces.

I twitched about a bit, shifting from one skate to the other. I'd have to move soon, and move quick, or I'd get a slump. Too much superfuel pumping round my veins with nothing to do and nowhere to go, and I'd get rooted to the spot, body frozen, brain a terrified blank, shaking like a bunny.

I bounced the ball a couple of times, giving me the chance to have a squint at the layout of the course, and let my gypsy compass try to take in every last shortcut, safe zone and danger spot.

I was hoping all those years of getting into trouble and then running away from it were going to come in useful. But I'd got another trick, as well.

I fixed an image of Snow's mask-like face in my mind. If I failed, I'd get kicked out, and that'd mean the mission was over. Then Snow would say, 'I told you so, he hasn't got what it takes.' And Wren would look disappointed and say, 'Yeh, perhaps you were right.'

Where was the respect in that? No, I couldn't fail.

'Ah, he's scared!' mocked Pierce from below. 'Poor lost boy! Let's get him!'

I screeched off the top path, leaped the barrier, and landed next to Pierce with a screech of metal on stone.

'Sorry, were you talking to me?' I said, and swept his feet from under him, then zigzagged away.

The game began. Except it wasn't exactly a game, not with twenty black-clad Draks after my blood. Fists flew, skates tripped me. They came at me full tilt, two or three at a time, and pasted me across the barriers.

'Bet that hurt,' growled Pierce. 'Give in?'

'What's a bruised rib or a scraped knee or two?' I said, trying not to double up in pain. 'It's still a cissy game.'

The Draks didn't like that, for some reason. Next thing I knew, one'd got the ball off me and was speeding away with the rest of the pack following him. Until Apollo flew down a ramp, grabbed the ball and rammed into the guy who'd been holding it. The unlucky Drak skidded and crashed.

The pack streamed after their leader, but I went faster and got by them, so I was level with Apollo. I lunged, and got the ball back.

He shot a glance my way, grinned, did a skidding turn using a railing as a pivot, and ran me down. Which left me sliding downhill on concrete. That hurt. It got more adrenaline flowing, though, sending it pumping through my veins like fire.

I got up, picked up some speed and elbowed assorted Draks out of my way, my heart racing, my muscles in fast-twitch mode. I ignored the crashing bodies, the grunts of pain. I had my own injuries, that knee was going to sting when the adrenaline wore off. But right now I was feeling no pain at all.

I came level with Apollo again, and nicked the ball.

Then left him behind.

Pumped the brake on my skate.

Did a crossover and screeched up a ramp towards the top levels to fool 'em all. It worked. The Draks peeled off, some braking, some trying to turn and running into each other instead. So I leaped a railing, leaped another, working my way to the line the quick way – straight down. I cleared one more railing and smacked on to the ground in front of Apollo again.

Showing off, that's all it was. If I was going to get a beating, at least I was going to go down with style.

But Pierce was coming up behind me, and my feet were skidding, and I was rolling over and over. I grabbed Apollo. If I was going down, so was he. We slid along the ground together.

'You've got a pretty good pulse for a dead boy,' I said. I had a grip on his wrist.

Apollo's mouth twisted into a grin. 'Worms moving under the skin, that's all.'

'Hey, treasure hunter with the big mouth!' growled Pierce, as I staggered to my feet. 'You want to give up now?'

'Who, me?' I said, trying not to gasp. 'I've not even warmed up yet.'

The thing was, I couldn't pull out all the stops. When I *really* go for it, the Hercules gene shows, and you can tell I'm a freak. Then Apollo might take too much interest in me and start to get suspicious about how I ended up in here. So I upped it a bit, but not all the way to Hercules level.

The Draks who'd kicked me were sitting on the sidelines, watching me closely now that I wasn't getting beaten to a pulp and some of their comrades were suffering. But I didn't care about them. It was Angel who was worrying me now.

She was a small black streak, veering in and out, leaping off terraces, hugging her doll, following every move I made. She was there at my side as I thundered down a ramp, and she grabbed the ball and skated off. But she was just a kid, and all

154

I had to do was speed up and take it back. It'd be like taking candy from a baby.

A figure streaked up to my side. It was Serpent Girl, and she must have read my mind because she said, 'If you tackle her, you'll regret it.'

I hesitated for a second, and that's how Pierce got the chance to zip by me and grab the ball, making Angel swerve. She hit the railings, ricocheted off the metal, and bowled over and over under the feet of the pack, who jumped and swerved out of her way.

I screeched to a halt. But she was tougher than she looked. She limped to the side, took the doll from her belt and hugged it tight. Her lips moved silently.

Still fleeing with the ball, Pierce suddenly jackknifed as though he'd been stabbed in the guts, and fell, pinwheeling across the concrete until he hit a railing near me. He lay still, out cold. I grabbed the ball as it bounced free.

Angel gave me that secret Mona Lisa smile, picked herself up and skated on, winding a strand of Princess's hair round and round her fingers.

But it didn't matter, because this was the finish. I was on the bottom level now. One more dash, and I'd be over the line. Good job, because I was starting to shake. The adrenaline was nearly used up.

Only problem was, Apollo was blocking my way. With a Drak at his side who must've stood two metres tall, and was built like a Shire horse. He was sweating like a horse, too. But so was I, and everyone around us. All of us were gasping for breath. Except Apollo – he was still ice cold.

'Give in?' he said. He fixed me with a dull gaze from under his hair.

'Never,' I said.

I had two options to get by him and reach the line. And he knew it.

'Which way are you going?' He was poised, ready to go either way. Ready to swipe my legs from under me. 'Whichever way, I've got you covered.'

I could pretend to go left, and then go right.

I could pretend to go right, and then go left.

Not much choice.

So I swerved left. And there must've still been some adrenaline left in my blood, because time slowed down and I saw Apollo's smile begin, and the muscles in his right arm pull back, and his left skate begin to slide forward. His body went a millimetre towards the right as he guessed I was faking.

So I did the one thing he didn't think I'd do. Time picked up speed again, and I pretended to go left, then went left.

And by a miracle, I sailed by Apollo. But the big Drak was there. And instead of tackling me for the ball, he got his fists up, and started jabbing out at me.

Seemed like the rules of the game had changed. Now that it looked like I was going to win, they'd decided to turn it into a boxing match. Fine by me.

He swung a punch at me. It hit me in the biceps, half paralysing my left arm. I blocked with the right. He swung again, so I aimed a punch at him. He didn't go down. He ducked it and hit me again.

But he didn't realize something. He wasn't dead if he didn't get the ball over the line. I was.

So I turned on the Hercules force and hit him. I wasn't showing off, honest. I swear to God it was only the one right hook, and I didn't use full force. But he fell backwards like a big oak tree going over.

There was a gasp from the other Draks.

Then I ran, ducked, swerved and slammed the ball over the line.

And the whole bay fell silent. All you could hear were the soft waves lapping the shore. And Spike, somewhere high on the cliff, howling into the wind like a lovesick wolf.

I looked around. The Drak was getting up off the floor, the back of his hand against his mouth. Angel was clutching Princess and staring at me. Usually it's easy to read someone's face, but Angel's expression was harder to fathom than Snow's mask.

The rest of the Draks were staring at Apollo. Some were grinning. Some were licking their lips, and looking from Apollo to me and back again. I think they were hoping there was going to be punishment for me daring to beat their boss.

Serpent Girl, nursing her ankle on the edge of a ramp, leant over and whispered, 'You've done it now. He'll get you for this.'

I raised an eyebrow. 'Sorry, no one told me not to beat him. I thought we were all playing fair and square. Are the rest of you not allowed to win, then?'

Now it was her turn to look surprised. 'Yes! We try to beat him every time we play. We just never succeed. He never loses.'

It seemed like everyone was holding their breath, waiting for Apollo to speak. So I walked up to him. 'Great game.'

The silence deepened. Angel came over and perched on the railing next to her brother.

'What does Angel think about the trespasser?' he said.

Her mouth moved silently. Apollo watched her closely, then gave his twisted grin. 'Angel likes the way the new boy fights. What's your name?'

'Freedom,' I said.

He looked at me and then grinned.

'Well, Freedom, you've earned your freedom. For now.' He held out his fist for a gangster's handshake. 'OK, fun's over for tonight,' he shouted to the Draks. 'Let's get some sleep.' He turned to me. 'Follow me. I've got a plan.'

Behind me, Serpent Girl skated close and said, 'You think they want to be friends? They don't. They're bored, that's all. They're playing with you. Do you really think they'll let you go when they're done?'

I pushed by her without speaking. I knew she was right. But I was in too deep now.

Chapter Twenty-Seven

'**I**mxi! Let's go meet Nana.'

We went up the zigzag road to the top of the cliff, the hot wind scraping our eyes like sandpaper.

'Are your mammy and daddy at home, too?' I said.

'No, mama died when Angel was little. Pa as well. The Draconis are a family with many early deaths. We don't make old bones.'

'You should become a Smith,' I said. 'We go on for ever.'

At the top I looked around.

'Where's the temple?'

Apollo gave his lazy twisted grin.

'Below the house. The temples in Malta are all underground. They're the oldest in the world.'

'So why did they put one of the entrances under six metres of water in the bay?'

'My Uncle Drago says the door was built when the sea was much lower. When the sea rose, the entrance got flooded.'

'Who did they worship?'

'Princess Lato,' said Apollo, quickly. But I caught the look that flashed across his face. It was only there for a millisecond, and I only caught it because my senses were on red alert, checking for signs of Java or the other Indigos.

Cold reading, my great-granny Kate called it, when she told fortunes. It meant flicking a glance at someone and, in a flash, reading all the little signs that show what they're truly thinking. For one heartbeat, Apollo had looked like a baby about to cry. His eyebrows went up in the middle, his mouth turned down at the corners, and his lips quivered. And then it was gone before anyone had time to see it. Except me.

And it was interesting, because boys who claim to be dead, and not to feel anything, shouldn't feel fear.

'All her temples are underground,' he said. 'Princess Lato is a dark goddess of the underworld.'

And there it was again. The tremor in his voice, the quick flash of fear.

We walked through an archway made of three massive stones, into a scrubby garden, smelling of ripe peaches and cats, and overgrown with vines and creepers that blew about in the wind. The Scirocco wind was fierce up here, like an industrial heater blasting in your face.

'Thanks for this,' I said.

He looked at me blankly. 'I'm not your friend or anything. I don't have a heart any more, so it's not kindness – you know that, don't you?' he said.

'About that,' I said. 'How long've you been dead?'

He shrugged. 'One morning I woke up in a coffin.'

'You're kidding, right?'

'No.'

'Come on!'

Apollo gave a wry grin. 'I had a death certificate and every-thing. Then they changed their minds. Doctors came and prodded me, they gave me stuff, they injected me, they got psychiatrists to talk to me, my nana came and shouted at me, but still I never moved.' His face went bitter again. 'You'd think they'd have let me rest in peace. So in the end, I couldn't stand lying there and rotting any longer, and I realized I was eternally damned to walk the earth, so I got up. That was seven years ago.'

That figured. The same time Angel stopped talking.

Everywhere we went there were cats – mean, skinny ones, slinking away and hissing at us as we walked past. Apollo tried to call one of them, but they ran away.

'I don't know why they're like this; usually they come to have their ears scratched.'

A rustling in the undergrowth, and Spike's tail waving above it, might've had something to do with it, I thought. But I kept quiet. My mind was on other things. Like how I was going to find Java.

The front door to the *palazzo* was wide open, with a white curtain blowing out like a ghost in the wind. As we went through, I was just thinking what a clever fella I was to get this far, and how impressed Wren'd be, when I got a head rush. You know, when you stand up quickly and your head spins? It was like that. I even grabbed for the doorpost.

Apollo was watching me through his hair. 'You felt it?' he said.

'Yeh, what is it?' I blinked, trying to stop the giddiness.

He pointed downwards. 'It's the temple underneath us. Makes some people dizzy. Not everyone feels it.'

The door slammed behind us. The Scirocco, I suppose. But it sounded final, like a tomb door closing shut for ever.

Apollo led me into the hall, the marble floor cool under my bare feet. It was full of furniture that might have been junk-shop rubbish or priceless antiques, I couldn't tell the difference. My mind wasn't on interior design, anyway.

'Isn't it a bit late to be visiting your nana?' I said. The last thing I felt like doing right now was trying to sweet-talk an old Maltese lady.

'No, Nana doesn't sleep much – she's been ill. But she likes to see visitors.' Apollo held a curtain aside for me. 'I want her to meet you.'

I followed him. The deeper into the house I went, the more I wanted to turn and get out. The place was a dark labyrinth. Twisting passages, doorways covered by curtains blowing in the breeze from the lazily whirling ceiling fans. And every now and then, the head rush, and me clutching a door frame.

We went by a row of pictures, those old oil paintings that look good from far away but really bad close up. One of them, over a dark doorway, was the wild-eyed man with long curly black hair who I'd seen a picture of at the briefing. He had the same crooked smile as Apollo. And in this picture he also had a thick gold necklace round his neck, a gold earring in one ear that was so heavy even my sister Crystal might've thought it was too much, and a gold ring on each of his fingers.

My head began to swim again just looking at the painting. Or it might've been the dark doorway below. It felt as if there was something inside, some huge power source in the shadows, that was sucking at my brain and pulling it towards the blackness. I leant my back against the wall and tried to breathe.

Apollo stopped and watched me. 'Head rush again?'

'Yeh.' I wiped my forehead.

He grinned nastily. 'It's only Black Michael.' He pointed to the picture. 'He's the founder of the whole Draconis clan. He's the one who made us our fortune.' A crafty smile appeared on his face. 'He gave us a secret that no one else in the whole world knows. What you're feeling is his power.'

'Yeh, well, I could do without it,' I said. I gave the painting a final glance and then followed Apollo down the dark corridor.

Gold, a secret, and old people living long lives. Something was nagging at my brain, something else besides Black Michael and his power. For some reason I got the feeling it was connected to my great-granny Kate. But for the life of me I couldn't think what it was.

'Imxi!' said Apollo, impatiently.

I shook my head to clear it, and followed him.

There were candles everywhere. It made it seem as if we were looking at everything in soft focus. The place was old and beautiful, but my mammy would have gone mad to see it in such a state. It had definitely seen better days. Wren had been right – something had happened to the family's wealth. Maybe Black Michael's power was running out. Whatever it was, the passages all smelt of damp and there were cobwebs everywhere.

'Concentrate, please!' said a man's voice from nearby.

My heart gave a thud. There were other people around, and they were close by. The man had spoken in English, which could mean—

'I *am* concentrating!' snapped a girl's voice.

Java.

Chapter Twenty-Eight

My heart gave a thud, but my face stayed the same. It was Java all right. And she was OK, by the sound of it. She hadn't sounded scared. In fact she'd sounded normal, which for her usually meant annoyed.

We went by another doorway and I slowed my pace, letting Apollo walk ahead. I pretended to be looking at another old painting on the wall. Then, as the wind caught the curtain and blew it open, I looked inside, casually, like I wasn't really interested.

And there she was.

Sitting at a table. No handcuffs, no crying, no bruises or cuts. Opposite her was a man who looked like he could have been Black Michael's mad older brother. The same gold earring and long greasy black hair, tied in a ponytail. The same crooked, wild eyes, except this bloke looked like he hadn't slept in years. His eyes were ringed in black, and one of them was twitching. His jacket was covered in black, yellow and brown stains and half destroyed by burn marks, as though he'd had an accident with a bunch of dangerous chemicals.

He was watching Java intently. His hands, stained like his jacket, were under his chin, making him look like a praying mantis. Suddenly, without moving his gaze, his right hand shot out, plucked a fluttering moth from the air and crushed it between his fingers. I shuddered. I wouldn't have been surprised if he'd then put the dead insect in his thin mouth and eaten it. Java didn't even seem to notice.

In the centre was a table lamp with the shade removed. They were both staring at it, their eyes glowing in the candle-light.

What made my heart give an even bigger thud was that the light bulb was flashing on and off even though the lead and the plug were sitting on the table next to it.

A hand reached out and drew the curtain shut. Apollo had realized I was missing and come back.

'Party tricks,' he said.

'Who's the girl?' I said, as though I fancied her.

'Foreign student, that's all.' He shrugged. 'My Uncle Drago's an inventor and a chemist. But he also gives lessons in Maltese and Arabic.'

'Are there any more students?' I said.

Apollo stopped and narrowed his eyes at me. 'What's your problem? Why the sudden interest?'

My heart skipped a beat. But I put on a big smile. 'Jeez, are you kidding? Girl students are hot.'

His glare got worse for a second or two, then he blinked.

'Yeh, right. Hot,' he said, like girls were the last thing on his mind. And then we carried on down the dark passage.

'Apollo? Angelina? Is that you?' said a quivering old voice. The hairs on the back of my neck stood on end.

Danger!

Something was wrong. My hackles started to rise. Something, some tiny noise, or smell, or movement in the air, had sent my senses on to red alert.

There were curtains ahead of us, and a strong smell of mothballs. But the mothballs hadn't worked: the curtains were covered in holes.

'Nana's in here,' Apollo said, holding the curtain aside.

I didn't move; just squinted into the gloom. There was something massive in front of me, but I couldn't make out what it was. I took a reluctant step forward. The smell of mothballs got worse, and the dark shape moved.

'Apollo, *hanini*, who have you brought me? Another Indigo?' said the weak voice. It was like the whine of a fly near my ear. I wanted to swat it away.

I forced myself to take one step into the room and froze, my hackles rising.

Predator here!

My reptile brain, warning me of danger. Picking up on a shadow, a smell, a small sound that I'd missed.

'Is someone else in here, besides your granny?' I said to Apollo, trying not to crouch and get my fists ready.

He smiled crookedly again. 'No, just Nana.'

I could hardly breathe now. But I had to be mistaken. I must be out of sync. I wasn't used to this country, the new smells, the stupid wind that never stopped blowing. The heat.

I thought for once I'd got it wrong.

A match sparked into light, a candle suddenly flared.

'Say hello to Nana Draconis,' Apollo said and smiled at me through his fringe.

Chapter Twenty-Nine

The feeble yellow light swept across the room. There was dust everywhere. Cobwebs hung from the chandelier. On a table, there was an old fish tank surrounded by candles and flowers, like an object of worship. Some kind of big fat lizard was scrabbling and slithering round in it. Nothing was normal in this house – even the lizards were bigger and fatter than they should be.

Next to it was a little statue of a young girl holding snakes in each hand, and with snakes instead of hair. Princess Lato again.

'*Santa Maria*, what have you dragged in now?' whined the voice.

'Relax, Nana. You know you mustn't stress yourself.'

'Don't fuss, Apollo, *hanini.*'

The fly-buzz voice beat into my head and made me want to put my hands over my ears for protection. I risked a glance – and had to stop myself jumping back.

There was a tattered four-poster bed. The moths had been

at that, as well, and its lace curtains were hanging in shreds. It was piled with tiny lace pillows. And the tables either side were covered with medicine bottles, spoons, tubs of pills and half-filled glasses. That was fine – it was what was reclining in the bed that was freaking me out. It was huge and shapeless, as if there was a walrus under the lacy covers. I squinted, trying to get my eyes used to the low light.

I could see a tiny head on top of the huge body, and gold glinting round its neck. There was a veil over the head, like brides wear, except this one was black. It was moving as the person breathed.

'Say hello to Nana,' prompted Apollo.

Dear God, she was bigger than Moose, my favourite sumo wrestler. She must have weighed two hundred kilos.

'Is this the trespasser, the one they fished out of the sea?' Her voice whined at my eardrums. 'The one who beat you at your game?'

Apollo grinned. 'Nana knows everything that goes on. She's amazing.'

Something moved on Nana's enormous lap, and I took a step back, but it was just cats, stretching and moving themselves as Nana shifted her bulk. The veil tilted towards us. I had the feeling of being scanned again. There was a tickle in my head, like a fly trapped behind glass, buzzing about, trying to find a way out.

It was all I could do not to shield my eyes.

'Hi. Pleased to meet you.' I managed to keep a tremble out of my voice, but my brain was shrieking at me to run. With reptiles it's flight, freeze or fight, and this time mine had decided to flee. This wasn't good.

'Stand forward.'

I had to force my feet to move. They seemed to have glued themselves to the marble floor tiles.

'Nana doesn't see very well,' Apollo said quietly. 'Bright light hurts her eyes; that's why we have candles. Our family's been plagued by health problems. But her other senses are very sharp.'

'You're dark for an English person.' Her head tilted back and the black veil rippled. Again I felt the tickle behind my eyes, as if something was scanning me. 'There's something else about you,' she said. 'Something different.'

'I'm a gypsy.'

I was trying not to back away from her but, Jeez, I wanted to. I wanted to be as far away as I could get.

An annoyed tut came from behind the black veil. 'Gypsy? Meh! I don't like vagabonds.'

I lifted my head and looked directly at her. 'No, I said I'm a gypsy.'

Apollo leaned over. 'Nana hates everyone – English, Italian, Chinese, American. She only likes Draconis. Don't take it personally.'

Her small hands clasped together. The veil blew out again. 'You're not an Indigo.'

I looked at Apollo, as though I didn't understand what she meant.

'She's just saying you don't have any paranormal gifts.' He was biting his nails, even though they were already bitten to the quick.

I felt the fly-buzz behind my eyes again. 'He's no use. Take him away!' she whined.

Apollo went and perched on the end of her bed. 'He is, Nana. You should see him fight!' He glanced back at me. 'I want him for a temple guard. We've lost a few recently, so we need new fighters.' He lowered his voice and leant closer to her. 'We need protection from our enemies. Angel needs protection. He's worth five of the Draks – they just play at being bodyguards. The temple guards have to be the best.'

Nana sniffed, and the veil turned my way. 'I'm sure he has people waiting in a hotel somewhere, wondering where he is,' she said craftily.

'No.' I crossed my fingers. 'I'm eighteen. I'm travelling on my own. I can do what I want.'

Apollo and Nana glanced at one another.

'Please, Nana.'

She grasped his hand. 'My pet, you know I can never say no to you!' she said, her voice all sweet and honeyed now. 'If you really want him.'

'Hey, you never mentioned that before,' I said to Apollo. 'I don't work for people. I'm a gypsy. I'm going to find my golden treasure and then go. Off round the world, maybe.' It wouldn't do to seem too eager. 'Anyway, how much fighting can the guard of an old temple have to do?'

Apollo's dead eyes narrowed. 'There was an incident years ago when some thieves tried to break into one of our temples. They damaged something precious to us. It brought us to this …' He waved his hands at the cobwebs and the tatters.

'Apollo!' said Nana sharply.

Apollo bit his lip. 'OK, let's just say it brought us bad luck. So we got our own bodyguards and trained them to guard our houses and our temples, so that it wouldn't happen again.'

'What happened to the thieves?' I said.

Apollo grinned. 'One fried in the explosion, one managed to run away, but he was badly burned. I don't think he survived long.' He looked at me. 'So, you'll work for us, as a temple guard?'

I gave a short laugh. 'Thanks, but no thanks.'

The veil turned my way, like a snake sighting a mouse. Nana's massive body shifted. Startled cats fled from the bed. Her shadow on the wall behind seemed to grow and writhe.

'You trespassed on our property, gypsy boy,' she said icily. 'You are lucky to be in one piece. But Apollo has taken a liking to you. So when we offer you a chance to be part of the Draconis temple guard, you don't say no. There is not a choice.' The veil tilted upwards. 'Do you understand?'

I shrugged, like I didn't care, but my heart was pounding. 'OK,' I said. 'I'm in. It'll be an education.'

Nana's veil rippled, and from behind it came a laugh. 'He's yours, Apollo. You can keep him.'

It was like she was talking about a pet hamster. And you know the life expectancy of most hamsters. But I didn't care. I was in the Draconis house and I'd seen Java.

But that wasn't the thing that was making my heart pound. It was Black Michael's face that kept swimming in front of my eyes as Apollo led me past the dark doorway. And as I went by I got the same feeling as before. As though there was a huge power source that was pulling at me, and drawing me towards it.

If Apollo felt it, he didn't show it. He carried on up the stairs, holding a candle in front of him and ducking the cobwebs. I followed him.

Ever since Wren and Bigley had told me about the family, with their fortune in gold and their long lives, something had been nagging at my brain.

Now, I reckoned I knew Black Michael's secret.

The only problem was, no one was going to believe me when I told them it was alchemy.

Chapter Thirty

'Alchemy? Alchemy!' Wren's voice buzzed distantly in my ear. 'Let me get this right. You're talking about the forerunner to science. The men who searched for a way to turn metal into gold, and find the elixir of life?'

It was way past midnight and it was still hot in the bedroom. I was sitting on the windowsill, trying to see if I could spot Spike out there amongst the bushes.

'Yes!' I whispered. 'I reckon Black Michael started it all. Afterwards the family had loads of gold and—'

'And you know about alchemy how?' he interrupted.

'My great-granny Kate, of course.' I'd got the glove jammed next to my ear to cut out the sound of the wind. 'If it was about getting gold out of nothing, she was the best. Only when she told people she could do alchemy it was hanky-panky. Other people's gold tended to disappear first, and then they'd call the cops.'

'Sounds like you might have stumbled on something

175

there, Freedom.' It wasn't exactly praise, but it did my heart good to hear it. 'Except for one thing.'

'Huh?'

'Alchemy has never worked. No one can change lead into gold. And there's never been anything that can prolong life. Not then, not now. So he must've been a fake.'

Someone started talking behind Wren.

'OK, OK. Bigley says I'm wrong. Apparently, in 1980, a scientist turned metal into gold. But it took massive amounts of energy to create only a few tiny grains of gold, so that still means—'

Wren's voice cut off sharply again. There was the sound of a distant argument, and then Bigley came on. She'd probably hit Wren with the crystal.

'Freedom, I think you're on to something here. Latest thinking is that if someone could get a massive enough power supply, then they *could* turn lead into gold. Have you seen anything that might be a new type of power supply, anything unusual?'

'No. But there's a temple beneath the *palazzo*, and I got a head rush when I—'

'That could be a side effect,' said Bigley. 'Listen, if this really is some sort of alchemy, then that power source is going to be massive and dangerous, and probably unstable. Remember the explosion twenty years ago? Maybe whatever is powering the alchemical transmutations blew up at the castle. See what you can find, but don't go near it. And be careful.'

'OK.'

Then Wren came back on. 'So what's happening over there?'

'I got caught; now I'm going to be a temple guard.'

'What's that? Like the Screamer?'

'Yep. Some sort of elite bodyguard. There's one at the castle, as well, so be careful.'

'OK, point taken. We're at present hidden in trees near the moat. There're no guards outside. But we'll watch out for any creeps who look like the Screamer.'

'I wouldn't mind learning a few of their fighting techniques,' I said. 'Like Dragon Fire.'

Suddenly Wren's voice was loud and clear in my ear. 'No, you don't! And don't go anywhere near those snake wristbands, either. Our lab tested the Screamer's. It works by shooting needles deep into the flesh of your arm and then stimulating tachyon energy points in the body.'

'What's so bad about that? It could be useful to us, Wren.'

'Don't even think about it, Freedom. Those wristbands will kill anyone who hasn't been trained to deal with the energy surge. It would take months of training to be strong enough to take it. The whole thing is dangerous, very dangerous. Our bodies were never meant to be put under that sort of strain. Understood?'

'Understood.'

'Good. So try and keep out of trouble — just observe and report back. Got it?'

'I could get Java out tonight, Wren. Then we'd be safe. I haven't seen any of the other Indigos.'

'No! Teamwork, remember. We have to be ready to rescue all the Indigos at the same time.'

I didn't say anything. Teamwork wasn't my strong point.

Look after my family, look after me, that's how it usually went. But I couldn't say that to Wren. Nor could I shift an image that had stuck itself in my mind and wouldn't budge. Harvey King, wheezing and terrified, and the puffer left behind on the bed.

'Yeh, OK.'

I squeezed my hand into a fist, and the call ended. Five minutes later, I slipped out of my room.

Time for a walkabout.

Chapter Thirty-One

I like prowling at night. Usually it involves a run across the city roof tops and an extra-hot takeaway eaten with only the stars for company. Tonight it meant prowling the dusty, dark passages of the *palazzo*.

It was three in the morning and everything was quiet, except for some insects that were making a hell of a racket out in the bushes, like a tiny out-of-tune orchestra. And the Scirocco wind, which was stealing round the house, flapping the rugs on the floor.

I moved silently, sinking into the shadows and fading into nothing when I heard anything that wasn't that wind. My mammy always says I'm a champion at disappearing. It's nothing to do with the Hercules gene, but everything to do with having seven sisters.

I wound through the passageways and peered into rooms. I found Angel's room and Uncle Drago's, which stank of chemicals, but no sign of a room that could have belonged to Apollo. Then I crept downstairs, flinching and freezing every time the wind blew or a shutter rattled.

There in front of me was Black Michael's picture. His crooked eyes stared down at me. Straight away I got a head rush again.

And beneath it, the doorway. It was still wide open and looked like a gateway into hell, although I guessed it was the way into the temple. A set of worn red steps led downwards. I forced myself nearer and a gust of hot air hit me in the face, like a beast breathing in my face. It smelt of roast chicken. I crept down a couple of the steps to a place where they turned a corner. I took a peek. Flickers of light were throwing huge shadows on the stairwell. The air around me was full of whispers, as though I was surrounded by ghosts.

I backed away, my heart pounding, my head throbbing, and hurried down the corridor, putting as much space as I could between myself and the red steps.

In the end I found the kitchen and raided the fridge. There was a choice between cake and spicy roast chicken. My muscles needed protein, not carbs, so I relieved the chicken of a drumstick. The chili coating would stimulate my blood.

Still chewing, I padded into the next room and—

'Do you ever stop eating?' said Java.

The good thing is, I managed not to jump. I kept cool. But, annoyingly, Java kept even cooler.

She was sitting at the table, with the lamp shining in front of her. No Uncle Drago with his stained praying mantis hands this time. Her only companion was a little silver moth, fluttering round the lamp.

'What a surprise,' I said, slumping down in the chair

opposite. 'Java doing extra homework so that the Draconis will be pleased with her.'

She ignored me.

You wouldn't think someone who looked like a pixie and talked like a princess could make me so mad.

'You don't seem surprised I'm here,' I said.

She carried on staring at the bulb. 'I saw you earlier, with Apollo.' The moth fluttered and bumped against the bulb. 'I knew you'd start creeping about.' She looked up. 'Are you crazy? This place might have all sorts of surveillance.'

My blood began to boil, and I don't think it was the chili chicken. It seemed that me and Java could never be in the same room for long before sparks began to fly between us.

'Think I didn't check? I checked – there's nothing.' My time at Phoenix HQ hadn't all been maths lessons. I knew how to sweep a room for bugs.

At last she looked at me properly. 'So what the hell do you think you're doing here?'

I stared back. 'Rescuing one of the Sparrow family. Again.'

She folded her arms. 'I seem to remember rescuing you, as well.'

'I rescued you more.'

Her foot began to tap. 'But this time I don't need rescuing. So why don't you go home and leave me alone?'

I spread my arms wide. 'Huh?' I said. 'You get abducted by some weirdo family who believe in dragon goddesses. And you want to stay? Have they brainwashed you?'

'No. And they didn't kidnap me. I came willingly.'

'What? That Screamer bloke turned up and you *agreed* to go

with him?'

'I made an arrangement with him.' She looked down at her hands. 'You don't understand.'

That got me mad. 'Oh no, I'm not smart like you. I didn't go to fancy schools. I was out on the road, the cops evicting us every other week, and the locals picking fights. And that's why I know danger better than you.' I looked around the gloomy room. 'There's something in this place that affects your brain. My head started spinning the minute I walked in.'

She looked up at me, her eyes bright now. 'You felt it, too? It's the Dragon Device.'

'What?'

'It's in the temple below us.' Her eyes began to shine. 'You might not believe this, but it produces this amazing elixir and—'

I leant forward. 'It makes gold?'

She leaned back. 'How the hell did you guess that?'

So I was right. *Take that, Wren.*

Chapter Thirty-Two

'It's this really amazing machine. Totally unique. Totally secret. It's the source of their wealth and power.'

I nodded at the cobwebs and the tattered curtains. 'Maybe they should get a new device. It doesn't seem to be working too well.'

'I know!' said Java. 'There's two of them. One here, and one at the castle in the UK. Neither of them works any more. That's where I come in. And all the other kids.' She tapped her forehead. 'Indigo brain waves.'

'I don't get it, love,' I said. 'What have Indigo kids got to do with a machine for making gold?'

'Nobody knows how Black Michael got the machines working in the first place. But they know they're very dangerous. The one in the castle nearly blew the place to smithereens twenty years ago, when thieves broke in.'

I got up and checked the corridor outside, listening for any movement in the house. The more I heard about the Dragon Device, the more twitchy it made me. But everything was still, except for the wind. I came and sat down opposite Java again.

'So what's the big deal if the devices are broken?' I said. 'The Draconis will have to work for a living like everyone else.'

'No! That's the amazing thing. There's a switch somewhere inside the device. But no one can reach it.'

'Not a good place for a switch, then.'

Java rolled her eyes. 'Black Michael was an Indigo, like me. He didn't want people tampering with the device, so he put it inside where he could move it with TK.'

I leant back. 'Jeez, love, what the hell is that?'

'Telekinesis. Moving things with your mind.'

Dear Lord, it was all becoming clear to me now. The Draconis family wanted the Indigos to restart the devices with mind power. But why hadn't they just advertised for paranormal people who could do TK and paid them a fee? A little voice screaming in the back of my brain told me the answer.

They *had* tried. And the result was three bloodless corpses. They'd resorted to kidnap because these kids weren't likely to survive.

'What'll happen when you get the device started again?' I said.

Java shrugged, as if she didn't care. 'Oh, you know, power and riches for all the Draconis again. Long life and health. Blah, blah, blah.'

She didn't fool me, though. I leant forward. 'And you. What will you get?'

She looked away and gave a laugh, as though this was a game to her. 'I want the elixir of life. Imagine it: the ultimate buzz!' she said. 'It's supposed to make you see things.'

Like she wanted to experiment with magic mushrooms for a dare. She still wasn't fooling me. She'd been hooked on cough medicine because it had reminded her of her mammy, and made her feel warm and safe. But her mammy's voice had gone silent. And now, suddenly, she wanted the 'ultimate buzz' again.

'This is about you speaking to your ma, isn't it?'

She stared at the moth. It banged against the lamp again, and a little shower of moth dust floated down on to the table. 'Might be. It's my only chance. See, Black Michael said the machine worked on "dragon power". He didn't know what else to call the power source. So the family began worshipping the Dragon Goddess, Princess Lato. But the Draconis now know it's powered by dark energy.'

'Which is what?'

'It's the invisible stuff that makes up the universe, the stuff that fills the spaces between the stars and the planets. Scientists have been trying to tap it for years. Me and Jamie've—'

'Jeez, I thought he'd be behind this, as well,' I said.

Java ignored me. 'Me and Jamie have been doing some research. The by-product of using dark energy is water.'

I laughed, but there was nothing funny about any of this. 'You don't have to do all this for water, love.'

She shook her head. 'Not just water. Supercharged water. It's what Black Michael and alchemists called the elixir of life.' She looked at me with her eyes glowing. 'It not only makes people live longer; it alters their minds. Which means it can be used to communicate with other dimensions, like the spirit world.'

'Like a drug?'

'Uh-huh.'

I leant forward, urgently. Between us the little moth continued to batter itself against the light.

'Listen,' I said. 'I'm not sure what happens after you die, not like you seem to be. But I reckon that if your mammy is looking down from above and she can see what you're up to, she must be going mental because of the danger.'

Java gave me one of her laser stares. 'As soon as the ceremony is over, I'll get out, honest. I just need this one chance.'

A few more molecules of silver dust showered down. The moth was going to kill itself. I tried to catch it, but it was too in love with the light and wouldn't be caught. Java blinked at the lamp and it went out. The moth, all forlorn now its love had gone, flew off.

'Neat trick,' I said. 'TK?'

She nodded, and wiped her nose. 'Walk down a street with me and watch the street lights go out.'

There was something red on her cheek.

'Why's your nose bleeding?'

She shrugged. 'It happens when I use Indigo thoughts to make things happen.'

'Jeez, are you mad?' I said. 'That's a warning – that what you're doing is dangerous, girl!'

'No, it's not. I'm just new to it, that's all. The brain is electrical, thoughts are electrical. So are light bulbs. So is the switch inside the Dragon Device. One can affect the other. It's not dangerous. It's easy peasy.'

'Easy peasy?'

'If you're Indigo, and you don't mind the nosebleeds.' But her mouth turned down at the corners. She wrapped her arms around herself in a bear hug. 'That's why I need to talk to Mum. I can do all this psychic stuff, and it's scaring me.'

'Let me scare you some more,' I said. 'Wren says they have evidence that the Draconis have been involved in sacrifice and bloodletting. And I don't mean just a nosebleed.'

Java shook her head. 'You've got it all wrong. They want our brain waves to help start the Dragon Device, that's all.'

'No, *you're* wrong,' I said.

She turned away. Silence fell again, except for the insects making all the noise outside.

I wanted to tell her that, even though she'd lied to me and used me to get the Screamer email, even though she was hanging round with Jamie Champion now, and me and her were finished, I was still worried to death about her being in danger.

But I'm not good at that sort of talk, I'm only good at fighting.

So instead I said, 'What in the name of God is making that racket in the bushes? It never stops.'

She stared at me for a second or two and then said, 'It's cicadas. They're like crickets: they rub their wings together.'

Behind the noise of the cicadas there was another one. I'd

been hearing it for a while. It sounded like someone wheezing. It was coming from the room next door.

'So, when are you going to introduce me to the other Indigos?' I said.

Chapter Thirty-Three

They were all there, fast asleep on old narrow beds. Curled up under sheets, with just their hair showing. Except for Harvey. He was sitting up, clasping his knees with his hands, wheezing and coughing.

'Who are they?' I whispered.

She pointed to each bed in turn. 'Jess, Tom, Sam, Navjit—'

'Yeh, I get it. Normal kids who've ended up running away from their families, because of an email.'

She flicked a glance at me. 'Don't feel sorry for them. They all think like me. This is a great chance for us to test our powers.'

Harvey heard us and looked over. 'Hi, Java. You couldn't sleep either?'

I went over to him. 'You got an asthma attack?'

He nodded. 'I lost my puffer.'

I turned to Java. 'The Screamer scared him to death. I saw it on tape,' I hissed.

She waved a hand like I was making a fuss about

nothing. 'They all got a scare. But now they know what's happening, they're OK. So don't go frightening them all again.'

Another figure stirred and said, 'Huh? Huh? Whazzup?'

'Shhh, Sam, go back to sleep,' whispered Harvey. Then he looked at me, his eyes shining in his thin face.

'This is the most exciting thing that has ever happened to me in my life, and . . .' But at this point he ran out of breath.

I sat on the end of his bed. 'I saw CCTV footage of you being kidnapped. It looked rough.'

His chest heaved, but his face broke into a smile. 'I was scared out of my wits. But now it's an adventure. And I know we'll be going home soon.'

'This is an adventure?'

'Yes. I've never had one before. No one ever really noticed me before. I was chosen.'

I blinked at him. 'You weren't chosen – you were forced here.'

He coughed and gasped, then looked closely at me. 'You're not Indigo?'

'Nope.'

'What're you doing here, then?'

'Rescuing you and all the others.'

Harvey's eyebrows rose. 'Why? We don't need rescuing.'

'You're enjoying this?'

'You don't understand what it's like to be Indigo,' he whispered. 'You think you're the only person like it in the world. And then suddenly you find you're not alone.' He grinned.

'The family are a bit weird, but they're OK, really.'

'They didn't get you any asthma medicine, though, did they?'

'They're busy. It's nearly time for the ceremony. Then I won't need medicine.'

Too right he wouldn't. He probably thought he'd get a chance to drink the elixir. But I reckoned it was because he'd be dead.

I looked around the room. It was getting lighter. The dawn was rushing towards us, and the heat was climbing. I could feel it stealing through the wooden shutters. Bright bands of light were streaming across the marble tiles and covering the beds in stripes.

I put the glove to my ear. I had to let Wren know that the kids were all here. And that I'd need help getting everyone out. Harvey glanced at me, then said 'Java?' quietly.

She came over. 'What're you doing?'

I should've been on my guard, but I wasn't. 'Letting Wren know that I've found you, and that we need help.'

'With a glove? That's a mobile?' She smiled innocently. 'How cool is that! Let me see.'

I held out my hand. She pulled. The glove came off.

'Give it to me,' I said.

'No.' Her eyes blazed. 'You have to go. You have to let us do this.'

'It's important,' said Harvey.

I looked at them both. The other kids were waking and sitting up.

'Huh? What's going on?'

'Who's he?'

I looked round at them. 'You're all going to die. The Dragon Device will kill you.'

'You're wrong,' said Java.

She threw the glove to Harvey. Then we stared at each other. And although half of me wanted to shake her and tell her she was crazy, the other half understood. Twice now she'd surrounded herself with danger. She might be a rich girl, her life so different from mine we could've been born on different planets, but she lived on the edge, just like me. And she thrived on it.

'Don't make me have to snatch it back,' I said, quietly.

'Try it,' she said.

But I never got the chance. From down the corridor came a wild rustling, not the Scirocco this time. And a few snufflings.

Spike. He must have got himself into the *palazzo* somehow.

'Jeez, that's all I need,' I muttered.

There was a muffled crash.

'Stay here,' I said to Java. But as usual she ignored me, and followed me out.

We crept down the corridor, following the snuffling, and peered through the curtains into Nana's room. The hairs stood up on my neck again.

The huge bulk in the bed was snoring ... and there in the middle of the room was Spike. At first I thought someone'd stuck a false Chinaman's moustache on him; something swollen and golden was dangling down either side of his chops. Then I realized he'd got a big fat lizard hanging across his mouth. The one I'd seen scrabbling about in the glass tank, next to the statue of Princess Lato.

'No, Spike!' I hissed. 'Drop it!'

He flicked me an 'Are you kidding?' look and gave a few massive chomps. Until all that was left was a bit of tail hanging out of his mouth.

'Oh my God, he's eaten the Gremxula!' whispered Java, behind me.

'The what?'

'It's their sacred lizard. The species is only found in this bay. It's sacred to Princess Lato!'

My heart sank. 'Can we get another one?'

'No! Get it off him and put it back.'

I crept into the room. But Spike saw me and gave a big, self-satisfied gulp. The tail disappeared. I made a grab for him, but he backed off. Straight into the glass tank. There was an almighty smash.

The snoring stopped. The mountainous body twitched, and struggled to sit up.

'Santa Maria!' moaned Nana. 'What's happening? Apollo, Drago!'

I grabbed Java's hand. We had to hide.

Nana's huge bulk lurched upright.

'The Gremxula's gone!' she wailed. Then her voice changed to a hiss. 'There's someone still here.'

The veil turned sharply and scanned the room.

'Snow? This is Wren . . . there's no Indigos in the castle. Bigley's certain of it. And no word from Freedom about whether he's found them with Java in Malta.

193

I've tried calling, but there's no answer. We need to try and wake the Screamer from his coma. See if we can get more information out of him. We've got twenty-four hours, and counting, to find them . . . '

Chapter Thirty-Four

I could hardly breathe. The smell of mothballs and the thick dust were suffocating me. And there was a big spider centimetres from my face.

Java was close beside me. Above us Nana's mattress sagged. Every time she moved, the springs bounced down, just above our heads.

'Oh, my poor heart!' Nana's voice whined.

I saw Drago's bare feet hurry in.

'Down! Down, I say! Damn this dog,' he shouted. 'Get out, you brute!'

I heard Spike's claws scrabbling on the stone floor as he made a quick exit, then an excited woof and more scrabbling. I think he'd decided that lizards didn't make a good breakfast and he'd gone outside to hunt for furry, squeaky little creatures in the bushes.

'Infiltrators,' Nana moaned. 'In this room. I sensed them!'

She shifted in the bed, trying to sit up. The springs bowed down. I flattened myself even more. The spider twitched a few times.

'A stray dog, that's all,' said Drago. 'It came in through the French windows. I keep telling you to shut them.'

All I could see were his hairy feet. Even those were stained, as though he walked around barefoot when he did his experiments. There was the clink of glass and the sound of a bottle being opened.

'Drink this.'

'I don't want your poisonous concoctions,' wailed Nana above us. 'I want the elixir. My heart can't stand much more, and I will not die now, when we're so close.'

'It's iced tea, for heaven's sake,' said Drago, and then began walking up and down. 'Now, calm yourself. Rest your heart. I've called Angel and Apollo – we'll decide what to do when they get here.'

I found myself a small moth hole in the bed hangings and watched. Drago came into view as he paced nervously up and down the room, his yellow and black fingers knotting together. From somewhere in the *palazzo* there was the sound of a shutter coming loose and banging against the window, followed by a door slamming in the wind.

'Damn the Scirocco,' Drago complained, walking to and fro. 'It will drive us insane this year. Will it never stop?'

'The wind is the least of our problems,' gasped Nana. 'My heart won't last much longer. We must act now.'

Drago whirled round. I could see his eyes staring, even from here. They were mad like Black Michael's.

'You think I haven't been trying?' he said. 'You know how I've tried over the years.'

Nana gave a toad-like, croaking laugh. 'I know! I had to cover your tracks when you stole those corpses.'

I turned and gave Java a look that I hoped said, *See? You've been doing experiments with a grave robber!*

Drago's feet paced angrily by, so close I could've touched them.

'I told you! I had to render them down for their essential chemicals and secretions.'

Jeez, no wonder he had wild eyes.

'Experiment after experiment. Night after night. It's a wonder I'm not insane,' he muttered. His feet paused and then strode over to a small bug crawling across the floor, and stepped on it.

'I know!' groaned Nana above our heads. 'We have to do everything! They never lift a finger at the castle.'

'You're right. Who found the link with the Indigo children?'

'You did, Drago. You did.'

'But did anyone thank me?'

'No!' howled Nana.

'I've tried harder than all those lazy English, who do nothing but sit around moaning about the good old days. They started all this. Letting thieves get in to take Black Michael's device!'

'I know!' said Nana, and her voice became suddenly crafty. 'So why should we wait until tomorrow for the ceremony? Why don't we do it now, before my heart gives out?'

Uncle Drago began tapping his fingers on the table.

'What? The ceremony has always been performed on the

Equinox,' he said. 'We can't break with tradition.'

'But if we start early, you will have the power first,' said Nana softly. 'No one else has struggled like you have to find Black Michael's secret.'

Drago began pacing up and down. 'The others won't like it.'

'Do we care?'

There was a pause. 'No,' said Drago.

The bed sagged and heaved as Nana began shouting. 'We are the important ones, Drago! This is Black Michael's house. This is Black Michael's device in our temple.'

'You're right. Why should we wait?'

I glanced at Java. This didn't sound good.

'We'll do it,' Drago continued. He glanced towards the door. 'Where are Angel and Apollo? Really, they are getting out of control. You spoil them.'

He strode to the door and shouted for them again. There was a distant thump from upstairs. At the same time, the spider decided to go for a run around. Right near my face. I jerked back, I couldn't help it.

'Shush, Drago!' said Nana immediately. 'There is someone here. I can feel a movement in the air of the room.'

The spider was two centimetres from my face. I flicked it, and it transformed into a ball of tangled legs and black hair and rolled out from under the bed.

'For God's sake, it's a spider!' said Drago, with a small laugh like a snake hissing. His feet moved silently towards the bed. There was a tiny crunch, like a small eggshell breaking. 'It's gone. Now let us concentrate on the matter at hand, my dear.'

'Don't mention the danger to the Indigos,' Nana said, quietly. 'You know how awkward Apollo and Angel can be.'

Uncle Drago gave a short laugh. 'Angel is dumb insolence, and Apollo doesn't feel anything about anything.'

I heard Nana sigh.

'Poor sweet Apollo!'

'Sweet?' snapped Uncle Drago. 'Sweet? He sleeps in a coffin in the catacombs.'

So that was why I couldn't find his room. But what the hell was a catacomb?

Nana sighed again. 'Even so, sometimes I think they are dangerously sentimental underneath. Just like their mama. She nearly ruined everything all those years ago.'

'They'll know the truth soon enough, when the ceremony is over,' muttered Drago.

I glanced at Java. Even in the gloom under the bed I could see she was frowning.

'What do we tell them if the Indigos die?' said Nana.

At my side, Java breathed in sharply.

'Anything we like. It's not for them to question how we get the device running again. If it proves too much for them, then we'll look sad and say—'

'Weak hearts! Yes, that's a good excuse,' murmured Nana.

'The Indigos are not important,' said Drago firmly. 'And if Apollo and Angel don't start acting more like Draconis, then they'll find they won't be part of the grand recovery of our family.'

The curtain billowed open.

'This had better be important,' said Apollo. 'I was dreaming

I had knives instead of fingers, and now I've missed the end.' He padded into the room, a sheet wrapped round him.

'You dream?' said Drago with a sneer. 'The dead don't dream.'

Apollo gave a sarky laugh. 'They do, Uncle. Being dead is one long dream where nothing matters.' He yawned. 'Nothing at all. So don't ask me to do anything. I'm not interested.'

He flopped down in a chair, one skinny leg hanging over the arm, the rest of him wrapped in the sheet, like a corpse in a shroud.

'There has been a disturbance in your grandmother's room. A stray dog got in and scared her. It has weakened her heart even further,' began Drago. 'She needs the elixir now, so we have to bring the ceremony forward.'

My own heart gave a thud. Jeez, so it was my fault. Not keeping Spike under control was going to scupper all Wren's plans.

'Which means you can't lie in bed all day as you usually do,' Drago finished.

Apollo yawned and stretched. 'Is it going to go wrong as usual, Uncle Drago?'

Drago's feet stopped right next to the bed.

'We have new techniques, boy, you know that.'

Apollo laughed. 'The email trick to collect the Indigos? Now that *was* a stroke of genius. Very dark. Black Michael would've been so impressed. But the ceremony? That stinks. We don't need to pretend to believe in dragon goddesses any more.'

'We follow Black Michael's rules. It is tradition.'

'But it never works. *And* it upsets Angel.'

Drago spun round. 'Always Angel this and Angel that! The ceremony is traditional, it's a ritual, it's what we Draconis do. She will attend the ceremony and so will you. And that's the end of it. Be ready for midday.'

Apollo yawned. 'It won't work,' he muttered.

'The girl, Java, will prove the turning point,' snapped Drago. 'The Indigo life force is very strong in her. Much stronger than in all the others put together.' Jeez, trust Java to be top of the class even here. 'This time, with her help, we'll switch the device on again. And our fortunes and lives will be revived.'

Apollo yawned. 'If you say so, Uncle, if you say so.'

He closed his eyes.

'About time,' said Uncle Drago sternly, as Angel wafted into the room like a little ghost.

She was in a white nightie, her hair hanging loose and curly to her waist. She sat down in a big chair, curled up her feet and hugged Princess to her chest.

'Put the damned doll down!' said Uncle Drago. 'And get ready for the ceremony. We're doing it now, this morning.'

Angel murmured something. Apollo opened his eyes.

'She doesn't want to take part,' said Apollo, watching her lips.

'She is Draconis; she will take part,' wheezed Nana.

The bed dipped above us, then a pair of legs like gigantic sausages appeared and thumped down on to the ground.

'Get me to my chair,' she said.

The light dimmed as Uncle Drago steered her, like a massive oil tanker, towards the huge wheelchair in the corner. She stopped in front of Angel, her veil heaving backwards and forwards as she fought for breath.

'We want only what's best for you, *hanini*,' she cooed.

Angel stared at the veil.

'Leave her,' said Apollo.

'Look!' said Nana sweetly, holding out a scrap of material. 'I've made a little ceremonial robe for Princess, see, with tiny little snakes.'

For a millisecond, Angel's face changed, just as Apollo's had. A look of fear flashed across it. Then she clutched Princess even tighter, ducked under Nana's arm and ran out. The veil turned towards Apollo.

'Listen to me, *hanini*!' said Nana.

Apollo opened an eye.

Her voice was like honey. 'Do you want Angel to be better, my love? Or do you want her to be like a silent ghost flitting around the *palazzo* all her life, never able to speak? Never going near anyone, always on her own, her head full of demons and voodoo? She needs the elixir of life, just like I do. It will cure little Angel.'

Apollo closed the eye. 'Yes, yes, yes, of course I want Angel cured — more than anything in the world.'

The veil nodded with satisfaction. 'Drago!' Nana wheezed. 'Take me to my dressing room. There is no time to lose.'

Chapter Thirty-Five

A split second after the sound of Nana's wheel-chair had faded, I was out from under the bed, followed by Java. She dusted the cobwebs off her hair.

'Why does this keep happening to me?' she muttered angrily, glaring at the door where the Draconis had departed. 'I always do things for the best. And then *bam*! People try to kill me.' She turned round. 'Remember the Bear Pit? Me tied to a stake, waiting for a monster to come and get me? And now . . . ' She stood there blinking furiously. 'I'm not a bad person, am I?' she whispered, taking a pace or two up and down. 'I've not done anything wrong . . . '

'Except steal a few grand from your daddy's company.'

She waved her hand irritably. 'Yes, yes, there's that, but that was just stealing. This is murder! Of *me*!' She swung round, her eyes blazing. 'Well, what are we going to do?'

'Escape,' I said. 'We get the others and we run. Wren won't be able to get to us in time.'

She frowned. It was the nearest thing to a smile I was going to get. 'Too right. Let's go.'

There was a movement in the passage. Java was nearest to the door. She froze. Then footsteps were coming close.

'Quick, back under the bed!' I whispered.

I reached out to grab her, but there was no time.

'One moment. I'll get it for you.' Drago's voice at the door now.

I faded into the curtains round Nana's bed. But it was too late for Java. She had nowhere to hide.

Drago walked into the room and picked up a blanket from the chair. Then he saw her.

'You!' he said, surprised. He clutched his stained hands together. 'What are you doing in here?'

'I heard Mrs Draconis cry out. I was worried,' said Java quickly. But she didn't look at him. Knowing he did experiments on corpses might've had something to do with that, I reckoned.

Uncle Drago pushed his long greasy hair aside and stared at her. 'Really? But how did you have time? We've only just left the—'

My heart missed a beat.

'Indigo,' Java bluffed. 'We move fast.'

Drago shrugged. 'Never mind. I'm glad you're here, actually. Come with me, please.'

'Oh, erm, I have to get something first.'

'No. Come with me.'

'But—'

'Oh, I haven't time for this.' Drago clicked his fingers, and

I saw a Drak swagger in and grab Java's arm. Then they left.

I faded out from behind the curtains. There was no chance of running now, no chance of Wren getting here in time. So I would have to find a way to delay the ceremony.

Which meant confronting whatever was in the temple below.

Chapter Thirty-Six

The goose bumps started as soon as I saw Black Michael's picture above the door, and felt the head rush.

I looked around – there was no one in sight. I crept down the steps. At the first bend, my hackles rose. I was like a dog sensing danger. By the second bend I was wiping sweat from my eyes; the air coming up the stairwell was super-hot, as though I was treading down towards hell. And that's exactly what it sounded like.

The voices of the dead moaned and wailed from the depths below. And something else, as well. Every few seconds there was a roar, like some kind of beast, and the ground shook ever so slightly beneath my feet. I wanted to clap my hands over my ears, but they were too busy making themselves into fists. That was my reptile brain kicking in. It was getting ready for a mortal enemy. But, from where I was standing, whatever was making the noise down below didn't sound mortal.

'This is the first time you might confront the paranormal,' Wren had said. 'No one will think any the less of you if you find it too much.'

It was alright for him to say that when we were safe and sound in Phoenix. It was different now I was thousands of miles from home and Java's life was in my hands.

My feet wanted to stay rooted to the spot, but I made them move. It was a long way down. The moans of the dead floated around me, and the roar of the beast never stopped.

Down at the bottom candlelight flickered, throwing vast shadows of monsters and ghouls against the stairs and the walls. A hot wind scorched my face. I narrowed my eyes against it. The shadows morphed and got smaller. Something was approaching. I dodged back up a couple of steps and then crouched and froze, trying to blend into the walls.

The roaring got louder. And the vibration of the floor ... Something was stomping towards me. Something big. The shadows leaped. The next roar was close, too close.

'LATO! LATO! LATO!'

The shadows solidified into one stamping, shouting horror. I swear, at first I thought it really was some kind of beast. Coming past the bottom of the stairs, appearing out of the darkness, an eight-headed monster, spider-like, making the ground tremble with each co-ordinated step, its roars echoing off the walls.

'LATO! LATO! LATO!'

Jeez, but it wasn't some creature bred in the temple, it was a group of men – fighters, judging by their build and stance – dressed in black robes, moving as one in a formation, stepping together, doing a routine like the kata that martial arts fighters do for training. This was the temple guard. Apollo's finest defence force.

Just watching them made the goose bumps rise on my skin again.

As they came by me, I could see they were spiky-toothed, like the Screamer, and tattooed. Snake wristbands glinted on their arms, and silver flasks at their belt. The roar of the beast was actually their battle cry of 'LATO!', like the shouts martial artists use to get themselves riled up.

I felt the heat coming off them as they stomped by, and I understood what they were doing. This was Dragon Fire training – these were fighters like the Screamer practising their deadly technique.

At each step and shout, the fighters made hand signs.

'LATO!' A hand to the forehead.

'LATO!' Their hands chopped near their throats.

'LATO!' A movement near their heart.

Then a last roar, and a clawed fist to their stomachs.

I'd never had much to do with martial arts – I couldn't stand the bowing and the discipline – so I had no idea what the hand signs were for. It could be nothing more than a practice routine, body shapes and moves that exercised the muscles. But the way I felt at the moment, I wouldn't be surprised to learn it was magic.

As the last of the fighters moved past, I let my reptile brain do what it had been wanting to do since I'd first reached the bottom of the steps. Turn and run back up them to the passageway, until at last I was wiping my eyes and leaning back against the wall beneath Black Michael's picture, hoping my head'd stop spinning.

Something icy cold touched my shoulder. My heart gave a random thump.

'The temple is off limits to you.' Apollo took his hand away. 'Until you've been sworn in as a temple guard.'

'You want me to be one of those guys doing the weirdo martial arts?'

Apollo nodded, leading me down the corridor. 'Dragon Fire practice. They train to fight as one, like a monster with lots of deadly arms.' He smiled. 'We'll never be troubled by burglars again.'

His cloak flowed out behind him, black as night.

'Cool outfit,' I said. If you could call a cloak like a vampire might wear, and jewellery with a snake theme, cool.

'I can't say the same about you,' he said. 'You're covered in cobwebs.'

I shrugged. 'My dog started barking. I went to find him. You've got a lot of spiders round here.'

Apollo stopped in front of the hall mirror and fixed a gold serpent necklace round his neck. I leant on the wall next to him.

'When do I get to join the temple guard, then? I want to learn their moves.'

'Later,' he said. He smiled into the mirror. Well, his mouth smiled, but there were no laughter lines at the corner of his eyes. And a smile that doesn't reach the eyes is a false one, even on a dead boy. 'First I want you to do something for me.' He turned to face me. 'Prove that you are for us and not against us. That you really want to be a guard.'

'You mean, like an initiation?'

'Yep.'

Initiations were gang stuff. And you wouldn't catch me joining a gang in normal life. But I nodded. 'OK.'

'Let's go,' he said, giving me a friendly smile. But this one didn't reach his eyes, either. 'Bring your dog.'

'Sorry, he's gone walkabout,' I said hastily.

Apollo swished by me, his cloak sweeping the dusty floor. 'He's out here,' he said.

Behind the house was a walled courtyard. Three of the walls were made of yellow sandstone – the fourth was part of the cliff, with a dark doorway cut into it.

Jeez, the light was blinding. And the wind blasted into my face like a blowtorch, plastering my clothes to my body and blowing hot dust down my throat.

The yard was deserted except for a few slinking cats and the orchestra of cicadas, so Spike wasn't hard to find. I followed a hissing cat and found him eating rotten peaches that had fallen from the tree over in the far corner of the courtyard. The little fluffball dog was with him. Seemed like they'd made good friends. I hoped Spike wasn't being a bad influence.

I put the belt from my shorts through his collar and dragged him over to Apollo. His stomach was rumbling horribly, and he was frothing a bit at the mouth. I didn't think lizard followed by peaches was a good breakfast for a dog.

Apollo moved back as we approached, keeping a wary eye on the dog. He nodded towards the dark doorway cut into the cliff.

'Let's go visit the dead,' he said.

'Wren speaking, what do you want? I'm knee-deep in a moat, so make it snappy . . . What? What?! . . . When did that happen? . . . I warned you that he was Psi, that he had some sort of mind control thing going on. Why the hell didn't you tell me before? You bet I'm angry! And for heaven's sake, someone warn Freedom. I don't care if he's not answering — keep trying. No, the local police won't be able to raid the place in time. The family are powerful and crafty, they've got their own guards. This needs stealth. Forget it, I'll sort it myself . . .'

Chapter Thirty-Seven

Compared to the temperature outside, it was like walking into a cold store.

'Natural air conditioning.' Apollo slammed the door behind us. 'It needs to be cool, like the grave.'

We went down some steps, the chill air bringing me out in goose bumps. Or it might've been the coffins giving me the creeps.

At some time, long ago, someone had hacked long passages and rooms far into the cliff. You could still see the axe marks. Then the axe bearers had fashioned stone shelves in the walls. And these were filled with coffins covered in cobwebs.

'What is this place?' I asked Apollo, hugging my arms to my body to keep them away from the webs. There was a smell of damp and rot.

'Catacombs. Where we bury our dead.' He patted a coffin. 'Centuries and centuries of Draconis dead.'

He pointed to a new coffin, shiny black with silver trims. 'That's mine. I had it made specially.' He clicked a switch. 'And

I had electricity installed.'

'I suppose even the dead need their PlayStations,' I said.

Apollo's mouth twisted suspiciously. 'How do you—?'

'It's behind the coffin,' I explained.

His stare became colder. 'You notice everything, don't you? But that's not all we need light for.' He pointed down the dark passageways radiating away from us into the airless depths of the cliff. 'It means we can skate through the catacombs.'

'So being dead's not always boring, then?' I said.

'It's OK,' said Apollo.

We kept walking. It was like a continuous horror show. The tunnel kept branching into side chambers, where shadows lurked, and sounds, of water dripping or small things scuttling about, echoed towards us. The air was damp and tasted of metal.

The further we got from the light, the more the coffins had rotted with age and split open, letting brown bones spill out on to the shelves. I kept a tight hold on Spike – I didn't want Apollo to turn round and see him chewing on the leg bone of a Draconis ancestor.

Mind you, I didn't want them turning round and noticing what I was doing, either.

The walls were made of soft sandstone, and each chamber and new passage looked identical. Which meant there was nothing for my gypsy compass to latch on to. So as I went I left patrins, in case I needed to get out quickly.

Patrins are how travellers and gypsies got messages to each other before mobiles were invented.

In the old days, when my great-granny Kate used to tell

fortunes, she used to watch out for special patrins left by other fortune-tellers, hidden outside houses, telling her whether it was worth knocking on the door.

My daddy had taught me how to do them. Sometimes, when he was working away, he'd leave me patrins by the roadside – a bent branch if we had to turn right, say, or a cross made from twigs to mark a good stopping place. A branch stuck in the ground, and then broken, meant the locals were dangerous and didn't like travellers being around. But mainly he invented his own: an old boot on a post, an Asda carrier bag tied round a road sign.

I'd picked up a piece of rock outside, and at every turn we made I marked a patrin on the soft stone of the wall. One stripe for left, two for right. To find my way back, all I had to do was reverse the directions.

'Wait here,' said Apollo eventually.

We were deep in the catacombs, and the coffins had given way to mouldering skeletons wrapped in faded, dusty old shrouds. Long hanks of hair were still clinging to some of the skulls. I shuddered as a mummified hand hanging from a shelf brushed my leg. Gold gleamed round its bony wrist.

There was a movement behind me.

I sneezed.

'Have you just pulled a gun on me?' I said, without turning round.

I heard him catch his breath. Then—

'You're smart,' he said. 'Turn round.'

Surprise, surprise, he had a gun.

He was holding it like a gangster, sideways, with a one-handed grip. It was a Glock, and it was pointing straight at me.

'So what's this all about?' I said, taking care not to make any sudden movements.

Apollo looked at me through his hair.

'I don't altogether trust you,' he said. 'So I want you to do something.'

'What?'

'If you are to be a temple guard for us, then you have to prove your ruthlessness and your loyalty.' He grinned. 'Blood in, blood out.'

I knew what he meant. It was gang talk. The rules went like this. You had to shed someone else's blood to get in, but if you wanted to leave it'd be your own blood you'd be shedding. In other words, if I tried to back out, I'd be dead. Blood in, blood out.

Apollo glanced at Spike. 'I think we both know your dog ate the Gremxula, the sacred lizard.'

'Huh?' I said, like I was surprised.

He put his head on one side and smiled. 'Shoot it.'

Chapter Thirty-Eight

This is why I'd never join a gang. Gangs are like a disease. They make you do something bad, and then that's it, they've got you. It's like you get infected with the gang behaviour, and you're caught. They own you.

Delay. That's what I needed. To delay things.

'OK,' I said, holding out my hand for the gun. 'I'll take him down that tunnel and do it. Don't want to get blood everywhere.'

Apollo gave his twisted grin. 'No, here. With me watching.'

I looked down at Spike, and he looked up at me with one of those daft expressions dogs have. One ragged ear up, the other down, his bottom teeth sticking up over his top ones, and his tongue hanging out the side of his mouth. I think he was going for the goofy-but-cute look.

'See, there's a bit of a problem,' I said.

Think, Fredboy!

Wren had said that Indigo brain waves were faster than normal. Well, I swear mine were running at hyperspeed just then, trying to get out of this.

'You'll have a problem if you don't get on and do what I say,' said Apollo.

'Thing is,' I said, at last, 'I don't like guns.'

That was the truth. Guns were trouble; they were for cowards. In any case, I wouldn't want to be sneezing over everything as I tried to shoot my dog.

'You got a knife instead?' I said.

Come on, Fredboy. Find a way out of this. Prove to Wren that you don't just charge around like a wild animal. Wild animal? Wait a minute, something's coming back to me . . .

'Here,' he said, pulling a knife from his belt and handing it over.

'Keep a hand on his collar for a second, will you?' I said, pretending to inspect the knife and running my finger along the edge to test for sharpness.

Apollo grasped Spike's big studded collar, trying to keep as far as possible from those teeth.

'Let's get this done,' I said at last. 'Let's not monkey about.'

Spike stiffened. His ears went down. His lips curled. His tail went between his legs.

I saw Apollo glance down at him, a bit worried. Then he went flying backwards, as a brown whirlwind took off like a train down one of the tunnels, its doggie brain full of memories of laboratories and tormenting capuchins.

I turned to Apollo. 'Aw, man. I said hold on to him!' I gave a sigh. 'Wait here, I'll go and get him.'

And I was off down the tunnel.

'Here, boy!'

Spike hadn't gone that far, but he wasn't happy. He was showing all his fangs and panting. There was froth on the side of his mouth. 'Maybe if you didn't go round eating people's sacred lizards, you might not get the bellyache,' I said.

I grabbed his thick leather collar and ran my fingers round it. There was a click, and the ultra-thin credit card mobile slid out. When I activated it, there was about a hundred missed calls on it.

'Wren—'

'Shut up and listen,' said a robotic voice, faint and crackling as it bounced into space, off the satellite and down to me. Snow.

'Abort the mission. Now!'

Chapter Thirty-Nine

Someone was shouting. Far off, but getting nearer. No, make that more than one person, make it a crowd of people shouting. And make it baying, not shouting – like a bunch of school bullies when they've spotted the little weak kid on his own.

Draks on the warpath.

'Get out now!' said Snow. 'The Screamer's escaped.'

Behind me, the sound of skates in the tunnels, getting closer now.

'Where is he?' I said.

'We don't know. But he'll warn the Draconis that you're a spy. Are the other Indigos there with Java?'

I swallowed. 'Yes.'

'Damn. We'll get a team out there. We've got a day.'

'No. They've brought the ceremony forward. It's in a couple of hours. And it could kill Java and the other Indigos.'

Snow was silent for a second or two. 'Then it's up to you, isn't it?' he said, his voice as robotic as ever, but with an edge now. He could almost have been gloating. 'You can either make a run for it, and save yourself − I'm sure a boy with your talents should be able to get himself free − or stay and destroy the device.'

My heart began pounding. 'It might be indestructible.'

There was a pause. Then he said, slowly, 'No, it's not. Water makes it unstable. The explosion at the castle was caused by the device being dropped into the moat.'

'How do you know that?'

There was another pause. 'I'm assuming it to be the case,' he said smoothly.

'One of the thieves died,' I said.

'Yes,' said Snow. 'But if you don't destroy it, Java and ten other Indigos may die. It's up to you.'

'What if I can't? Am I getting help?'

But the phone went dead. And it was like his words were right there in front of me. *It's up to you.* Which meant I could get out and live, or stay and get blown up by the device.

Yeh, but this is your fault, Fredboy, a little voice in my mind whispered. *You let Spike run wild. He frightened Nana into bringing the ceremony forward. You didn't think it through.*

Somebody began shouting. The skaters were getting closer. 'Freedom!'

It was Java, appearing out of nowhere, scaring me out of my wits. She was creeping down the tunnel towards me, fear on her pixie face, her hair damp with sweat. All dressed in white now, like she was going for her first Holy Communion.

'I'm in big trouble. I've just kicked Uncle Drago to the floor and pushed Nana's chair down the steps.' She winced.

'And she was in it at the time.' Then she put a hand on my arm. 'But you're in even bigger trouble. They're on to you.'

'I know!' I checked behind her. The tunnel was empty for now. 'How did you find me?'

She blinked, like I was stupid. 'You told me about patrins. So I followed the scratches on the wall. One for left, two for right.'

So much for the secret Smith code.

Then she said, quietly, 'I didn't need them, though. You're easy to track. I could find you anywhere. I've got you here.' She tapped her forehead.

Our eyes met. I could say what I wanted about us being finished, but for this moment it was like we were back in the fight game again. When both our lives were on the line. And it didn't matter that we came from different worlds; we still knew each other better than anyone else did.

A pair of skates screeched by the bottom of the corridor.

'I think we'd better—'

'Run?' I said. I grabbed her hand. 'Good plan.'

Chapter Forty

It was too late. The passages were echoing with the sounds of Draks on the warpath. I could hear Pierce and Apollo urging them towards us, bellowing to them that we weren't far away. There was the sound of metal on stone as skates skidded towards us.

'Seek 'em out, Spike!' I said urgently.

He began to patrol up and down, growling to himself, trying to figure out which way they were going to come at us first.

A Drak face peered round a far corner. 'Imxi! He's here,' a voice called. More faces appeared.

I got Spike between my knees, and pointed his muzzle towards the faces. 'See the Draks? They're bad, Spike. Seek 'em out!'

He began straining against my hand. His stomach gave a terrible rumble.

'Go get 'em, boy.'

I let him go, and he shot off like a bow-legged bullet, his

double row of teeth in a permanent snarl. Jeez, he was bad-tempered at the best of times. So God help the Draks who tried to stop him now, when he'd got the bellyache. He looked like he was on a mission. A mission to rid the world of Draks.

The faces backed off round the corner. Spike followed them, his legs skittering on the floor, his nails clicking as he cornered fast, his tail going like a propeller. Furious barking floated back down the tunnel, followed by swearing and cursing.

I pulled on Java's hand. 'Imxi, let's go.'

I chose a passageway. We raced down it, hit an intersection, picked another route and ran on, moving as though we were reading each other's thoughts. We cut right and left, we followed the least-used passages. When one of us stumbled, the other pulled them up, and then we were racing off again.

Still the sound of skates followed us. Less of them now, because Spike had got most of them. But there were enough to make us run like the devil was on our tail.

'Down here!' I pulled Java's hand and we sped down another passage. And another, and another.

This time I thought we'd lost them all, but I caught the metallic rumble of a single pair of skates behind us, and someone cursing as they skidded round a corner. I glanced back, and a flickering shadow licked against the wall as the skater closed on us. Every now and then a rasping breath echoed around us.

We swerved into a smaller passageway, and swerved again, and, worst luck, the tunnels got tighter. And the skater behind began to gain on us, the screech of his skates echoing closer and closer.

'Roof fall!' The way ahead shrank to a crawl space. Java never faltered. She skidded on to her knees and went through like a ferret down a rabbit hole.

I dropped to my knees to follow her. But that rasping breath was right behind me now, and I felt long nails grabbing at my heels as I forced myself through. I kicked back like a mule, my skin crawling at the touch of those talons. There was a brief *ooph!*, Then I was off and running faster than I'd ever done, dragging Java with me.

Jeez, a couple of hours ago I'd had no idea what a catacomb was. Now I knew it was a place of endless tunnels going ever deeper into the cliff. The mouldy shrouds gave way to decaying mounds of bones lying on the shelves, cobwebs draping them like dirty lace curtains. We had to drop our pace and start worming our way past fallen rocks and clambering over stacks of bones.

Behind, only a corner away now, the dark figure was closing on us.

'Oh, my God,' Java murmured as we pushed our way through. She picked a bone up off the floor. 'No wonder my head feels like pigeons are nesting in it!' She glanced round. 'There's lost souls everywhere. I can feel them.'

I kicked a skull out of the way. 'Please, I've enough with the bones and the spiders, without ghosts as well.'

'There's lots of pain and suffering.'

'Forget it and run!' I hissed, as the skates closed on us again. 'Or it'll be me and you feeling the pain and suffering.'

We turned a corner. And Apollo's lighting system ended. Dim grey natural light was feeding in through air vents. We were far from the scorching sun and the Scirocco now.

These tunnels were old – they could have been from the Stone Age. The sandstone walls pressing in on us were painted dark red, the colour of old blood. It was like being in the mouth of a petrified beast. Over and over again we fell into dips in the ground, or tripped on something that turned out to be a heap of bones or skulls scattered by rats. Around us the walls ran with red water that seeped out of the rocks. The trails of damp cobwebs stuck to our faces and hands.

And there was no sound this far inside the catacomb, except the sound of the lone skater on our trail. A dark figure, a robe billowing out behind him, seconds behind us. And Java gasping for breath, and me trying to pull her along. But I could hardly breathe down here, either. The air was stale, and full of dust that gagged my throat.

'Keep going,' I said, trying not to touch the walls with their blood-red stain, nor fall against the corpses that lay mummified on either side of us. And all the time a whispering in my mind, like the souls of the dead were trying to catch my attention.

Until at last . . .

'Light!' gasped Java.

A tiny square of white at the end of a long tunnel. We swerved towards it. It got brighter and bigger as we rushed towards it, until we could see sky and hear the waves rushing and crashing on to the rocks.

I began to fret. 'Wait!' I said.

Java stopped in the doorway and grabbed on to the rocks either side, as though she'd suddenly gone dizzy.

'Yikes, dead end!' she gasped.

I squeezed by and leant out. The wind was a furnace blast, scorching across my face and eyes like sandpaper. I looked down. Way below there were jagged rocks and a wild sea. To one side of the doorway there was a ledge. But it was no use to us – it was maybe fifteen centimetres wide, and it ended where a thorn bush was growing out of the cliff.

Behind our backs, the sound of a skate braking. I heard a hissing laugh. I turned around, trying to hide Java. No need for both of us to get a beating.

'See, we meet again, gypsy boy, praise Lato in all her moods . . .'

It was the Screamer, his black robe ripped and torn from Spike's fangs.

'Thought you would've learned your lesson last time,' I said.

Sweat was dripping down his face, and strings of spit hung from his pointed teeth. He spat and wiped his mouth on the back of his hand. 'No one captures me, no one betters me,' he said. 'I'm the collector and I'll collect you, dead or alive.'

'Not today you won't,' I said to him. 'My dog's right behind you.'

The Screamer laughed as if he didn't believe me. 'Really?'

'Yeh, really,' I said.

His face turned savage, and his forked tongue licked out. 'You shouldn't try to trick me. Pity you didn't see what I did to your stupid guards at Phoenix. A few words from me and they would've helped me kill their own mothers if I'd asked.' He laughed. 'The mind is a simple thing to control, when you've got my skills.'

'Makes no difference to my dog. Hypnosis won't work on Spike. And he's got a taste for Draks now.' I nodded to a point behind the Screamer. 'He's right there.'

Without taking his eyes off me, he undid his razor-tipped belt and made a loop in one end.

'Can't hear him growling.' He swaggered forward a few paces. I reckon he thought it was a ploy. That I just wanted him to turn round, so I could attack. I did. But it didn't mean Spike wasn't there.

'He's deadliest when he's silent,' I said. 'Go get him, Spike!' And the dog leaped.

The Screamer never even twitched. Just half-turned casually, held out the looped belt and, as Spike leaped, he dropped it over his head. A second later the dog was straining against his new leash, which was now hooked on to a jutting rock.

Seemed like me and Spike'd met our match.

'OK, let's talk about this,' I said. 'Let the girl go. I forced her to follow me. Then I'll come quietly.'

The Screamer grinned. 'What girl? You're on your own.'

I glanced around. Then up, down and sideways. Doorway empty, rock ledge empty. Java had disappeared – quite a feat when the only options were to do a high dive on to rocks, climb up a vertical cliff face, or grow wings and fly away. Looks like she didn't need Indigo brain waves to be amazing.

The Screamer made a move towards me. I stepped back.

'You might as well give up,' he growled. 'There's nowhere

to run. You've got the cliff behind and me in front.' His lip curled. 'Unless you're Spider-Man.'

I shrugged. And moved away again, until my heels were hanging over the drop to the lethal rocks at the bottom.

He froze. His pointed tongue flicked out like a lizard's. 'You won't do it—'

'But I like cliffs,' I said.

And stepped backwards.

Chapter Forty-One

'**S**tupid kid!' I could hear the Screamer muttering to himself. 'Bashed his brains out on the rocks rather than face me. Scared of the Dragon Fire. Dead for sure.'

I wasn't. I was hanging from my hands, my fingertips jammed into a tiny crevice. My arms were beginning to feel like spaghetti, and my leg had gone numb where I'd smacked my knee against the rock ledge as I jumped.

'May Princess Lato take his soul and torment it for—'

I waited until his pointy-toothed face appeared, peering over the edge. Then I swung myself up, nearly ripping my arm out of its socket, jackknifed so I could lock both legs round his scrawny neck, and half-pulled him over the edge.

'Give up or we both go over,' I whispered, my face close to his ear. 'Or do you fancy dying today?'

He hissed and spat for a second or two. Then I felt him gather his muscles.

'Clever,' he gasped. 'But not clever enough.'

He gave a twist, the world changed, and suddenly it was me hanging over the edge, and he'd got the neck hold on me. I clawed my hand round his neck, trying to release the hold.

'Stop struggling, gypsy boy!' he growled.

'Not while there's a breath left in my body,' I grunted, trying to find purchase so that I could turn the tables again.

Far beneath me, the sea beat against the rocks.

'Soon there won't be.'

He knelt on my arms, freeing his hands, and grabbed for his wrist.

No, Fredboy, whatever you do, don't let him go into Dragon Fire.

'May Princess Lato fill me with—'

Which was as far as he got before a human thighbone appeared behind his head and smacked down on his tattooed skull. His head shrank into his neck.

'Pervert,' said Java, as though she'd materialized out of thin air. And hit him again.

He said 'Mmmph,' looked surprised, and nearly rolled over the edge. I caught him and pushed him back inside. Then, without letting go, I dragged him over to Spike and bound him with his own belt. Mind you, I had to drag Spike away from him. I don't think the dog had been taught not to attack a fallen opponent; he didn't know about fighting rules.

Java watched, still swinging the thighbone. 'I didn't kill him, did I?'

I rubbed my neck where I'd been half strangled.

'No,' I said. 'But he's out cold.'

'Java to the rescue in the nick of time!' she said, her eyes alight. Jeez, I swear I'd never met a girl like her. I thought gypsy girls were smart and tough, but Java was way out in front.

I hid my smile and shrugged, like it was no big deal. 'Not a bad hit. But I'd got it covered. I was just about to knock him out myself.'

Java's mouth curled into a smile that made me forget my sore neck. 'Yeh, right. Another thirty seconds and they'd have been scraping you off the rocks.'

'Me? You're joking, love. All under control,' I said, quickly. 'Now show me how you managed to vanish into thin air. I suspect there's steps somewhere?'

She smiled. 'I'll show you.'

'Hang on.'

I grabbed the Screamer's scrawny arm, unclipped the wristband and put it in my pocket. Then Java led the way along the ledge outside, and squeezed by the thorn bush. 'Look, steps up! I hid here.'

Calling them steps was false advertising; they were nothing more than a series of tiny footholds cut into the rock and leading up the cliff. But they were enough to get us up to the top in record-breaking time, even with me carrying a growling, complaining Spike over my shoulders, weighing something like a hundred tonnes and getting heavier with each step. But I could've sprinted up Everest with him in my arms when we clambered over the top, and I saw where we were.

We were metres away from freedom.

A short scramble in the teeth of the burning wind, and we would be at the perimeter wall. Barbed wire glinted on top, but after the corpses it looked about as dangerous as a string of fairy lights.

I put Spike down and took a step towards it. Then stopped. Then another step towards it. Every cell in my brain was screaming at me to run for the wall and get out. Leave the Screamer behind. Leave the Draks behind. Just get out with Java and survive.

'We could jump the wall,' I said. 'Make a run for the nearest village. Contact the Maltese police, and they can get the other Indigos out.'

Twenty paces, that's all, and we'd be free.

To hell with Wren, telling me it was teamwork that mattered. He wasn't watching out for me now, was he? He'd not even bothered to keep in contact. He'd just let Snow take over.

Ten paces, then Java'd be safe.

To hell with Snow. He'd got no right to tell me to stay here. I'd rescued Java, that's all I cared about.

The wall was a couple of paces away. I stopped. I took another step. A flash frame of Harvey's thin face ran through my mind. His eyes alight as he told me how exciting all this was. How he'd been 'chosen'.

'Go on ahead, ' I told Java.

'Why?'

'I've got something to do. Get over the wall, then contact the cops.'

She didn't budge. 'No. This whole thing is my fault. I'm not going.'

I looked around. We were safe for now, but it wouldn't be

long before the Draks started patrolling out here.

'Please, get over the wall,' I said, urgently. I made my hands into a stirrup. 'I'll give you a leg-up. Then I've got to go and sabotage something. I won't be long.'

Would you believe it, she still hadn't moved. 'No.'

'Yes. This is my deal. It's nothing to do with you.'

Don't think I'd gone soft. Don't think it was Snow making me do this. Don't think it was because I was a loyal employee of Phoenix. I was doing this to avenge myself on the Draconis, and because of Harvey and the other kids, and their hopeful faces. Jeez, don't even ask me why, I just knew I had to try to destroy the device.

'Look, someone will see us in a minute. I need you to go and call the cops. Please,' I urged.

Spike was sniffing at the base of the wall, and cocking his leg. Then he gave a howl, leaped half a metre in the air, and smacked down to the floor and lay still.

I looked around wildly.

'What the hell's up with him?' said Java. Then she clutched her head and fell to the floor.

That was all I needed.

Angel. Somewhere near.

Chapter Forty-Two

he came out from behind the wall.

Her hair was in dozens of plaits now, blown by the wind, like snakes writhing. The doll, Princess, was hanging over her arm. I think she must have got dressed up for the ceremony, because she was in a cloak and long dress with a little dagger in her belt. She looked just like the model of the Dragon Goddess on Nana's table, except that Princess Lato probably didn't wear daisy flip-flops underneath her robe.

This was the last thing I needed, a wicked little girl and her evil doll.

'I swear to God, Angel, you really know how to ruin a day, don't you?'

The Mona Lisa smile vanished. She didn't realize I'd grown up with girls who'd specialized in giving me grief. Even with her freaky doll she stood no chance.

As Java groaned and tried to sit up, Angel began to mutter to the doll again.

'No, don't do that,' I said. 'That's bad.' Like I was talking to Whitney Jade or little Ant. 'Give me the doll.' I walked towards her.

'What the hell?' Java staggered to her feet.

Angel whispered to Princess again. And Java keeled over and went, 'Ow, ow, ow!' Behind her, Spike yelped and did a barrel roll.

I got the message. The voodoo wasn't affecting me, but come any nearer and Java and Spike'd get it.

Beneath the plaits, Angel's eyes were like dark pools. No light escaped them, just like Apollo's. Something had happened to both of them seven years ago. Something they couldn't handle, so Angel had stopped talking and Apollo believed he'd died.

'What's bugging you?' I said. 'Did something happen when you were three?'

She blinked, and began twisting the doll's cloth arm round and round. Maybe I'd hit a nerve. But I wasn't going to get any further until I managed to get the doll away from her.

And to do that, all I had to do was keep her attention, because I'd noticed what Spike was doing. Every time she whispered and he got knocked down, he managed to do a barrel roll that took him closer and closer to his latest object of hate. Angel's doll. Whenever he saw she wasn't looking, he crept a bit farther on his belly.

'Things that happen when you're a kid can really mess with your mind,' I said. 'Strangers were watching me when I was little, and I used to have nightmares about it. I never knew what was real and what was a dream.'

She screwed the doll's arm harder.

'Did your mama die when you were three?'

Her eyes widened for a second. She nodded, and Spike saw his chance. He went from nought to light speed in half a second, and rammed into the back of her knees with his bullet head. She fell forward, dropping the doll. Spike didn't need a second chance. He grabbed it in his slobbering jaws and went prancing off with it, shaking it like a rat and flinging it in the air.

'Drop it, Spike! Leave it!' I shouted. But he took no notice of me, until suddenly the doll fell in two halves, and he started tearing at the bottom half, the stuffing flying like confetti. I grabbed the top half.

'Hi, Princess,' I said, shaking it. Just as I'd thought, it was too heavy to be just a rag doll.

Angel picked herself up, her bottom lip quivering. Then she stuck out her hand and made the sign of the devil, with her little finger and forefinger pointing my way, like horns.

'Jeez, love, are you trying to hex me?' There was something hard inside the rag doll. I gave it a shake. 'I don't reckon the world works like that. There's always a simple explanation.'

A tiny transmitter fell into my hand. I held it up.

'Clever girl. I reckon this gives out high-frequency sounds that'd knock a dog over easily, and any human that's had the right brainwashing.' I threw it as hard as I could, and it sailed over the wall. 'Not voodoo, after all.'

Angel's hands crunched themselves into two little fists. Her eyes began to glitter dangerously. So did Java's. She scrambled to her feet and came over.

'Damn, damn, damn. I'm so stupid!' She plucked at her earlobe, and held out a tiny metal stud. 'Apollo gave it to me. He said it would help with the ceremony, help concentrate the dark energy.' She threw it angrily away. 'Tune me in to high frequencies, more like.'

'I hate you,' swore a voice no louder than a mouse squeaking.

'So you *can* talk!' I said.

Angel's face was red, her eyes screwed up. Her chest was heaving. Then she threw herself at me. It was like being attacked by one of my mammy's chihuahuas. They might not be big, but they had a terrible nip and could get everywhere at once. Angel didn't just nip — she kicked, scratched, bit, clawed and spat at me. I had to put my hand on her head and keep her at arm's length to survive the attack. She didn't like that. It turned her into a furious windmilling devil girl. I don't think anyone had ever challenged Angel since she was three years old.

When she'd had enough of trying to hit me, she started doing hand signs. The ones I'd seen in the temple. Her little fist tapping her throat and chest, copying the guards. Maybe she thought it'd make her stronger. It didn't.

Another tiny poisonous whisper.

'Huh?' I said.

'Give Princess back.'

A rabbit could've made a bigger noise. I took my hand off her head. For a second it looked like she was going to fly at me again.

'Don't even try fighting me. You won't win. And I can't

give Princess back. She's broken now.'

'Mend her.'

I let my half of Princess fall on the floor, then I pointed over to where Spike was standing, sneezing, in the middle of a whirlwind of Princess's stuffing. The doll's clothes were blowing about the cliffs and getting stuck on the cactus spines.

'No more Princess,' I said to Angel. 'You'll have to speak to us now, instead. Who put the transmitter inside?'

Angel's eyes were huge. She looked around wildly, but there was no one to help her. No brother to stick up for her. No Draks to protect her. And Princess was destroyed.

'You can talk to me,' I said. 'I won't tell. I'm in loads of trouble as it is.'

Her lip trembled. 'Apollo.'

'Why?'

'To keep me safe from the Gremxula.'

I frowned. 'From the little fat lizard?'

She nodded. Her eyes were fixed on me. 'Lizards are tiny,' I said. 'They can't hurt people.'

She shook her head. 'The Gremxula in the temple is big.' Her eyes widened in fear. 'Bigger than an elephant.'

She looked like she believed it. She looked like she expected a giant lizard to claw its way over the cliff top any second and eat her. A kid of ten should know what's real and what's make-believe. But I let it go.

'Why did you stop speaking to people?' I said. 'You could whisper to your doll, so there's nothing wrong with your voice. Why can't you speak up?'

Angel looked around, like she was worried someone would hear her, even out here on the cliff top with only the wind for company. She shivered, despite the heat. 'I'm evil.'

I nearly smiled. 'I don't think evil wears daisy flip-flops and is shaped like a little girl.'

She frowned. 'The Gremxula can make you die, too.' Two lines appeared between her eyebrows in a killer frown. 'It'll curse you,' she insisted, her voice getting a bit stronger now, more like a small rabbit's than a mouse's.

'Sticks and stones, love – they're the things that kill you. Not words,' I said. I went closer to her. 'I know all about curses from my great-granny. And they don't exist, except in your head.' I grinned. 'Because if they were real, half the police in England'd be suffering by now. She was always cursing the cops.'

There was no answering smile from Angel. I crouched down, making her taller than me, so that I didn't appear to be a threat.

'Lizards don't grow as big as elephants. It's not possible,' I said. 'Who told you about it?' Someone had been playing with this poor kid's mind. Frightening her half out of her wits.

Angel began winding one of the plaits around her fingers. 'I saw it,' she whispered, and there was terror in her voice now.

'Tell me,' I said.

She shook her head. 'It killed my mama. In the temple.'

A single, glittering tear appeared at the edge of Angel's eye, and hung there without falling.

'You better get me another doll.'

The doll was her security blanket, and she was scared without it.

I sat back, cross-legged. 'I've got a niece called Whitney Jade and she was frightened of dogs, until we gave her a special dog whistle and a dog-training hat. And as soon as she put the hat on and held the whistle, she wasn't scared of dogs any more. Next time you feel scared, wear your cloak and be Princess Lato. I bet a dragon goddess isn't scared of anything, not even a big fat lizard monster.'

The single tear fell. Then her face changed, and she took a few steps backwards.

Coming along the cliff was a black swarm of Draks.

'This time, run,' I said to Java. 'You can make it to the wall and be over before they're halfway here.'

She shifted her balance, ready to run for the wall, then shifted it back, her eyes going from the approaching Draks to me. Her face took on a stubborn look.

'No. It's too late, anyway. They'd just climb over and get me back.'

Maybe she was right. The heat rising off the cliffs was making the Draks shimmer and waver, but they were close enough for me to catch their shouts to each other. Could I fight them, all of them, here and now? Was there any way I could beat them?

I took the Screamer's wristband out of my pocket. I twisted the tail and poked the eyes. About fifty lethal needles shot out. If it had been wound round my wrist, the needles would have gone so far into my wrist they'd have nearly met in the middle.

I could try Dragon Fire, see how many Draks I could take out. It'd give Java enough time to get away. But Wren had ordered me not to use the wristband. Said that it would kill me. I put it back in my pocket.

From behind me, footsteps crunched on the sharp rocks. Seemed like Java was right – it *was* too late. They'd circled round and come up behind us, as well.

I sneezed. They'd got guns.

Chapter Forty-Three

The cliff top sizzled in the heat. Dry balls of brushwood were tumbling about in the wind.

Two against twenty. Me and Java, our backs to the wall. In front of us, and spread out along the cliff, taking up positions, Apollo's black army.

Don't even think that Spike was making himself useful and going round biting them all. He'd snarled for a while, but then his doggie brain had decided that hunting little lizards in the cactus was the best way to help us.

The sun beat down as though it was trying to hammer us into the ground.

'Ah, look at 'em,' sneered Pierce. 'Two of them against all of us. And we've got the guns. What do you bet they're going to try to be heroes, and we're going to have to shoot them?'

'Maybe we're waiting for reinforcements,' I said.

'The cops?' jeered Pierce. He pumped a few rounds from his AK-47 into the wall. 'We ain't bothered. They won't get in here. They won't rescue you.' He looked over towards the cliff steps. 'But I think someone else wants a word.'

Coming over the top was the Screamer, and he didn't look very happy. He'd got a big lump on his head now, and it hadn't improved his looks. His eyes never left my face as he approached and held out his hand.

'Give me my wristband,' he said.

I would've argued, but twenty guns were pointing my way. I handed it over. He began to pace back and forth, winding it round his wrist.

'What do we do now?' whispered Java.

I could've told her there was nothing we could do. We were facing too many of them, even though I was a freak and had the Hercules gene. You only won fights like this in films, when your enemies didn't have guns, and were polite enough to stand in line and come at you one by one. If either me or Java made one wrong move, then this lot would attack all together. And they'd make mincemeat of us.

But I reckon I must have been born with terrier genes as well as the Hercules one, because there was something in me that refused to give up when things looked really bad. Wren had told Snow that I didn't do well when life was too easy for me, and I think he was right.

There was nothing we could do to get out of this situation, but that didn't mean I couldn't learn something that might be useful in the future.

'Try to get him to talk about Dragon Fire,' I muttered, watching him swigging from his little silver flask.

'Sorry if I hurt you back there,' I jeered. 'Sorry you've got to swig booze to get over the pain.'

He moved fast. A second later his fist was rebounding from my stomach.

'Jeez, is that it?' I said, trying not to double up in pain. 'Is that Dragon Fire, the big big secret of the temple guards?'

'Looks more like kiddy karate to me,' said Java. 'For the under-fives. I thought you had killer moves.'

The Screamer came right up to Java, centimetres from her face, invading her space. She pulled her head back, trying to keep a distance between them, but that's just what he wanted. He thrust his face even closer and grinned. 'You want killer moves? I've got them, girl.'

'Course you have,' she said, in that sweet but evil tone of voice my sisters use when they want to drive me mad.

It worked on the Screamer, too. Muscle power is nothing compared to the power of a girl making fun of you.

'Want me to prove it, then?' His face got even closer. 'Huh? Huh? Want me to show you Dragon Fire?'

I saw his fingers tapping and turning the golden snake. Then his eyes lit up, and he started to pant as the energy in every cell of his body began to burn, all at once.

Java turned her head away. 'It's a con,' she muttered. 'There's no such thing.'

For a second nothing moved except a falcon wheeling in the sky above, and a ball of tumbleweed blowing through the line of Draks surrounding us. Then the Screamer hissed out a burning breath and leaped towards me.

In one lightning-fast move, his arms were swinging round to get me in a bear hug that crushed my chest. And even with the Hercules gene I couldn't move. I could feel his breath scorching my face. He began to squeeze. It felt like a hydraulic press against my ribs. But I never moved, never tried to stop him, because I knew what Java was doing.

'Make fun of Dragon Fire, would you, girl? I could tear you limb from limb with this,' he spat, talking fast now, as the heat burned through his blood. 'I've awakened the dragon that sleeps curled round my spine.'

'Ew!' Java pulled a disgusted face. 'You're on drugs, more like it. I saw you drink that stuff.' She pointed at the silver flask on his belt.

'That's sweetened liquid. To fuel the Dragon Fire.'

So I was right. He was drinking chocolate milk.

'If you say so,' said Java, rolling her eyes. 'Still looks like drugs to me.'

The Screamer's arms tightened round me, squeezing the last drop of breath from my lungs.

'Do you know how old Dragon Fire is?' he spat. 'It's thousands of years old!'

Java looked at her nails. 'Whatever.'

His eyes narrowed. 'It was invented by the Yellow Emperor of China. The Japanese Samurai improved it. The gladiators used it in the Colosseum to defend themselves against lions and tigers!' Spots began to appear in front of my eyes, but his arms just squeezed harder. 'The Barbarians and the Berserkers used it to fight the oppressors. Even your puny British tribes fought off the Romans using it.'

Java shrugged, her eyes flicking back and forth from me to the Screamer. 'That's all made up. I've read history and I've never heard of it.'

The blood was singing in my ears now. Over the pounding of my own heart I heard him say, 'That's because it's secret! It's known only to the few.'

'Yeh, right,' said Java, so, so sweetly, like she was talking to a little kid who can't stop making stuff up. 'Course it is.'

I could almost have felt sorry for him, except I was suffocating to death.

'All across the world, fighters kill to learn the secrets of Dragon Fire,' he howled.

Java put her head on one side. 'I don't think so. It's just martial arts. But I expect you think it's something special.' She folded her arms.

The Screamer let me go. I fell to my knees, gasping for breath. When I looked up he'd pushed Java against the wall, and was hissing at her.

'Stupid girl, the wristband activates fifty pressure points. This releases the energy in every cell. All at the same time! It makes us burn!'

'No, *you're* stupid!' she gasped, as his hand tightened on her neck. Jeez, she was brave, because the Screamer was fired with some sort of holy rage now, and the worst people to fight against are those defending their religion. 'That would kill you.'

The Screamer's eyes were nearly popping out of his head, he was so mad. 'Hand signs on pressure points! They open the gateways. That is why the training is so long and so dangerous,' he said, trying to calm his voice. 'We have to learn how to take the energy and let it flow through our muscles and our brains.'

His hand flew up, curved as if he was about to make a fist, but instead he tapped Java on the forehead, between her eyes. 'Head gateway, opened by the Hook.'

He flexed his hand. This time he had his little finger and first finger outstretched to make horns, like Angel had done when she tried to hex me. But he didn't threaten Java with it; he jabbed at her throat. 'Throat gateway, opened by Horns.'

These were the hand signs I'd seen the temple guard practising. This was how someone could learn to control Dragon Fire. Angel must have seen the guards practising and copied them.

The Screamer moved his hand and thumped Java's chest. 'Heart gateway, opened by Fist.'

He hit her in the belly with his fingers bent. 'Solar Plexus gateway, opened by Claw.'

Java doubled up as I staggered to my feet.

'Interesting,' I said. 'Thanks for the lesson.'

The Screamer whirled around and laughed in my face.

'Oh, you think I've given you the secret?' he jeered. 'Go try it, gypsy boy. You'll still fry. No one has ever taken less than half a year to get it right.'

'We'll see about that, shall we?' I said, swaying around like my Uncle Shady after a night in the pub. I was so far gone I didn't even see him move.

Something hit me hard across the head, and the world switched itself off and shrank to a dot.

Chapter Forty-Four

S–h-tik!

I opened my eyes. I was in hell, with a throbbing head and a pounding heart.

S–h-tik!

A nasty little grating noise, putting my teeth on edge. To make matters worse, one of my hands was chained to a stone pillar. It left me half hanging, half crouching, swinging like a monkey.

I blinked a few times to clear my head, then looked around. It didn't look good. If this was a computer game, I'd be on my last life, with no health, and time running out at any second.

I was in the temple below the house. It was dark, hot and smelt of smoke, death and roast chicken. The chicken was close by, blackening on top of a fire in an iron basket. A sacrifice, I guessed, because there were feathers and innards smoking in the flames as well. A hot wind blew the smoke my way, along with the sound of the sea lapping and splashing.

My pillar was near one wall. I wasn't the main attraction; I was guessing that the centre of the temple, surrounded by a circle of stone seats, held the Dragon Device. But at the moment it was shrouded in shadows.

'Hey, Screamer! Apollo! Anyone!' I shouted, making my head pound even more. 'Let's talk. Where's Java? She better be OK.'

There was a click, and spotlights sent shafts of light streaking through the smoky air. One cut straight across my face, half dazzling me. I shaded my eyes.

'What are you going to do about it if she isn't?' said Apollo, walking towards me. He held his hands out. 'So what do you think of Black Michael's temple?'

One glance and I wished he'd left the lights off.

When I'd stood at the top of the red steps, I'd thought I could hear the sound of the dead moaning, and in a way I was right. The burning Scirocco wind was whining and singing through holes in the walls. And the walls were made of human bones.

One wall was made of skulls, piled on top of each other. Straight ahead was another, made of leg bones stacked close together from floor to ceiling. Finger and toe bones had little shelves of their own. It was like being in a supermarket stocked by cannibals. Looked like Black Michael had raided the catacombs when he'd decorated this place.

Worst of all, I swear the floor was made from millions of human teeth, stained red. Except for the patch of ground beneath me. This was where the noise of the sea was coming from. I was standing on a thin metal grid over a pool of frothing blue sea water.

'Amazing place,' I said, as Apollo came nearer. He was as pale as ever, even in the gloom down here. He had the cloak wrapped round him, to stop it flying about in the wind. 'I like the Jacuzzi.' I stamped on the grid under my feet. 'I didn't know they had them in temples. Or is it somewhere for the blood to drain?'

Apollo winced. 'It's the—'

S–h–tik!

He peered into the shadows on my left. 'Angel! Is that you?'

There was no reply, just the little grating noise, metal on stone. It was coming from my left. A statue of Princess Lato loomed out of the shadows. Golden snakes writhed around her head. In each hand she held two more snakes.

Whoever had carved her out of the block of stone had worked very hard on the scales and claws and teeth. Her face was half hidden by the coiling snakes in her hair. But underneath, you could just about see a girl with a fierce look. Like one of my sisters, if you stole their lip balm for a laugh.

Curled at the foot of the statue was Angel with the pieces of her destroyed doll, talking to herself in her little voice. Every time she whispered she was hitting the stone base of the statue with the little knife she'd worn on her Princess Lato costume.

'Hey, Angel,' I called. 'I don't see any big lizards in here. I think someone's been telling you lies!'

'Leave her alone,' said Apollo. He strode over to her and

took the two halves of the doll from her. He turned to me. 'Did you do this?'

'Yes.'

He strode forward. His hand connected with my chin before I could swing out of his way. Point taken. Don't upset Angel.

'She thinks a giant lizard killed her mama,' I gasped, trying to get my breath back. 'How did she die?'

Apollo screwed his eyes closed. 'Long time ago. Don't remember.' He walked away.

S—h-tik!

It was scary, watching a little girl strike again and again with a knife.

I tugged on the old rusted chain attached to the pillar. Being tied up was definitely cramping my style. And I owed Apollo a punch in the jaw, to make him realize you don't hit people who are chained up. I pulled again, putting all my weight behind it. The chain creaked where it joined the stonework, but the pin holding it was solid. I'd have to pull the pillar down if I wanted to escape.

Remember what old Hercules used to say, Fredboy? Never let them put a chain on you. Smiths don't take kindly to being chained. When a bunch of thugs decided to chain Hercules to a wall, he pulled the wall down.

I put my free hand on to the pillar and pushed. Nothing happened.

I'd been in some kind of trouble all my life, so that sometimes at night I wished I didn't live on the edge. But wishing had never got me out of danger. Asking nicely had never got me out of danger. Only the Hercules gene had.

I bunched my biceps and pulled on the chain again. This time it creaked louder.

Keep pulling, Fredboy. What's a stone pillar and iron chain compared to the Hercules gene? You've got the muscles, now use 'em.

I gave a massive pull. Stone grated against metal. Then I swung from my shackle and lurched over towards the chicken sizzling on the fire, and managed to tear a drumstick off with my fingertips. I only did it to annoy. When people get annoyed they make mistakes. Of course, I was also starving and the protein would come in useful.

'That's a sacrifice to Princess Lato,' said Apollo, throwing down the doll and coming over. 'You really believe in getting on people's nerves, don't you?'

'Sorry,' I said, waving the chicken leg. 'I thought this was dog chow!'

The wind whipped my words away. I imagined them swirling up the red steps and out into the open air, where Spike was roaming, still trying to find his lizard snacks.

'I can't believe you go along with this Princess Lato stuff,' I said, chewing on the chicken. 'My Auntie Star always wants us to be born again and go to church, and we just tell her yeh, yeh, yeh, then scarper when she's not looking. You're letting the side down, doing what the old folks say.'

He stared at me, his eyes dull. 'I don't want to do this any more than you do.'

'Simple. Don't do it, then.' I threw the chicken bone down.

'Your fault. The police are on to us now. They won't ever prove anything, but it's a bore. This might be the last time we can do the ceremony.'

'So? Let me, Java and the other kids go, and we'll say no more.'

'You don't get it, do you?'

He walked over, hugging the cloak round him like he was cold.

'This might be the last chance I get to try and make Angel better.' He gave his twisted smile and looked over at his little sister curled up at the feet of the statue, chipping at the stone with her knife. 'See, it all comes down to making Angel better. When she's OK, I can rest at last.'

He picked nervously at the hem of his cloak. For a dead boy, he was pretty twitchy. Which was fine by me – the more he jabbered on, the more I could swing from my shackle with all my weight and make the pin holding the chain move and weaken.

'Can't say I think much of the interior design,' I said, nodding towards the walls of bones.

Suddenly Apollo was right by my side, really close, and murmuring in my ear.

'The temple is Stone Age. Michael just borrowed it. It suits the Draconis because we're bad. Bad blood. The bones are the bones of Princess Lato's victims. She's always been a thirsty goddess, demanding lots of sacrifice. When Michael invented the Dragon Device, he decided Princess Lato was our saviour and began worshipping her. He liked a ceremony, especially if it contained blood.'

He held up a skull and ran a hand over it. It was polished as smooth as a billiard ball. I think he was aiming to make me think he was so evil that there was nothing I could do to make him feel sorry for me and Java and let us go. It didn't work, though. His hand was shaking and he was talking too fast.

'In the old days, the priests would drain the blood from the victims whilst they were still alive. Then they would cut the flesh from the bones and boil the heads up. Then keep them here as a tribute to the Princess.' He tossed the skull from hand to hand and watched my reaction.

Damned if I was going to let him read me that easily. I gave him a blank stare.

'And now we have all of you,' he said. A light clicked on overhead, illuminating the centre of the temple.

There was a gasp.

It was Java. And with her the other Indigos. A circle of pale faces and intense eyes. Their hands outstretched before them, as though they were warming themselves by a bonfire. But the thing in the centre was no bonfire.

Chapter Forty-Five

'd thought the Dragon Device would be big, monstrous. I was wrong.

It was a small iron machine, crouching in the light now filling the temple. It was no bigger than the generators we gypsies used for power when we were travelling. It looked a bit like a baby dragon, curled up asleep. But more like a small, pot-bellied stove, the kind my great-granny Kate had in her wagon. It might've been a thousand years old, it might've been made a few months ago. Its sides were red with rust, or it could've been dried blood.

Huddled around it were the Indigos. I could see Harvey, not struggling to breathe now, but smiling instead. And next to him, Java, her white dress torn and covered in dust, as though she'd put up a fight outside. She turned and blinked in the light.

'Freedom? 'S that you?' She sounded confused. Maybe they'd hit her round the head, as well, to get her down here. 'It's beautiful. We got it so wrong.'

'Move away from it!' I shouted.

She shook her head. 'No. It's like all the energy in the world in one place.'

I stared at the device. It was covered in swirls, zigzags and dots that seemed to move on their own. They sucked at my eyes, making my head spin. The patterns seemed to join on top to form two shallow bowls. One to collect the gold, one for the supercharged elixir, I guessed.

'Even switched off it's dangerous,' said Apollo, keeping his distance from the circle.

He was right. It looked as if it could sit there for another billion years, or explode in the next second, vaporizing everyone in the temple.

He hugged his cloak around him like a comfort blanket. 'When we get the machine started, everything will be OK again,' he said.

There was a noise from the stairs; it looked like we were going to have company. Apollo peered through the gloom.

'I have to go and help,' he muttered.

'Yeh, that's right. Run to Nana and Uncle,' I jeered. 'And I thought you were cool and dangerous when I met you.'

He glanced at me through his hair. 'This is for Angel,' he said, and walked off.

I glanced over at Angel, but she was still lost in her own little world, murmuring to her doll and hacking the base of the statue with her knife. So I swung towards the circle. Java glanced at me.

'Java,' I said, urgently.

'What?'

'Do you trust me?'

'Yes.'

'How much?'

Now her eyes had become like headlamps. 'I'd trust you with my life. You know that.'

I tried to swing closer, nearly ripping my wrist apart. 'Then, please, please, get away from the device. Run. Take the others, and run.'

A tear began to slide down her cheek. 'I can't. I'm sorry.' Her hand hovered over the device. 'It's got me. It's got us all. This was meant to be.'

Footsteps echoed from the far side of the temple. Apollo was on his way back.

'Nothing is *meant* to be,' I said desperately. 'You want to die?'

But she wasn't listening. Anger rose up inside me. Java, the danger girl, the girl with the edge, had been tamed by a stupid pot-bellied machine.

The footsteps were getting closer. It seemed that whatever had been stuck on the stairs wasn't stuck any more.

'Nana's coming,' said Java. 'They're going to start the ceremony. So leave us be.'

We'd see about *that*.

A giant shadow bobbed along one of the bone walls. It was the size of an elephant. For a second I thought of Angel's scared face, and her tiny mouse voice: 'The Gremxula can make you die.' A lizard the size of an elephant. Had Angel seen a shadow, like this one?

Another thought flashed through my mind. This wasn't the

shadow of a monster, it was Nana's shadow, as they somehow carried her into the temple.

'You wait till you see her,' said Java, dreamily. 'All dressed up in her golden lizard-skin gown.'

Lizard-skin? Nana looking like a lizard? Dear Lord. Was that the answer? Nana dressed for the ceremony. Nana huge and glittering. The size of an elephant, to a little chavvy of three like Angel. Doing something so frightening that Angel had blocked it out of her mind, and made up a story about a monster instead. Did I think Nana could kill someone? Yes, I did.

S—h-tik!

The little knife was still hacking at the base of the statue. 'Hey, Angel,' I called. 'Remember I told you that you won't be scared if you're wearing your Princess Lato outfit?'

The little girl stared at me, and nodded.

'I think the person who hurt your mama is coming along now, and this time they won't be able to hurt you. Because this time you're as fierce as Princess Lato.'

Angel's eyes were enormous. She glanced over her shoulder in terror. A procession was making its way from the stairs; something big was being carried at shoulder-height. Something so heavy it was making the bearers stagger and curse.

'You know who it really is, don't you, Angel?'

The knife struck again. Angel began to shiver.

'Nana,' she whispered.

'She can't hurt you this time. Not if you tell everyone what really happened. Can you remember what happened?'

Something in Angel's face changed. It was like the expression on the face of the statue above her.

'Princess can remember,' she whispered again.

'Your doll?' I said.

Angel's eyes were fixed on the shadow coming towards us. 'No. Princess Lato, the Dragon Goddess.'

She turned her head sharply. Drago and the temple guard, like a priest and his choir, were parading into the centre of the temple.

At their side, the Screamer whirled and thrust his thin arms into the air, as if he was raving to the music singing through the skulls and bones. The ceremony was about to begin.

Do something, Fredboy. They're coming to start the device!

A shadow flickered at my side. Apollo. I grabbed him.

'Don't do this.'

He pulled away. 'I have to. Maybe this time it will work.'

A shadow fell across the altar.

Angel's knife went S—h-tik!

A fly buzzed behind my eyes. Nana was here.

It was too late.

Chapter Forty-Six

he blocked out the light. I swear the ground trembled as she approached.

The temple guards were carrying her on a sort of movable bed, like an Egyptian Pharaoh. They were sweating and tottering under the weight. Java was right: she'd got herself dressed up for the occasion in a gold robe that shone like snakeskin. She was holding a long steel rod, the sort a cheerleader might twirl around, except this one was engraved with snakes, and the end was a snake's head with an open hissing mouth.

The veil swept from side to side as Nana surveyed the temple. When she passed me, she stopped and pointed. 'Abomination!'

I gave her a salute. 'Thank ye, love.'

The veil rippled. 'Gypsy spy!'

'Sticks and stones.'

Then, in a low hiss, 'You'll die for what you've done.'

'We'll see, shall we?' I said, not looking away from her,

even though I wanted to. 'The Smith family has a habit of escaping from tight spots. My great-great-great-granddaddy escaped from hanging after they'd put the noose round his neck.'

The veil began to shake. 'You insolent—'

'For heaven's sake, ignore him, he's nothing!' said Drago, fussing at the side of her like a tugboat helping an oil tanker to dock. Nana thanked him for this by lashing out with her stick.

He glared at me, as if he'd relish the thought of an angry goddess coming down and blasting me with a thunderbolt. He'd got himself dressed up as well, down to pointy snake-skin shoes, but even his ceremonial robes had chemical stains and burns all over the front.

I turned back to Apollo.

'Please, put a stop to this,' I whispered. 'Ask Angel. She's remembering about your mama.'

He'd been watching Drago with his dead eyes. 'Too late. The Draconis like worshipping the goddess, they've always killed, and the police can't do anything. They've been trying for ever to stop us, but there's never any evidence. See, Michael gave us wealth, but he gave us bad genes as well.'

'You're wrong,' I said. 'Genes can affect the colour of your hair. Or they can make you strong, or weak. But nothing we're born with makes us act in a bad way — take my word for it.'

Apollo looked away, following Nana's slow progress across to the thrones. 'Ych, like you'd know.'

'I do,' I said. 'I had a sort-of brother called Leon. He'd had a poor hand dealt him from birth. And he went bad. His boss made him fight me. He nearly killed me, but in the end he made the choice not to be bad any more.' Not that it had saved him. He'd died anyway. But I wasn't going to tell Apollo that.

He stared at me for a moment and then turned and looked at Java, who was crouching by the Dragon Device, hugging herself with her arms and rocking backwards and forwards.

'It's too late,' he said, and turned away.

The temple guards heaved Nana up and lifted her on to the biggest throne. She sat in it like a gold-clad sumo, her veiled head scanning the temple, her hands resting on the snake stick. Uncle Drago sat next to her, pulling his cloak around him and rubbing his stained, restless hands together. He looked impatiently across at Apollo and beckoned him to take his place on the stone seats.

'Is someone burning stevia?' I heard him say. 'This is not the time for visions.'

I had no idea what stevia was, but I had a feeling it was something to do with a little figure that had crept over to the fire and was piling leaves on to it. A cloud of smoke billowed out. I coughed and my eyes began to sting. Whatever stevia was, it made your head spin.

Through a blur of tears I saw the temple guard march by me. Each had the snake wristband. Each had a little silver flask swinging on their belts, like the Screamer. They took up positions round the circle, facing outwards, their arms folded. Even they didn't risk going too near the Dragon Device.

The Screamer came over. His mad face loomed close to mine. 'You better start praying for mercy from the Princess,' he gloated.

Then he hurried back into the centre, and raised his hands like a priest before his congregation. His sleeves fell back, leaving his scrawny, scaled arms reaching upwards.

'Now let us call the Goddess,' he proclaimed. 'To come and bless this ceremony before we switch on the Dragon Device.'

Nana's veil blew in and out, as though she was breathing heavily with anticipation. 'Get on with it, then!' she said, impatiently.

The Screamer threw back his head. 'I invoke you, Goddess, in the ways that the ancients called you!' he began.

His voice rose against the whine and moan of the Scirocco wind.

'We praise you, Princess Lato, dragon power of the earth, fiery goddess.'

Come on, Fredboy. Keep thinking, keep plotting. If you can't fight 'em, use your brains!

I wound the chain around my knuckles, did my monkey swing and pulled. Used the strength the Hercules gene had given me.

The pin screeched again. I felt the stone shift.

'I don't know about praising her,' I shouted. 'Why don't you ask her to tell Angel's story? That'd be more interesting.'

The Screamer stopped for a moment and gave a signal with one skinny arm. A guard took a few quick steps and hit me hard across the face.

To my right, something stirred and rustled.

'Emerald-eyed, fleet-footed, bloodthirsty ruler of the minds of men, protector and empowerer of the Dracon—' continued the Screamer.

Nana's veil puffed out, and her hand reached over to Drago and nudged him.

'For heaven's sake. We haven't time for this mumbo jumbo!' she complained in her fly-buzz voice. 'I'm dying, remember?'

She shifted her massive bulk and sat up straighter on the throne. Her gown rippled, making her look like a walrus struggling up a beach.

'We've wasted too much time on this Princess Lato nonsense,' she declared. 'Let's get the device going!'

She signalled to Drago.

'Wait!' said a small but determined voice.

Nana's hand froze in midair. Everyone stopped. A few guards wiped their eyes and coughed. But then silence fell.

'Did someone call me?' said Princess Lato.

Chapter Forty-Seven

The flames of the sacrifice fire leaped higher, filling the temple with smoke and the smell of burned chicken. It writhed over the statue of Princess Lato. The Screamer fell to his knees.

From within the smoke, I thought I saw the statue of Princess Lato shimmer like the air above a hot road. The stone snakes in her hands became real, curling and twisting. The face stopped being stone and became flesh. The eyes moved. A foot appeared beneath the long robe and took a step forward.

Jeez. Maybe the smoke was drugged. Maybe we'd gone mad. Maybe the temple did things to your mind. Or the device was making us see visions.

Princess Lato walked forward, through the shaft of light that cut across the floor, the snakes squirming in her hands. The Screamer scuttled backwards, on his knees, to get out of her way. I thought for a moment that dragon wings flickered on her back, but they might have been shadows caused by the flames of the fire. Claws glinted on her fingers. The snakes looped about her wrists and writhed through her hair, hiding her face.

Apollo was frozen, staring wide-eyed at her. Uncle Drago leant back, his praying mantis hands clasped under his chin in horror.

I was guessing that this normally didn't happen when they invoked the goddess. Like most gods, I don't think she usually put in a personal appearance.

Nana's fluttering hands dropped on to her enormous lap. The silence lengthened.

Princess Lato took a few more steps, until she was centre stage.

'Well, someone say something!' she said, stroking the head of the snake coiling round her wrist. 'I'm getting bored, and I don't like being bored! It makes me cross.'

'Is this a joke?' stammered Nana. Her veil swivelled in Apollo's direction. 'Did you do this? Is it a special effect? Is it your idea of a joke?'

Princess Lato stamped her foot. 'You called me, Nana Draconis. So what do you want?'

The veil twitched and puffed out a little. 'This isn't happening. This is an impostor; we are surrounded by impostors. Do something, Drago!'

Princess Lato folded her arms. 'Not listening, until you say my real name!' And she stared off into the distance, and began humming.

'Stop that,' said Nana, weakly, clutching a hand to her chest as though her heart was failing.

'Shan't.' Princess Lato could've given my sisters a run for their money in the sulkiness stakes.

'Hey, Princess, why don't you tell us Angel's story?' I shouted. One of the guards left his position and kicked out at me, but I dodged and his foot caught the edge of the fire basket, making it flare up and the silver dish holding the sacrificial chicken tilt to one side. 'Tell 'em all what happened to Angel.'

Princess Lato turned and smiled at me.

'Yes, that's a good idea!'

She turned to her frozen audience. The eyes of everyone in the temple were firmly fixed on her. And when everyone is concentrating on something else, that's the time to get up to no good. I swung towards the fire.

No one noticed. They were all watching Princess Lato.

'Let me tell you. My mama was Tiamet,' she said.

She stared proudly round at everyone. 'My mama made the whole world!' Her mouth turned down for a second or two. 'She was always busy, busy, busy.'

Even the guards were watching open-mouthed. So they didn't see me swinging myself gently, gently, in the shaft of light, and edging the silver plate, with its scorched and charred chicken, closer and closer to me with my foot.

'And my father?' She shook her head sadly. 'Never there. Went off before I was born. Said he was going to make the mighty oceans, or something.' She rolled her eyes again. 'If you can believe that.'

'Is this you, Angel?' snapped Uncle Drago. 'Dressing up and talking nonsense like this? You're upsetting your grandmother with this silly charade!' He leant forward and tried to peer at the goddess's face, but the snakes never stayed still – they were continually writhing, making an ID impossible. He turned to Nana. 'This shouldn't be happening. The invocation is just a ritual!'

'Angel can't speak, so I am telling her story for her,' Lato snapped back. 'It is an exciting story of murder and blackmail.'

Nana's jaw dropped. She cowered back against the throne. 'Drago!' She took tiny wheezing breaths, but the effort made her whole body shake. 'Stop her!' she whined.

Princess Lato took another step forward. Right in front of Nana.

'It happened a long time ago for Angel, but it's a mere speck of time to me,' she said. 'Seven years.'

Apollo caught his breath and leant forward on his throne. His eyes were fixed on Princess Lato.

The old woman began to tremble. 'She's lost her mind!'

Princess Lato moved closer to Nana.

'When Angel was three years old, she crept into the temple while you were trying out your experiments to call the dragon power. The stuff you now call dark energy. You!' She pointed at Nana. 'You didn't want to die, so you tried the experiments too soon. You killed Angel's mama.'

Apollo half stood up, then sat back. 'What?'

'No,' croaked Nana. 'She wanted to take part. She wanted to start the Dragon Device. To save the family.'

'Shut up!' snapped Princess Lato, the snakes in her hair lashing around as though they were angry as well. 'You always tell lies. Angel saw lots of things. She heard you tell her mama to put her hands on the Dragon Device. You knew it might kill her. When Angel's mama cried out in pain, you ignored her.'

'Lies!' gasped Nana. 'You cannot know this!'

'And Angel shouted to you to help her mama.' Princess Lato moved closer to the throne, until the snakes in her hands were writhing right in front of Nana's veil. 'You didn't, did you? You did something worse.'

Nana was leaning back as far as she could and still the snakes were just millimetres from her face. She lifted up the silver stick and held it in front of her like a barrier. 'My heart! My heart! Stop her, Drago!'

But Drago was frozen to his seat.

'You told Angel that it was her fault her mama died. You said you'd kill her if she ever told anyone what had happened. That's why Angel didn't talk,' said Princess Lato.

The wind had picked up. I don't know whether it was from the Scirocco outside, or the device. A vicious gust swirled around Nana, blowing her veil back. I saw her face for the first time.

Her eyes were all white, with just a tiny black dot in the centre. She was blinking as though even this dim light hurt them. Her mouth was open as though she was silently howling. If you had to make a Halloween mask that showed ultimate fear – the sort of dread that you'd get, say, if you'd lived a cruel, sinful life and were now frightened that you were about to die and go to hell – then the best model would be Nana's face at this very moment.

I heard Java gasp. Everyone's eyes were glued to the old

woman. I used the time to pull the silver plate nearer to me with my toe.

'Yes, so you should look frightened,' said Princess Lato, not even flinching before Nana. But then a shudder ran through the old woman's huge body, and the mouth clamped shut and the fear disappeared, replaced with cold anger. She leant on the snake stick. Her white eyes fixed themselves on the young girl. She licked her lips.

'Angel is just a stupid child, she didn't understand,' she spat. 'I – we need the elixir. We must become glorious again and live long lives—'

'No, you mean you want to live longer,' said Lato, brushing away a snake that was getting in her eyes. 'You have done so many wicked things, no wonder you're afraid to die.'

Something moved next to Nana. It was Apollo, his cloak billowing in the wind, his face even paler than usual, his mouth a thin line. His eyes were round with fear.

'I was there, too. I never forgot – I just made myself not think any more. That was the night I died.'

He looked hard at his grandmother, and she shielded her eyes. 'I was hiding in the temple, too. When Mama touched the Dragon Device and screamed, I tried to pull her away. But there was a flash and something threw me across the temple.'

He reached over and stroked one of the snakes in Lato's hands. 'I thought the dragon had bitten me. That's all I remember, until I woke up in a coffin in the catacombs. The Dragon Device killed Mama, and did this to me, and you never told me!'

'She is a wicked old woman!' said Princess Lato. And

turned her back on Nana.

The old woman began to shake with anger. 'This is not a goddess – it is a lying abomination sent by the devil!'

Princess Lato folded her arms. 'Not listening!'

Then Nana reared up and stood, huge and dangerous, tottering under her own weight. Her feet were tiny below the big balloon of her body. 'Apollo, move away or suffer the consequences,' she hissed.

Jeez, Nana was going to kill Angel.

The smoke was curling thickly now, stinking of burned chicken and hot metal. Through the smoke I saw Nana lift her snake stick.

'No!' shouted Apollo, lurching forward. But Drago suddenly reared up from his seat and grabbed him from behind, trapping his arms.

I reached down and grabbed the silver plate, knocking the charred chicken flying, then angled it in the shaft of light dancing across the temple. And a beam like a laser lanced out and struck Nana in her light-sensitive eyes. She screamed, dropped the stick and crumpled back on to her throne.

'My heart!' she said weakly, and then lay still.

'Oh my God,' shouted Java. 'She's dead. I saw her spirit leave her body.'

In the blink of an eye two of the guards were at my side. Two fists were jammed into my ribs, stopping me moving again.

Princess Lato swayed for a second or two, then fell back and lay on the floor, her arms outstretched.

Apollo ripped Drago's arms from around him, leaped

forward and crouched by the unconscious little figure.

But Drago was already moving. Without another glance at Nana he strode forward, and shouted, 'Oh for heaven's sake! This is turning into a fiasco!' He kicked Apollo. 'You! Take Angel out of the way. I'm sick of both of you. Go on, get out of my sight.' Then he whirled around and grabbed Java.

'We start with her. Put her hands on the device, see if anything happens. Come on, let's get this over with!' he shouted to the Screamer.

'No,' said Java, pulling away from him. Her face had lost the star-struck look. She was frowning, and that meant trouble for Drago. 'The device is beautiful. It's amazing. But you're not worthy of it.' Her lip curled. 'You can't make me start it!'

The Screamer moved so fast he was a blur. The two guards fell back. Then I felt his breath on the side of my face, and the cold steel of a knife at my neck.

'Better start concentrating, Indigo,' he spat at Java. 'Or your friend is going to become our latest offering to the gods.'

I felt the blade dig into my neck.

'No!' I said, my eyes fixed on Java's. But her gaze was on the knife at my throat. 'Don't. Please,' I began.

As though it was happening in slow motion, I saw her turn and raise her hands and drop them on to the device.

There was a flash.

Chapter Forty-Eight

Did I say there was a way out of everything? Well, I swear to God I couldn't see a way out of this. Not before Java was killed.

The guards were surrounding the circle of Indigos, facing outwards, their arms folded, legs braced, like bouncers guarding the stage at a rock concert. Their snake wristbands gleamed on their wrists.

Drago, his long hair streaming out, was clinging on to a pillar, watching avidly, like a kid waiting to get into a sweet shop. His eyes were as greedy as Black Michael's. He kept licking his lips.

And in the circle a glow, and Java shaking. I felt rage surge through my blood.

'It's on. I felt the switch move,' she shouted. 'Now let him go!'

The Screamer kept his grip on me. The knife never moved.

'I'm OK,' I shouted back. 'Just move away from it!'

'I would if I could, but I can't!' she screamed, her hands

pressed on the rusty iron sides.

The device began to hum. Drago began to smile.

Java jerked. Her hair came alive and stood out like a dandelion clock. Harvey blinked and leant back out of the way as static sparks shot between Java's fingertips. His smile faded and his chest began to heave.

Java started shaking. A spot of blood appeared on her face.

The rage in me had reached boiling point. Time to move.

I threw my head back, and it connected with the Screamer's face, hard enough to knock a normal man senseless. I heard something break. His nose, maybe, not that there was anything I could do to ruin his looks. He gave a howl and staggered back, clutching his face, So he never stood a chance of seeing my elbow as it headed for his stomach. The knife shot from his hand and skittered across the floor. As he slumped down I grabbed the snake wristband and pulled. No more Dragon Fire for him.

In the few seconds before anyone could react, I bunched my muscles, swung and pulled against my shackles with all the strength of the Hercules gene. Stone chips rained down, but the chain held.

I looked round wildly. There were two figures standing near me, holding hands. Angel and Apollo. Their eyes fixed on the device.

'It's electrocuting her,' I shouted to them. 'Angel's better now; she's told her story. You don't need this any more! Pull the plug!'

'There is no plug,' said Apollo, as if he was numb. 'It's part of the grid of dark energy now. Nothing can stop it.'

The red spot on Java's face became a trickle. I couldn't reach her.

The Screamer began to untangle his limbs, like a spider, and climb to his feet. I kicked him down again.

'The girl's brain waves will be in sync with the device now,' Drago shouted over the moaning wind.

'We'll see about that,' I said, and heaved on the chain.

'Neural networks in her brain are rerouting themselves, her endocrine system's shutting down.'

Dust was blowing in from outside now, like a sandstorm, whirling round the temple, making strange shapes, like ghosts and phantoms, lit by flashes of static electricity.

'Iron in her blood will be in flux, the electromagnetic aura around her body will fuse with the device and pull in a few atoms of dark energy from the universe around us. Once that small stream enters, then she doesn't matter any more!' shouted Drago.

The wind's voice moaned and howled around him.

'Like siphoning petrol from a car, it will keep flowing into the temple.' He looked at me, his hands twining around each other like Lato's snakes. He smiled. And then looked straight into my eyes with glee. 'You're. Too. Late.'

Sparks flew from bone to skull, from the statue to the device, ricocheting off the ceiling and the thrones.

'Don't listen to him, Java! You turned it on, so you can turn it off!' I shouted, swinging on my chain, using my weight to rock the pillar. 'You're the one with the Indigo brain. Tell it to switch off!'

Her eyes were fixed on the device. 'I tried. I can't!' she cried.

Tears of blood were running down her cheeks. And my heart was breaking, because I couldn't do anything.

A movement caught the corner of my eye.

Something weaving through the dust storm. A tail, sticking straight up in the air, sailed by.

Spike. About time.

'Here, boy!'

He spotted me and wagged his tail. 'Come on, I've got chow!' I cried.

I picked up the chewed chicken leg and put it against my handcuff.

'Chow!' I braced myself.

I felt his jaws clamp round the chicken leg – and my wrist shackle. I got my free hand on his collar.

'OK, Spike. Me and you are going to play tug-of-war against this pillar,' I said. 'Your reward is the chicken leg.'

He'd still got his jaws clamped round the chain, but he managed to give me an evil red-eyed look. I put my feet against the pillar, leant back till I was almost lying straight out, and then began to pull on the chain.

Screek! And a shower of dust.

Spike took the hint and began tugging, as though he'd got a rubber ring clamped between his teeth and was having a game with his owner.

The stone pillar shook, and the pin slid out halfway and jammed.

'Pull, Spike!' I bunched my muscles, twisted the chain round my fist and heaved.

He dug his paws into the floor and pulled in sharp tugs,

shaking his head, like he was worrying it. But the pillar wasn't budging. A boy and a dog couldn't pull a stone pillar down.

Come on, Fred, Hercules pulled a wall down, for heaven's sake. Are you his heir or what?

I closed my eyes. Wound the chain one more time round my fist. Bunched my biceps, triceps, pecs, lats, the lot.

'Pull, Spike!'

Screek! And the pin flew out, and so did we, flying backwards across the temple.

Sailing by the guards, who watched with their mouths opened. Sailing by Uncle Drago as he stared with greedy eyes at the Dragon Device that was killing Java. Landing, tangled with Spike, and skidding along the tooth floor, taking the skin off my knees again. I scrambled to my feet. Spike was still pulling on the chain.

'Bite!' I said.

And with a last chomp of his enormous jaws, he bit through the metal handcuff.

The Screamer scrambled to his feet and leaped out of my way. He wasn't looking at me with contempt any more. In fact, for the first time, he looked scared. Maybe he'd never seen a boy pull a stone pillar down before. He wasn't the only one.

When he was too far away for me to reach him, he wiped his bloody nose and sneered at me. 'You think you're a prime fighter? Let's see you beat the temple guard.'

I took a look and sized up the situation. It wasn't good. Eight against one. Eight fighters, with their secret Dragon Fire moves, working like one monster, coming towards me, their feet perfectly in step, ready for attack.

The circle was lit up like a bonfire. The device inside was glowing cherry red. The blood was dripping down Java's face and on to her hands. A blood sacrifice. Differently performed from the old days, but it was going to end the same way it had for all the people whose bones were piled up against the walls.

There was only one thing I could do. I looked at the snake wristband in my hand.

You think I've given you the secret? the Screamer had warned me. *No one ever got it right in less than half a year.*

Too late to worry about that now.

I began to wind the wristband on to my wrist. It seemed to coil round of its own accord, like one of Lato's snakes.

I heard the Screamer start laughing. 'You're dead!' he crowed.

He didn't realize I had no option. Out of the corner of my eye I could see Java shaking, her hands glued to the device, her eyes fixed on me.

My fingers moved on the wristband, activating it. There was a nasty little sound, *snick!* The wristband went rigid and tight. I felt needles pierce my skin.

Then pain exploded in every cell of my body.

Chapter Forty-Nine

The inside of my skull was on fire. My nerves sizzled. My mind howled like the Scirocco.

I couldn't see through the pain. I was being burned alive. I had one chance: open the gateways, let the energy flow into my muscles like blood through my veins.

I knew how to do it. I knew how to save my life. There was a problem, though. I couldn't move because of the pain. I couldn't do the hand signs to channel the energy that was killing me.

Fire surged through my brain. And all I could hear over the roar was the sound of the Screamer and the temple guards laughing at me. No respect now. No respect from them, no respect from Snow. And no respect from the one bloke who mattered to me. Wren. Where was he while I was burning? Where was his teamwork now?

The world blurred and began to spin. Too late to worry about Wren now. I fell down. Might as well burn on the temple floor. I wished Java'd stop yelling, though.

'Somebody better help him!' she was shouting. 'Or I'll destroy this stupid device. I'll stop the Indigo waves; I'll kick it over.'

Good bluff, but no one took any notice. They knew she was doomed. They knew I was doomed.

'Don't wait for them, Freedom,' she shouted, when she saw no one was moving. 'You can do it. You've got the Hercules gene.'

Too late. Hercules might've been able to do it. I couldn't.

And I thought I heard Snow saying, *What happened to Freedom?* And Wren saying, *He was always too headstrong. Thought he was invincible. Thought he'd try Dragon Fire, even though I'd warned against it. Even though it took months of practice. No wonder he never got any respect . . .*

'Look at him burn!' shouted the Screamer, gleefully. And I heard the laughter of the guards all around me.

Come on, Fredboy. You're not going to let them take the mickey, are you?

OK, good point. I did want respect. It wasn't much to ask.

I got to my knees. Java was still shouting, at Apollo now. Shouting at him to help me. Some hope of that.

I got to my feet. It was the hardest thing I'd ever done. My heart was going to explode any moment. Something touched me on the shoulder.

'*Santa Maria!* You've got the snake wristband on!' said Apollo. 'You're dead. Welcome to my world.'

'Help me,' I gasped.

He backed away. 'I don't know.'

I took a deep breath. 'Would your mama want you backing

away? She died. Do you want this thing to kill more people?'

'No.'

I gritted my teeth. 'Then help me. Redeem yourself.'

His dull eyes stared at me. 'I've seen the guards practising, but I never took any notice of how they do Dragon Fire.'

'Angel knows!' I said.

There were black spots in front of my eyes now. I wasn't even sure I was speaking out loud. Maybe I was only imagining Apollo here with me. Maybe it was too late, after all.

Then I felt a little hand on my forehead. And a croaky whisper.

'Forehead, like this.' She made a hook. And hit me. 'Throat. Like this.' She made the devil's horns sign. 'Heart. Like this.' I felt her hand against my chest. But the pain never let up. 'Stomach, like this.' She hit me square in the stomach with her clawed hand.

The pain peaked. Then it fled. And my reptile brain took control. The Screamer might have a dragon wrapped round his spine, but I had a reptile. It didn't know anything about gateways, but it knew about the energy that runs round the body. It coiled itself, it wrapped itself round me, it channelled the energy into my muscles.

I leaped to my feet, my breath like fire, my eyes burning.

The reptile brain works fast, noticing everything, finding everything a threat, watching out for the one small chance, watching out for the way to survive. If I'd had a tail I would've lashed it.

I felt as if I could have lifted the temple up all on my own and thrown it across the sea like a discus.

And all around me, snick, snick, snick, snick. Eight wristbands shooting needles into the guards. So we all had Dragon Fire now. But they didn't have the Hercules gene.

'OK, let's finish this,' I said.

Chapter Fifty

rago was still clinging to the pillar, taking no notice of anything except the Dragon Device. His eyes were fixed on the two bowls on the top. One had a tiny trickle of gold in it. The other was glistening.

Jeez, it was working, which meant Java was dying. A sharp pain stabbed through my heart.

No way. She was my love. I couldn't stand it. At that moment I'd have wrecked the world to save her. The temple guard stood no chance.

'Do something!' I shouted at Harvey. 'Or it'll be you next.' But what could he do? This was real life, not a film. There was no magic wand to make things better. Only my fists, and the temple guards moving like one monster towards me.

Eight heads, sixteen arms and legs. But it was no sweat. I felt as if I controlled the space around me and everything in it. So that I could go back and re-edit a kick if it wasn't hard enough, or speed up faster than an eye could blink. I could spin a guard round whilst he was still thinking about his first move, and throw him against a pillar so hard that he ended up with the pattern of the stone on his face.

Their downfall was that they'd been trained too well. They'd only practised against themselves. They thought I'd fight like them. Move and countermove, like a killer ballet. I fought like the gypsy boy I was, using the weapons I'd been born with. Elbows, fists, knees, teeth and feet.

And when my strength dipped, there was Apollo, handing me the flasks he'd taken off the fallen guards, and I was drinking a magic potion that tasted like chocolate milk.

Then the fight ended and the eight-headed monster was slain and lying groaning on the floor, its energy gone.

I blinked the sweat out of my eyes and looked over to the circle. The device was still glowing, but now all the Indigos had their hands on it. Ten heads were bent over it, their hair sticking out, their noses bleeding, sharing the pain.

Harvey had probably saved Java's life for the moment. But much more of this and they'd all die. There was only one thing I could do.

Chapter Fifty-One

'Run!' I shouted, tottering under the weight of the device.

My eyes vibrated, my stomach writhed. It was like holding something that was alive. It seemed to squirm in my hands, melting and reforming. My bones felt as though they were warping.

I'd never seen people move so fast. I'd run into the circle and grabbed it from the hands of the Indigos. Then I'd got a grip on it and heaved it against my chest, my knees cracking and my arms nearly out of their sockets.

Apollo screamed, 'It's unstable! Put it down!' Then he'd grabbed Angel's hand and fled up the stairs.

Any of the guards who were conscious had started to scuttle away from me as fast as they could, dragging their pals with them.

'Harvey!' I yelled, taking two steps forwards and one back as I tried to get enough momentum to make it across the temple. 'Get everyone out!'

The Harvey who answered wasn't the same boy I'd seen in the CCTV footage. This one had the same growling look as Java. He leaped to his feet, his nose still pouring blood.

'Hold hands!' he ordered. The next second, he was dragging the other Indigos across the temple.

Only Java didn't get up. She was left behind. Curled up on the floor as though she was dead.

The world stopped.

No. Not dead. I couldn't let her die.

I swear, I forgot all about the squirming weight in my arms. If Java was dead ...

Don't think. Don't just stand there – do something!

I staggered over to her. I tipped the device forwards. A sickly smell rose from it, making my stomach churn. Then I saw the little drop of liquid in the bowl run over the edge, down the side of the device, and drip into her mouth.

'Drink!'

She twitched, then licked her lips. I blew out a breath, and took another. She was alive, at least. I could breathe again.

'No,' said Drago, appearing from nowhere, his eyes fixed on the device. 'Put it down. Or I will kill you.'

He didn't realize. I'd had a fright. I'd thought Java was dead. Nothing was going to stop me destroying the thing that had done that to her. I took a better grip on the device and headed towards the little pool.

'You cannot ruin everything we've worked for!' he howled.

But he had no power now. He couldn't stop me. The device writhed and seemed to melt my bones, but the frothing blue water was there at my feet.

I lifted it high above my head.

'No!' said Drago again. But then the look of fury on his face turned into one of cowardice, and he turned and ran for the stairs. The device crashed down, smashed through the metal grid and hit the water.

You've done it, Fredboy. Now run for it!

There was only one problem. My legs wouldn't move. There was no energy left in my cells, nothing to burn. I'd used it all.

For a couple of heartbeats, nothing happened. After the moaning wind, the screaming and the shouting, suddenly there was nothing. It was as though a god had reached down from outer space, put a finger out and stopped the world spinning.

A hand touched my arm. Jeez, I thought it was Drago come back. I flinched. But it was Java's face swimming before my eyes. If I'd had even one atom of energy left in my body, I'd have hugged her and never let go.

'Got any more of that elixir?' she said, and tried to smile. 'It's dynamite.'

'Get out of here,' I gasped.

The water in the pool was beginning to boil.

Java took a step back. 'The device is in there?'

'Yes!'

'We better move.'

'Yes!'

Then there was a sound, like the feedback from a microphone.

And the world around us exploded.

Chapter Fifty-Two

There was a black flash the very opposite of light, like the world had become a negative. And a spout of water burst into spray and sizzled down on to our skin.

The black light expanded, burning our eyes, sucking our minds, frying our eyebrows, and filling the temple with blackness as though we'd been catapulted into the far reaches of another universe. We threw ourselves to the floor, and covered our heads.

The walls began to cave in. Stone creaked, bones showered down. Rubble came crashing around us.

Everything was going wrong! I thought we'd won. Nana was dead, the guards and the Screamer had fled. And now, with the sound of stone grinding on stone, the roof started bowing in the middle. We were in mortal danger again.

'No, no, no. It shouldn't end like this!' I said.

'Come on!' said Java.

'No energy,' I gasped.

She staggered to her feet, shielding her head with one hand. She grabbed my hand. 'Lean on me. I'll do the walking!'

She grabbed my hand and pulled me back a few metres, so that I was out of immediate danger. But then Spike appeared through the smoke and dust again and began sniffing round, looking for chicken.

'Bad Spike! Scram!' I yelled.

But he saw me and thought I was calling him. And he came running, like he wasn't a dangerous freak, like he was one of Whitney Jade's spaniels ready to go for a walk to the park. And he had a look in his eye that said he was coming over to me because he wanted to, not because I was his owner or anything.

But the roof above him was starting to sag, like a tarp full of water.

'Move! Getoutofit! Shoo!'

Stupid mutt! He stood there, his tongue hanging out, dust and stones falling all around him. His tail was still wagging when the patch of roof fell in on him with a screech.

'No! That's not how it ends!' I shouted into the dust and smoke.

'Leave him! We've got to go!' Java screamed back at me.

'No!' I said.

But she was dragging me along backwards, as though I was a rag doll. Jeez, I felt like a rag doll. 'Not fair!'

'Christ's sake, Freedom. You can't save everything.'

I'd got no strength to fight her. Then there was a big crash up ahead, and dust was blasting at us from all angles.

'No, no, no.' She said it quietly, sadly, in the midst of the devastation. 'We're stuck. The steps are blocked. There's no way out!'

And in my head I was imagining Snow's voice again, saying, 'What happened to Freedom?' Then Wren's. 'The usual, got away with the Dragon Fire, but hadn't the strength to think his way out. Old Hercules would've done it. Obviously the gene's become weakened over the years. The Smiths are not what they were. Oh well, I suppose I better go and tell his folks . . .'

No way — my mammy'd go mad if I died. And I'd got something to say to my daddy first.

I pushed Java's arm away, and tried to stand on my stupid weak legs.

'Can you swim?' I said.

'Snow? It's Wren. I'm nearly there. Estimated time of arrival — hang on, I'll ask the captain . . . Is that our bay? Yeh, we're here. You bet, we made good time. Almost supersonic. I can see action up ahead. We've got the local cops joining us . . . and . . . Holy Moly, what the hell was that? . . . I just saw some sort of waterspout near the coastline . . . looks like something went bang!'

Chapter Fifty-Three

'**T**he pool leads to the bay. I reckon there's an underwater tunnel.'

Now half the roof had gone, there was an ominous quiet, and a distant rumbling. The temple was getting ready to demolish itself entirely.

I let go of Java's arm and half fell, half jumped into the water. The Dragon Device lay shattered and sizzling at the bottom. I let myself sink. In front of me was a tunnel. I was right. It looked new, and clear of sand, as though the explosion had cleaned it for us. I surfaced. The rumbling was getting louder.

'It's a long way to swim without a breath, but it's the only way out,' I said urgently.

Java nodded. 'OK.' Like I'd invited her for a paddle in the pool at the Leisure Centre.

'Can you swim underwater?'

'I'm in the school synchro team. You have to hold your breath for ages.' She looked at me. 'You OK? You look shaky.'

I nodded. 'Bit weak. But no Smith's ever died of drowning. I'll be fine.'

She stood on the side and took a few deep breaths. As she dived in, a rack of bones exploded outwards as the walls began to collapse.

Skulls rained down around me. I took a deep breath and followed her. And the world changed from a choking, exploding one full of supersonic bones, to a cool silent paradise. I opened my eyes. Far away, a small square of blue showed where the tunnel ended and the sea began. Far, far away.

That was the problem. There was no way I was going to make it.

Chapter Fifty-Four

ee the fish! Fish everywhere. Never seen so many! Green, red, electric blue. Pretty fish, like you'd have in a tank. And a crab – I swear to God, a crab with a shell on its back, scurrying out of my way.

Concentrate, Fredboy. Stop looking at the fish, or you're going to die!

I reckon the seaweed's not as pretty as the fish. The tunnel's full of it, waving and brushing across my face and tangling round my legs.

Help, it's got me prisoner!

Rip it away. It's the only way through! Stop being so pathetic!

Not my fault! My head's cloudy, and I can't think straight. The Dragon Fire must've put a massive strain on my body. We only use a third of our muscle power, usually. The brain makes sure we don't use any more, so our muscles don't get destroyed.

Use a technique like Dragon Fire too often and you'd end up dead. Like I was going to, probably.

Swim, damn you!

Wow, who'd have thought there'd be a hairy caterpillar down here? Must be a sea caterpillar. Hi, little fella! Damn, it stings! But that woke me up a bit. Good sea caterpillar!

Knuckles bleeding on the barnacles and corals covering the walls. Weirdo sea plants waving about like ghosts. And the end of the tunnel a long way away. The trouble is, I've only gone about halfway. Must drag myself one more metre. Legs useless now. I'm pulling myself along by my arms. One more metre. But it's no good because there's maybe another fifty to go, and I can't even pull myself one more centimetre.

Knuckles stinging, eyes clouding. But here's a strange thing. There's someone at my side. No, make that something. A statue, shining like gold, wrapped in waving seaweed? Still, can't hang around looking at statues, because I've got to breathe, right? Just got to breathe.

And for a second I thought the water around me was cold blue air, and I gave in to my dearest wish, and breathed in.

It looks like the Smiths do drown.

Chapter Fifty-Five

There's stars exploding behind my eyes, and my chest's full of sea water instead of oxygen, and I'm choking, but only on more sea water. There's a pain in my head, and I think that's done it, I've caught my hair on the rocks and I'm stuck here with lungs full of sea water, and I'm going to die.

Pull away!

But instead of going forwards I've started to go upwards. Hallucinating, obviously. But still going upwards. Surely not to heaven?

Get a grip, Fredboy. Someone's pulling you up.

Then there was air on my face, cold air, but it was too late because I couldn't breathe with the sea water filling my lungs, so air didn't really matter. But it was nice to hear Java again, even though she was swearing like my Uncle Shady after an argument in the pub. Seemed she'd been struggling to drag me out of the water. Maybe we were both dead, and this was how you got to the afterlife.

The afterlife had dry land, that's for sure. I was lying on it. I couldn't see anything, though. Either there was no light, or I'd gone blind. But I couldn't think about that now, because Java began thumping me on the back, and I started to cough out about five litres of sea water. It came gushing out of my mouth and nose.

She kept saying, 'Ew! Gross!' but she kept thumping.

After about ten years of coughing I finally took stock of my surroundings. We were in a cave, judging by the sound of the echo. With no way out except through the water lapping at our feet, leading back into the tunnel of death.

No, it wasn't a cave. I felt around. The walls were smooth. So was the floor we were sitting on, except it had a coating of little pebbles. Maybe we were in an old room that had led off the tunnel before it got flooded. There was something else on the floor, as well. Something that felt the same size as the pebbles, but was smooth, and clicked together like metal.

I held Java's hand.

'That was scary,' she said. 'I thought I was going to die. Then I saw the bottom of the statue by the tunnel wall. I think the explosion must've cleared the sand away from it. But I couldn't see the head. So I followed it upwards, and found air.'

I carried on holding her hand. She put her head on my shoulder. She was crying.

'What's up?' Stupid thing to say when we'd nearly died. 'I mean, besides us being stuck here?'

There was silence for a moment, with only the water plopping and slooshing. 'Just finally letting my mum go,' she said in a small voice. 'No chance now of talking to her again.'

'She's moved on, love. One day you'll meet up, I bet.'

I put my arm round her and we huddled together in the echoing darkness. She put her head against my chest. I picked up one of the smooth metallic pebbles and rubbed it. For some reason it felt familiar and comforting.

She wiped her eyes. 'Did Angel and Apollo get out?'

'Yep.'

'I never thought Apollo would turn against his family,' she said.

'Nana had screwed his head up. Then he'd got used to getting his own way, and having his gang do everything he ordered.'

Silence again. I stared into the blackness. I'd got something to say. And it'd be easier said in the pitch black.

'Look, you know when I said it was all over between us, and—'

There was a splash beside me. And a faint gasp, like something gulping for air. In the blackness Java and I squeezed our arms tighter round each other.

A hand grabbed my leg. I froze. Something had surfaced from the tunnel.

Chapter Fifty-Six

The darkness was shattered by a bright light. Dazzled, we both closed our eyes, a rainbow of colours flashing behind our eyelids.

When I opened my eyes again, our dark prison had turned into an old room. Damp walls, stained with sea water and patterned with barnacles, surrounded us. And a big figure was stumbling out of the water, wearing a wetsuit, weight belt and tank. His flashlight strobed round.

'Wren?'

The figure clambered out, swearing as his knee hit a rock. 'No, the monster from the black lagoon. What do you think?'

Java sat up. 'That's not possible. How did you find us?'

Wren unhitched the scuba tank from his back and stood it down. 'We were coming into the bay, when suddenly—' He swung his arms out and his eyes popped. '*Whoosh!*'

'What?'

'Big waterspout shoots up! Right near the coast. And I thought, hello, underwater explosion. Looks like things have already kicked off. Pity Freedom couldn't call me, and—'

I raised an eyebrow. 'Jeez Wren. Things were a little tricky. They were trying to kill us.'

Wren shook his head. But I caught a glint of his gold tooth. 'I said surveillance only.'

'It didn't happen like that.'

He grinned. 'It rarely does.'

'So how did you figure that we were here?' said Java.

Wren plonked himself down between us. 'We came into land. All hell's let loose on the beach. There's weirdos everywhere, screaming that the temple's collapsing. Then the good old Maltese cops turn up and the weirdos start to scarper like the cowards they are. And we've got the Draconis family appearing from the temple, covered in dust and looking like death. And a crocodile of Indigo kids holding hands and going on and on about how you saved 'em and how you're bound to be dead. And I thought, yeh, right, not very likely if I know Freedom and Java.'

'It was a close call,' I said. I was only half listening, though, because I'd discovered something interesting about the smooth metallic pebbles. And my brain had begun thinking up some hanky-panky.

'So we hare down into the ruins of the temple,' continued Wren, in full flow now. 'And, hey presto, you've disappeared. No dead bodies. Nothing. So I had a hunch.' He tapped his forehead and winked at Java. 'You wait till I tell Bigley. I think I might be getting some of those Indigo brain waves.'

Java pulled a face. 'Poor you. They're nothing but trouble.' She shivered. 'Right at this moment I can feel the memories of people who must've used this room thousands of years ago, and they're not happy memories. They're giving me the heebie-jeebies.'

Wren looked around. 'My God, what is this place? I thought it was a cave when I swam in.'

'It's part of the temple,' said Java, squinting around with a look of distaste on her face. 'But it must have been built before the last ice age, when the sea was lower. Which is impossible, because we learned at school that there were no buildings before the ice age.'

Wren ran a hand over one of the stained walls. 'The world never ceases to surprise me. Our historians and scientists think they know everything. But really we only see little bits of the picture. They find a bit of blue and think that means there's sky. But it might be the sea, or someone's blue jumper, or the eye of a blue-eyed god.'

Java looked around. 'I'll be glad to get out of here.'

'Good idea,' said Wren. Then he looked at me. 'What're you up to?'

'Huh?' I said, putting on an innocent look. 'Nothing.'

But Wren had turned the torch my way.

'Oh, lordy, lordy,' he said. 'We found gold! We found some of the treasure!'

I'd found it, more like. There was a small heap of coins next to me, and a handful of others scattered and gleaming on the floor.

'We're taking this with us.' He unclipped a neoprene bag from his weight belt. 'The Maltese police will be very interested. So will the archaeologists.'

See, that's what happens when cops find gold. They want to hand it in. Me, I'd had other plans for it. But I sighed and said, 'OK.'

I held up one piece. My mammy would've called this heaven. The Smiths love gold. I put it against my own lips, feeling its beautiful smooth coldness. I picked up a few more coins, and let them run through my fingers. Reluctantly I began to fill the bag.

'Got it all?' said Wren.

'Uh-huh.' I handed him the bag.

'Let's go.'

'How? It's too far.'

Wren put the tank back on his back and then a hand round each our shoulders. 'We buddy-breathe. Stay together and share the regulator.'

Then he leaped back into the water. We followed him in.

He gave me a suspicious look. 'You OK? You keep sinking.'

'No, I'm fine. No problem. Just tired,' I said quickly, kicking hard to keep myself afloat. But it wasn't tiredness that was sending me to the bottom. It was reverse alchemy.

All I can say is, never try to swim with your pockets full of gold.

Chapter Fifty-Seven

The beach had become a temporary holding pen as the Maltese cops arrested everyone in sight. No more murderball on the terraces now. Most of the Draks had scarpered, but there were a few left. They were in handcuffs, like the Screamer and the temple guards.

I should've felt triumphant. We'd returned to the light from our watery prison under the cliffs. I was alive. Java hadn't died.

Don't think about that! Don't think about seeing her curled lifeless on the floor.

But now we were safe, I didn't feel anything. I just watched the proceedings as though I'd taken no part in them. I think the Dragon Device had left some sort of shiver in my bones. A vibration that wouldn't go away.

Apollo, peering through his hair and looking unsure of himself, came over with Angel. Her plaits were half unravelled and her robe covered in soot. They both looked as if they'd woken up after a long nightmare and weren't sure where they were.

'I think I'm alive again,' he said. It was the first time I'd ever seen his eyes shine.

'Looks like it,' I said.

He kept looking back towards the smoking ruins of the temple. 'When the device exploded, maybe it restarted my heart.'

Maybe it had, but it could've been because the secret of his mama's death had been told at last. Maybe secrets can weigh heavy enough to make your heart feel like it's stopped. I looked around. 'Where's Drago?'

'The *pulizija* have him.'

'How do you feel about all this? Your family is gone. The temple's gone.'

Apollo shrugged. He looked around. 'It's a long time since I felt anything. I was thinking I might copy you.' I thought I caught a smile on his face.

'Huh?'

'Search for the treasure that's around here somewhere.'

'Good for you,' I said, my hand hovering guiltily over my pocket. 'I bet there's loads of gold down there.'

He wasn't having mine. He owed me that at least.

Angel was biting her lip, watching Nana's body being brought up the steps.

'You OK?' I said to her.

She looked at me with her Mona Lisa eyes. Except now she didn't look mean and mysterious – she just looked like a little girl. Like Whitney Jade.

'Yes,' she said. Her voice was still quiet, but I could hear what she was saying.

'It was you, wasn't it? Being Princess Lato?'

'You said if I was scared I should pretend to be like Lato.'

'How did you do the snakes, love?'

She gave a secret smile. 'Uncle Drago puts special leaves on the fire during ceremonies. They make you see things. So I put more on.'

The stevia leaves must have affected our senses. Coupled with the weird light in the temple and Angel's performance, it had been easy to think that we were looking at the real goddess. I don't know what the others saw, and I'm betting we all experienced the incident differently, but I think Angel had a career ahead of her in films.

Apollo grabbed her hand. 'Come on – we have to talk to the *pulizija*.'

Angel hung back for a moment. She grabbed Java's arm. Her eyes went hazy, and a bit crossed, and for a second her face looked like Princess Lato's.

'Your mama says you will meet again,' she said in a dreamy voice. 'She says, "Cheery-bye for now."'

Then they both walked up the beach and out of our lives.

Java looked like she'd been turned to stone. But there was no time to wonder what had just happened; Wren was next to us, shouting that we were to get the other Indigos and go down to the shore.

Java moved off, still in a daze. I stayed where I was.

Wren went to move, then frowned at me. 'You OK?'

I shrugged. There was something on my mind. 'I still feel odd from when I picked the Dragon Device up.'

Wren's eyes opened wide. 'You picked it up? In God's

name, why?'

'To throw it in the water. Snow told me that was the way to destroy it.' I screwed my eyes up and looked at him. 'Did you know that?'

Wren pulled a face. He was hardly listening, he was too busy checking that he'd rounded up all the Indigos. 'No. He must have been guessing.'

I stared out to sea. The powerboat that had dropped me off here was skimming over the waves towards us. I turned back to Wren. 'I didn't think you were coming for us.'

He stopped in the middle of lighting a small cigar, and glanced at me. 'Snow told you.'

'No.'

He blew a smoke ring. 'If you're joking, I don't get it. Why would he not tell you?'

I kept my eyes on the boat. 'I swear, he didn't. I thought we were on our own.'

For a second, Wren looked puzzled. Then he grinned and slapped me on the back. 'Let's just say that satellite communications are not the best. Heat of the moment, you must have misheard him.'

'Yeh, that must be it,' I said, like I'd forgotten all about it already.

I should have slapped myself on the back for that. I was learning. No more ranting and raving. I'd bide my time on this one.

And then the Cruiser powered towards us, the captain swinging it round like a joyrider doing a handbrake turn.

'OK, let's go home,' said Wren.

Chapter Fifty-Eight

We were high above the blue Mediterranean. It looked as if we were in someone's private jet. Wren seemed to have lots of friends in high places.

Java and the other Indigos were in the seats behind, filling up on little trays of food and cans of Coke. Everybody on the plane was fussing over them, fetching them first-aid kits and tending to their scratches. Nobody was fussing over me. I'd had to go and find my own plasters. Now I was sitting on my own, and I think everyone could tell by my face that I wanted to be left alone.

It wasn't the shiver in my bones from the Dragon Device that was bothering me. It was Spike.

We had all survived except him. And no one seemed to think I should be upset. Just a dog, right? Dogs weren't humans. And Spike wasn't even a good dog; he was an untrainable, evil, fanged monster dog, who was down to be euthanized anyway. But that was why I'd made a friend of him. He was the dog equivalent of me. Trouble, but true to those he admired. He'd saved my life, and Java's. And I hadn't been able to save his.

I stared out of the window and said goodbye to him as we left Malta way behind. They'd made him bad, they'd made him a killer, but in the end he'd chosen differently. He'd become a good dog. OK, one with more teeth than usual, but still a dog, not a killing machine.

'See ya, Spike,' I muttered, and raised my can of Coke to him.

'Freedom?' said a wheezy voice.

It was Harvey. He slid into the seat next to me.

'Thanks. I think what you did was amazing.'

I looked at him. This was the face that had stirred my conscience. All my life I'd thought it was just me and my family, they were my only concerns. Our little gypsy world. Why should I care about anyone else? They didn't care about us. But it didn't work like that. Harvey had made me realize we were all connected, wherever we came from.

I'd been at school with loads of kids like Harvey. It had never worked out. Gorjer kids hated us. We hated them back. Even the ones that had wanted to be friendly, I'd pushed away. Didn't they realize we were different?

Java was right: I was as prejudiced as they were.

So I put a smile on my face and held out my hand to Harvey.

'Hey, let's do it again. It was fun.'

He grinned at me. 'Where are you from?'

I shrugged. 'All over.'

'Me, too,' he said. 'I'm at boarding school. My parents live abroad. I'm always on planes.'

So I was right. We weren't that different at all. It wasn't only gypsies who were nomads.

Thirty minutes into the flight, Java came and sat by me. She looked amazing. I looked like a dog's dinner.

'You OK?' I said.

She twisted the rings on her finger. 'Yep.'

'You think Angel really got a message from your mammy?'

She nodded. 'She said, "Cheery-bye". That's one of the things I remember about mum. When I used to talk to her in my mind, she always used to say "Cheery-bye" when we parted.'

She wiped her eyes and rubbed her face. Then she smiled at me.

'Let's see your wrist.'

I held my hand out. Fifty tiny holes were tattooed round it in a snake pattern. It looked as if you could tear around the dotted line and my hand would fall off.

'Does it hurt?'

'Not much.'

She twisted the rings again. 'I was wrong to mess around with the Screamer email. Thanks for coming and sorting it.'

'No problem.' A silence fell, and I couldn't think of one thing to say to break it.

'The things we've shared will always give us a bond,' she said.

We touched knuckles, like gangsters. Then she tapped her

heart, and reached over and tapped mine. 'Always.'

I didn't say anything. The silence stretched again. Eventually Java broke it.

'What were you going to say in the underwater chamber, before Wren arrived?' she asked, in a small voice.

I'd hoped she'd forgotten that. I looked out of the window at all the blue.

'Freedom?'

The thing was, I'd got a problem. I couldn't forget seeing Java lying lifeless on the floor. I'd thought she was dead. I couldn't go through that again. Having my heart torn apart. Or feeling jealous of rich boys like Jamie Champion because he could hang around with her, when her daddy would throw me out on sight.

I needed to be on my own again, free, sitting on roof tops, eating takeaways, making life up as I went along. Grow too fond of things, and all you get is heartache.

'I don't remember,' I muttered.

Java looked at me for a few seconds. 'Well, it couldn't have been that important,' she said. Then went and sat on her own.

That was sorted, then.

Chapter Fifty-Nine

It was raining in England – fine rain that you knew would last all day.

'What's up with him?' said Wren, who was driving us home in the black BMW.

We'd said goodbye to Harvey and the others at the airport. They didn't need us now. They'd got a crowd of mammies and daddies ready to greet them.

'Who knows?' Java was sitting beside him. She turned slightly, and gave me a cool glance.

They'd been yak-yak-yakking for ever. About the Dragon Device. About being Indigo. About the temple, the snake wristband. About what I'd done. *'He did what! Are you mad? You need more training, boy. Just wait till I get you back to base.'*

Yak, yak, yak. I was fed up. So I was sitting on my own at the back, flicking one of the gold coins from finger to finger, not talking. Looking out the window, continually seeing people walking dogs that looked a little bit like Spike.

At last we roared up to the gates of Phoenix HQ.

'Who the hell's put that there?' said Wren. There was an old boot stuck on the gatepost.

'Hang on,' I said.

I got out of the car, took off my trainers and tied the laces together, then hurled them into the air, so that they caught on the telephone wires high above the gate. I padded barefoot back to the car.

'What was that all about?'

'Nothing.'

Inside the HQ, the first thing I noticed was that a few of the smaller statues, the ones made out of plaster, now had their hands missing. The Tunnel Crew and a stolen snake wristband, I suspected. I followed Wren down the hall. So did Java.

'Shouldn't you be going home?' I said. The sooner I didn't have to see her, the sooner my heart might heal.

'You've both got to debrief,' said Wren.

Java just stared at me, like she couldn't figure me out at all.

'OK, but then I'm off,' I said. I needed to go to Costalot, to sit outside around the fire, to jaw with Joe and play with the little kids. 'We're all going off up north to see my cousins.'

Wren stopped dead. 'We've got another mission on the board for you.'

'But I've only just finished this one,' I said. He must think I was a slave or something. 'Don't I get time off?'

Wren looked horrified. 'What? You want a holiday? You get weekends off. Isn't that enough?'

I didn't answer. Just stalked off down the statue-lined corridors.

A cop came up to Wren and handed him a phone. He carried on walking, saying, 'Huh? Really? You're kidding!' Then he clicked it off. We walked for a while longer.

'What actually happened to the mutt?' he said, as if he'd just remembered about Spike. He hadn't even bothered to ask before.

There was a twinge of pain in my heart. 'He didn't make it. He was crushed when the temple collapsed.' Jeez, imprisoned all his life in a lab and, just when he gets out, he perishes.

Wren stopped. 'Really?' he said, folding his arms.

Maybe he thought I'd not looked after him or something, the way he was glaring at me. 'I swear to God, I couldn't save him.'

Wren's foot began tapping. 'Funny how that bag of gold you collected for me turned into pebbles when we got back into the daylight.'

'Don't know what you're talking about,' I muttered.

Wren held out one of his big hands. 'Come on, let's have it.'

'Huh?' I stuck my hands in my pockets. 'No way. It's mine. Treasure, fair and square.'

The foot kept on tapping. 'That was a call from the police in Malta. They've started clearing the rubble of the temple. They found something of yours.'

'What?'

'Spike. He's in the local jail in Valletta, eating his way through the bars.'

'You're kidding!' I hadn't smiled since I got out of the

water. Now I did.

'Looks like you're not the only one with the Hercules gene,' said Wren. 'They want it out of the country by tomorrow or they're going to put it to sleep.' His mouth twitched. It might've been a smile. 'Khampal in Accounts won't stand for it. It's going to cost a fortune to crate it up and fly it here.'

'He,' I said. 'He's a he. He's a mate. Of course I'll pay. Here. It's only money.'

I handed over the gold. Mind you, I had to force my hand to let go of it.

'One day, maybe I'll make some money that I can actually keep,' I muttered, trotting after Wren, down the spiral stairs to the Ops room.

A quick glance at the board showed the Yeti mission was still unsolved. But mine had a line through it, and JD scrawled next to it in Wren's writing. Job done. A glow started up in my heart, though you wouldn't have known I'd done anything fantastic by the amount of praise I got. I thought maybe there'd be flags out and people cheering me. I thought maybe I'd get a bit of respect now. I was wrong. I suspected I'd have to wait for Spike to get back here. He'd greet me properly.

A techie left his computer and came over. 'Dark energy. Did you connect with it?' he said abruptly.

I shook my head. 'Ask Java.'

And Snow was there, leaning on his stick, his mask-like face avoiding mine. Time slowed as I walked by him. Maybe, one day, I'd figure out why he hated me so much. I knew by the look in his ice-chip eyes that he wanted me to lose it in front of the others, to go up to him and ask how he knew about the Dragon Device and the water.

And he'd say, 'I never said anything of the kind. You're lying.' And he would be believed. He wore the suit. He had the job and the title. He was head of something. Who was going to believe me, however much it was true?

Well, I wouldn't give him that satisfaction. I wouldn't let him tell the others, 'Freedom can't think things through. He's always flying off the handle.'

Not this time. This time I'd think it through. And I'd get to the bottom of why he wanted to do me down.

'Well, here I am, back safe and sound,' I said. I held out my hand. 'Thanks for the support.'

He never moved. I went to walk off. Then I stopped.

'I was wondering how you got your burns,' I said innocently. 'Were you in an explosion?'

He just stared at me. I smiled and walked on.

Before the mission I'd thought about leaving this job. Gypsies didn't work for people, and they definitely didn't work for the cops. But leave Phoenix now? No chance. Not while Snow was breathing.

I started to follow Wren, but a cop came up to me. He was one of the ones who'd muttered when I'd been given the mission.

He said, 'Not bad, kid,' then thumped me on the arm.

It was a start.

Ant came running up and fixed himself to my leg like a limpet mine. 'The monster's back!' he squeaked. I didn't know what monster he was on about. Probably one he'd made up in his head. But at least he was pleased to see me.

Then a second cop came over. But all he said was, 'We've got a message from your father. He wants you to get in touch and meet him.'

'No problem. I've already arranged it,' I said. The two patrins at the gate. One boot for *Meet me*. Two shoes for *See you soon*.

After that, everyone ignored us and got on with their work, until Bigley came over. Wren plastered a big grin on his face, but she ignored us both.

'Java!' she said. 'You've got incredible gifts! I need to talk to you about Indigo powers. I think we could use them on the Psi team ...' She lowered her voice. 'Your mother's maiden name, it wasn't Fairchild, was it?'

Java blinked in surprise. 'Yes, why?'

But Bigley just narrowed her eyes and gave a secretive smile, then led her into the next room.

Java, helping Bigley, here at Phoenix? Jeez, did everything have to go against me?

'What's Ant on about?' I said to Wren, who was watching Bigley go, looking like a disappointed puppy-dog. 'What monster?'

He shook himself, then clapped me on the back. 'I told you we had a mission for you.'

He plucked a photo off the desk.

'We've got an ID now of the monster in the sewer.' He handed it to me.

It was a fuzzy picture of a large tunnel. Water ran down the centre, and in the distance there was a figure, turning as it ran away, its face caught in the flash of the camera. It looked like—

The photo fell out of my hands.

'Freedom? You OK?'

I picked the photo up and looked again. No mistaking it. Leon, my brother.

'It needs investigating,' said Wren. 'Are you in?'